Lulu in Babylon

Allison Silver

Lulu in Babylon

Allison Silver

MARMONT LANE
BOOKS

Marmont Lane
BOOKS

For information address Marmont Lane Books
139 South Beverly Drive Suite 318
Beverly Hills, CA USA 90212

www.marmontlane.com

FIRST EDITION

Publisher: Bobby Woods/Marmont Lane Books
Design: ♡x☕=⚡
Cover Illustration: Matt Mahurin
Chapter Illustrations: Matt Wuerker

ISBN 13: 978-0-9905602-8-9
Library of Congress Control Number: 2018932642

ALSO BY ALLISON SILVER

20th Century Travel

(co-author)

For

HELEN PALTIS SILVER

who always thought I should write.

Lulu in Babylon

Allison Silver

MARMONT LANE
BOOKS

PROLOGUE

B EN ROBBINS CIRCULATED WITH A FINESSE that came from years of working a party. He played tennis regularly, was a serious student of martial arts, but this was his strongest sport. Usually, he was aloof – which he knew was key to his allure as the head of a studio. Tonight, however, he was feeling demonstrative. So he was.

He didn't move more than a few steps in any direction without reaching out to someone – and he was a master of the nuances and calibrations of movie industry relationships. He understood the minuet of manners as well as any courtier at a levee of the Sun King.

Some, particularly Oscar winners and big directors, he greeted with a bear hug, ending with an extra few slaps on the back using both hands. Others, including influential directors, producers and the most powerful agents he dealt with regularly, got the hug, but pats from only one hand. Longtime colleagues or in-demand younger agents got the hug, but no accompanying pats. For older agents who handled actors he might need soon, as well as some of these intense younger actors who played both action and art movies, he would laugh a greeting as he grabbed both elbows, and a variation involved clutching both forearms. With some of the most gamine of actresses, he would stand close enough so that he could put a hand affectionately at the back of their neck as he kissed their cheeks, often standing on his toes to do so; others, including the sylphlike young actresses swanning about the garden, received a kiss as he held one of their elbows. He would also use that affectionate back-of-the-neck grab with some younger actors, since he regarded this maneuver as almost shorthand for a hug.

Ben felt so relieved his party was working that he extended his physical repertoire down the food chain. If some people were worth only a handshake, he reached out with two hands. Or he enclosed the person's wrist with his other hand. Wives got a hug in addition to his ritual air kisses. It was all about creating the illusion of close contact. And maintaining his presence at the top.

There was no way Ben could have known how bad the timing of this party would be. The director of the Los

Angeles County Museum of Art had called more than eight months ago, asking if Ben would host a dinner at his Brentwood house for the opening of the Bruce Nauman exhibition. Ben said "yes" so quickly it didn't occur to the director that the studio head had, as always, weighed his options.

Nauman was such a big deal that Ben was sure this would raise his profile in the art world. It might help get him to MoMA — all he really wanted. He could end up being approached not just to lend Hollywood glamour for fund-raising, but as a serious player, worthy of respect.

Nauman was important. Ben expected at least some of that to rub off. In the nano-seconds before saying "yes," Ben had calculated that most other artists of Nauman's stature were dead. They wouldn't be coming to any opening party.

When the LACMA director called, Ben was still seething about being shut out on a Gursky photograph the week before. By an L.A. art dealer — that was the infuriating part. Not some Chelsea dealer who couldn't place him in the social strata. Yet the dealer, whom he had started cultivating only recently, had promised all Gursky's best pieces before Robbins could get a look.

She was already aggravating, as far as he was concerned, because she smoked. A messy weakness, Ben felt. She had said, between drags on her cigarette, that her long-time clients had first claim. He smiled. It was a trick he adopted long ago — to smile when most annoyed.

She promised he would get an early look at the next show. He tried cajoling. When he got no traction, Ben moved on to threats, though his tone was never anything but friendly — something else he had learned years ago. It scared people more, he found, when you didn't raise your voice. Especially in Hollywood, a town filled with screamers — people who practiced a scorched-earth policy in their daily lives, setting flamethrowers on high over a missed call or not enough ice in a diet Coke. There were former personal assistants all over town with charred psyches, burnt to a crisp, still fragile years after the fact. It was when Ben lowered his voice, however, that even studio vice presidents shivered.

His voice had fallen to a whisper talking about the Gursky, but the dealer hadn't moved. She didn't understand how serious he was. He knew he would ultimately get her, though. He'd also make sure to leave fingerprints.

Subtlety didn't work in Hollywood. The town was too shameless. Besides, it didn't give him the degree of satisfaction he needed. It was like irony. Wasted in Hollywood. Certainly Ben didn't subscribe to it. That was the turf of his longtime associate, Fred Hirschberg. Fred had nothing but irony. Ben had no use for it.

The art world offered a now-unfamiliar challenge to Robbins. At this point, there were few things beyond his reach in Hollywood. He was considered irresistible – but without the charm that word implied. His negotiating position was to get what he wanted. Nothing else was on the table. It was the way he talked. His arguments registered as self-evident. People sitting across the table came to see it was a fool's game not to agree. Ben's voice was invariably calm, but the steel was there, unsheathed.

Nauman was flying up to Los Angeles for the dinner and Ben was planning a high-octane affair. His aim was to lace the L.A. art scene liberally with his Hollywood power base, and a touch of the Downtown L.A. establishment.

He knew how difficult it was to get movie people to talk to anyone outside the business. Their insularity, an essential narcissism, was encouraged. People from other professions were so eager to hear about the film business that movie people never had to talk about anything else. Ben knew he could rely on a Pasadena lawyer to ask about life on the set. But you could not count on industry players to have any interest in civilians – non-industry people. They had no conversation for outsiders. In any case, he focused on the industry because he wanted the party buzz to reach West 53rd Street in New York. He pulled out all the stops – major military invasions hadn't been strategized as carefully.

He had wrangled three of the biggest stars – two Oscar winners, and a third who could open a picture and give it room to breathe for a week or even more. Two of the three had housekeeping deals on the lot, and the third, notoriously elusive, was negotiating for the studio's big summer movie.

Ben was also expecting Nick Copley, a big-time action star who, a lifetime ago, had been a respected, serious actor. He had leveraged commercial success on a big action movie series (Part 4 and counting) to become an Oscar-winning director. Copley was not a friend exactly — but Ben made sure to have dinner with him roughly every six weeks. They had made a lot of money together on two projects — which, in Hollywood, translated as friendship.

To round it out, Ben had asked two major action stars — both, he was sure, had never been in a museum. They had done business with him, though, and each promised to come.

He'd also asked Dianne to call friends she made through the kids. He couldn't remember ever socializing with the people she'd suggested, since they were execs at other studios. But he wanted to include more of the town.

Ben had called in chits from two big comedy stars, "Saturday Night Live" alumni from different eras. A good 20 years separated them. The older was the most passive funny guy Ben knew. His personality felt like a black hole — sucking in the life force of all around him. Yet Ben made three calls to make sure he came. He was an important art collector and smart — if he decided he wanted to talk.

He was hanging out with the younger comedy star now. Ben hoped he wasn't coaching the younger man on how to walk away from a deal. The younger star would be bringing his posse, three witless friends dating from high school. "Entourage" manqué. A minor inconvenience, though, if it meant he would show.

Ben had worked hard to insure the evening would be notable. But it turned into something unexpected — since it was also the start date of his new career.

A few months ago, Ben had finally decided he could no longer work with Harry Lefferts, the owner of the studio. His relationship with Harry was complicated — but not so different from anyone else who worked with him. In fact, few people at the top of any company Harry controlled had stuck it out as long as Ben.

Even in a town filled with screamers, Harry stood out. You could do a healthy trade in stories about his venality. Since Harry's divorce and this new marriage, his third, he had calmed down a bit. But he had recently started interfering in deals he would never have cared about before.

About three months ago, when their conversation grew caustic, as it did with greater frequency, Ben had played his usual card — insisting he was too old and too rich to put up with it. He could leave tomorrow. He expected Harry to back down — as bullies usually do when pushed. The studio had to move forward and approve another sequel for one of their biggest franchises, even as the budget sailed north of $225 million and the script made no sense. If they wanted it for Memorial Day, they had to pull the trigger now.

Ben usually got what he wanted with this sort of threat. But, for the first time, Harry had said, "Fine, go." Both men blinked. If only because shooting had to start. But Ben decided he'd had enough.

He called Louis, his old friend on Wall Street, who'd been telling him for years he ought to set up an independent production company. Even in this economic climate, the line of credit wasn't hard to secure.

He had long talked with Dianne about making a change — usually during Mach-10 fights with Harry. This caught her off guard, however. There had been so many fights, he realized, over so many years, that Dianne had decided this day would never come. She flinched when he told her, inhaling with a sort of gasp. But all she said was "What?" As if she hadn't heard correctly. Now, months later, Ben sometimes caught her with a dazed expression — as if she had walked into the living room and found the chair legs all sawed to three-quarter height.

It had been a strange three months. Especially when Ben found out that Fred was taking his job. This was not what he expected — which was that Fred would come with him to the new company.

Ben finally decided it was all good that his long-time associate would be running the studio — though it would be odd sitting across the table from him. Irritating as well. It bothered Ben that he hadn't seen how close Fred had grown to Lefferts.

Ben finally remembered the LACMA opening about two weeks after his deal was announced. It was so random, he thought, that the party was the same day his new company officially launched. But he decided it was fine. More people would come, he concluded, since they would want to see how he was holding up. They would see nothing had changed — in fact things were better.

The party started like so many others he had hosted over so many years. First, cocktails on the back patio. The antique Italian terra cotta tiles, from a monastery outside Padua, lit by lanterns and candles. There were tall heaters scattered throughout, to warm the chill June night air. It was silly to call it cocktails, though, since most guests drank water — exotic brands of fizzy or still water, but water nonetheless. But tonight as he looked around the garden, he realized people must actually be drinking. Voices a little too loud. Perfect!

Ben surveyed the crowd and realized that one person talking too loudly was Nick Copley. With his second Jack Daniels, Nick usually started his cartoon imitations. It looked like he was on his third, but things wouldn't start to go south until his fifth. He was going to begin looking for a date right about now, though. His wife, Hannah, always stayed out in Trancas with the kids, so Nick was, as usual, on the loose.

Ben looked around and saw Cyd Townsend, a young vice president at a production company on the lot. She was a statuesque brunette with a sense of humor. Ideal for this. He went over to kiss her hello. "Nick seems at loose ends," he said. "I'm sure he'd love to talk to you." She understood.

As she walked over to the director, Ben assessed the crowd again. Everyone he wanted was here. He was particularly happy that all three Oscar winners had shown up. For this alone, he felt the evening qualified as a success.

He was also glad to see that the biggest agents in town — power players from four different agencies — had come. They were longtime regulars at his parties. Most were big art collectors, since that was an easy way to network in Hollywood — far cleaner than politics.

Yet even as Ben circled the garden, laying on hands, he couldn't let go of the fact that Fred and Hailey weren't coming. Fred's assistant, Martine, had called about 45 minutes before the party, to say he was tied up at meetings. That was it.

This would be Ben's first big party in more than 20 years where Fred was in town but not there. Ben wondered if people knew. He thought there was a muffled "Hirshberg" off to the right. He was probably hearing things though, since it was on his mind. Then, he distinctly heard "Hirshberg" on his left. People knew.

"Benjy, Benjy." He heard Milo Flintridge's voice as his shoulders were grabbed from behind. Milo, lean and burnished, and a good six inches taller that Ben, turned him around to give him a bear hug. "You're lookin' good, kid!"

Milo had directed so many hits for so many different heads of production that he cut through the power games. He was immune to the drama of studio musical chairs; his father had been an important movie executive from the mid-50s through early '70s until, one day, he wasn't. The studio bosses back East fired him when they decided he had lost touch with the audience. Milo had been navigating Hollywood's stratified social milieu since childhood — as a toddler, he drank his bedtime Ovaltine onboard Sam Spiegel's yacht, and he later played hide and seek on studio sound stages. The father of one of his close high school friends had been an embittered, if outwardly genial, blacklist survivor.

His own success had been a long time coming — he had honed his directing skills on years of commercials and episodic television. When he started out, he was just the son of a guy who had once had a career. Until he hit it big, then did it again, and again. He had too many successes for it to be luck. But he worked hard at wearing success lightly. He knew how easily it could all be lost.

Ben pulled Francesca, Milo's wife, toward him and kissed her on both checks. Francesca Frateli had been a star in Italy, but her first big Hollywood film, an action movie, had just opened. Her lush voluptuousness worked well in the cartoon action beats. If her Hollywood career had been a question mark before — there had been tentativeness in her two earlier Hollywood roles not evident in her small yet soulful Italian movies — it looked assured now. Her enticing sexiness was finally connecting to mainstream American audiences.

Ben had known Milo over many years, through two earlier wives, as well as innumerable girlfriends, and he had a good feeling about Francisca. It must be two years since they had married and she still seemed smitten with a director twice her age — 52 to her 26. Though Ben felt she never seemed as young as she actually was. It could be because she had been a star in Europe since age 17 and, he remembered, living on her own since 15. There was an undercurrent of experience in her voice, no matter how helpless she might appear. Milo clearly adored looking out for his much younger wife, but Ben always felt she was more than capable of taking care of herself.

Ben was so focused on congratulating Francesca on her strong numbers that he didn't notice the teenager until Milo turned to pull her closer. She had been standing, pale and diffident, off to one side.

"Lulu's here for the summer," Milo said a little too heartily. "She came on Saturday. You remember my little girl, Louise? Would you believe she's 15!"

Ben looked at the girl and, though it was at least 10 years, saw Claire Sturges, Milo's first wife — almost as if he were looking at a hologram. She was tall and slim, with Claire's luminous skin and halo of Botticelli red-gold hair. She was just at the brink, where coltish and gangly turned graceful and willowy. Her features, which must have been outsized on a child, probably had only recently settled into proper proportion.

Milo had been making a picture for Ben when his marriage to Claire blew up, so Ben remembered her all too well. Ben had just taken over the studio, so it was his first big crisis. Every detail was etched into his brain. Claire had finally figured out that Milo was playing around — and had been for years. The picture was about 20 days into production when she decided this was it. Ben still remembered those fights. Milo calling at all hours, and Ben trying to help him smooth things over. He didn't want the shooting schedule to fall behind. But the production went off the rails for almost two weeks, while Milo tried to persuade Claire to stay.

Ben took Lulu's hands in both of his and smiled hello. The teenager was already taller than he was. "Not so little," he said to Milo. "I'm glad you brought her."

He looked at Lulu. "Are you having fun here?" he asked.

Lulu's smile got nowhere near her eyes. She paused before she spoke, though Ben didn't notice. "Sure," she said, "It's so nice to spend time with my dad."

Ben heard only Lulu's first words before he saw, over her shoulder, someone he needed to talk to. The Grossmans had arrived. He excused himself.

Milo put his arm around Francesca as Ben walked away. He made sure to speak loud enough for Lulu to hear. "He looks like he knows that Fred isn't coming," he said. "This is going to be quite a night." He shook his head, with a faint smile.

"Why exactly didn't Fred come?" asked Francesca.

"He doesn't have to anymore," Milo replied, as he leaned down to kiss her temple.

Off to the right, Milo saw Nate Levinson and Gwen Hedges heading their way. Milo prepped Lulu. "Nate and Gwen are getting the boat with us this year," he said. "Nate's a producer. She's a terrific costume designer — won an Oscar for "Devil's Playground.""

Levinson was slight yet doughy, with pale, thinning hair and an unassuming, almost gentle demeanor. His manner was hesitant, even shy. His small mustache only made him look more cherubic — like a fake mustache on a baby. But behind thin black wire-rim glasses, his eyes were sly and shrewd. They were the only giveaway that he controlled a major independent production company, which now had five TV programs, one on Amazon, one on HBO and three on the networks, and also regularly churned out action blockbusters.

Hedges seemed his opposite, a tall, angular woman with jet-black hair, cut in an architectural shingle. There was a dramatic streak of white running through it, starting just above her right eye. Lulu thought it seemed part of her ensemble, since she was wearing all white — a straight white sail-cloth skirt that almost grazed her ankles, a crisp long-sleeved white cotton shirt with a floppy silk chiffon pierrot collar and cuffs, an oversized white silk cardigan with large black buttons, lacy white anklets and white buck jazz shoes. Around her neck she wore at least a dozen strands of pearls, all sizes, colors and lengths — long loops of blue-gray gumballs, strings of tiny pink petit pois and everything between. Lulu wondered if she changed the streak in her hair to match the color of her outfit.

Milo turned toward the couple. "You talked to Freddy?" he asked. Levinson was close to Fred. Unlike Ben, Fred had legendary people skills and many, many friends. "So happy not to be here," Nate said.

Milo looked for Lulu, who had again edged off to the side. "Lulu, you know Nate and Gwen," he said as he pulled her into the circle. They both smiled at her in recognition. Lulu was sure she had never met them. "Lulu came in from Boston on Saturday," Milo continued, "I know she and Emma will have a good time together on the boat."

"Hi, Lulu," Levinson said, as he held out his hand. His tone was almost apologetic, his handshake soft.

"Our daughter Emma is so looking forward to meeting you," Gwen said, as she kissed Lulu's cheek. Her voice was gravelly, honey on sandpaper, though not as dramatic as her clothes. "How do you like being in L.A. so far? You having fun?"

Lulu decided this was the question everyone asked in Los Angeles — as if they were worried the city was failing to measure up on the fun front. She answered a beat faster this time. "Course. It's nice to spend time with my dad."

Milo reached out to hug her as she spoke. "When did you get back from Santa Barbara?" he asked. "How was the house? How crazy was it?"

Nate and Gwen, Milo explained to Lulu, had stayed with a couple named Tom Steadman and Shelia Adderman last weekend. They had finally finished work on the weekend house they had bought almost two years ago. Milo told her that Tom ran Magnum Pictures, where Nate had a picture set up.

"Not my taste, but good — if you like early American," said Nate, who favored urbane 1940s French. "Lots of Sheraton highboys and way too many quilts. All in that Spanish hacienda." He made a slight face, shaking his head, his eyes heavenward. "But the weekend was beyond crazy. You know her friend, the one who's always around?" He reached out, pretending to put his hands over Lulu's ears. "He's fucking her."

"You mean her best friend from college?" Milo asked, "The one she convinced him to hire?"

"She got the job and now she's doing him."

Francesca gasped before both she and Milo started laughing. "Does Shelia know?" Milo asked.

"She's too obsessed about her father," Nate said. "He's dating someone younger than she is. That's all she can focus on."

"That's all she talked about when we had dinner," Milo said. "But I'd date someone younger than her, too. Who wouldn't? She's what, 37?" Francesca elbowed him, but was laughing. "Believe me, she looks like she's 1,000."

"It's all that coke she does," Nate said. "All weekend, she'd get coked up and then go out for a run. She'd be gone for hours. It's like she's in training for a marathon. But he doesn't miss her. He just sits in deep discussion with her friend. Insane!

"It felt like I was in an Edward Albee play," Nate continued. "But not 'Who's Afraid of Virginia Woolf.' One of the bad Edward Albee plays."

"Did you see their little girl? Fiona, right?" asked Francesca. "So adorable."

"We spent more time with her than either of them did," Nate said. "I don't want to think of the therapy bills when that kid gets older. It will take her a lifetime to recover. If she ever does. Neither of them even seems to think about her. He's too obsessed with the friend and she only talks about her father and her producing career — for what it's worth."

"Doesn't she have a picture starting?" Francesca asked.

"Yeah, she has it set up at Sony," Nate said, "It's a good script but she has no idea what to do with it."

Milo was laughing. "You don't think anyone knows what to do," he said, "except you."

"She's clueless," said Nate, "But she got Connor Ericson to commit. So now they put it on the fast track. He's happening."

"Connor?" Francesca said. She ran her fingers through her thick, tousled mane of dark hair, pushing it back off her face. It cascaded down her back.

"Yeah, he won't know what hit him," Nate said, "Three weeks into production with her, he could probably claim justifiable homicide."

As Ben walked toward the Grossmans, he kept thinking about Fred. It bothered him that his longtime partner hadn't called himself. He returned every call — that was his trademark. So it left a weird aftertaste that Fred hadn't found time. So out of character.

Dianne hadn't said anything when he told her Fred and Hailey weren't coming. She was in the middle of getting her hair and make-up done, and knew better than to talk in front of her beauty team — they took care of half the Westside and had appointments with at least three of her guests tonight after they left the house.

Yet, as Ben looked around the garden, right before the guests started to walk back to the front lawn for dinner in the tent, his spirits lifted. He hadn't realized how tense he had been these last two weeks. This thing with Fred was worrisome. As Ben surveyed the guests, however, he decided it would all work out.

Ralph and Evelyn Grossman were probably Fred and Hailey's oldest friends — literally as well as figuratively. The couple, now in their mid 70s, were starting to shrink with age, and Evie was petite to begin with. But she still stood out in her trademark day-glow caftan. This one was electric blue, worn over bright yellow raw silk Capri trousers, and she was carrying a stoplight yellow ostrich Hermes Birkin bag. She was hard to miss, swimming in this sea of black.

Ralph had been producing hits longer than Fred had been in the business. Yet when Ralph decided to direct small projects, Fred was the executive he called. The directing was nowhere as successful as Ralph's producing — which was legendary. He had built a major franchise. It offset his directing efforts, which were "cappuccino" movies. Ralph, however, had left the indie sensibility behind years ago.

Even with this slight stutter, Grossman was valued as a Hollywood elder statesman. Besides, he was due to produce another sequel next year and it was expected to wipe out all his losses and then some.

Ben wanted to give them a heads up that they were at Nauman's table. Dianne was going to be seated there, and he knew she would find out what was up with Fred. But he wanted to suss it out himself first.

He did not take it as a sign either way that the Grossmans had come. Ben could not think of an evening they had stayed home in the last 15 years. It was probably at least that long since they'd had a private tête-à-tête. Maybe that's why they were considered one of the happiest couples in Hollywood — they knew each other only in public.

He walked toward them with every sign of delight, giving Evie an extra tight squeeze. Then he got right into it. "What happened with Fred?" he asked, "What's up?"

"He got stuck in a meeting," Ralph said. Clearly, Fred had talked to Ralph. "He was trapped in a long conversation with Lefferts," Ralph said, "and it screwed up his day. He was telling me how sorry he was that he couldn't get here."

Ben realized he had stopped motioning people into dinner and returned to that mode. But he now thought he heard the words "Fred Hirshberg" from two different directions. It was spreading. "Hirshberg" seemed to ricochet through the night. Ben's smile felt like a pasted-on rictus.

To get to the tables, the guests walked under the pergola beside the house. They could look into the side gallery, to see some of his collection, including a Robert Ryman, a fairly good Johns and a notable Rothko in yellow, orange and green. But Ben felt too many guests seemed more interested in getting to the front lawn than in looking at the art. Not often the case — and unexpected tonight.

Out front, a large white tent covered almost half of the lawn. There were more than 25 tables, with starched white tablecloths and centerpieces of white and green orchids. The wait staff wore short white jackets and green bolo ties. Like so many other evenings at the Robbinses.

Until it wasn't.

Once inside the tent, Ben knew something was off. Tables were partially empty — only to be expected since guests were still circulating. But there should have been more people standing and talking, or trying to locate their seats. It looked like there were fewer people than at cocktails — and it wasn't because the lighting was brighter. There were not enough people standing to fill all the empty seats.

Ben realized the very people he had been so delighted to see earlier in the garden, who had assured the evening's success, were no longer there. It took him a beat to grasp that many guests, regulars at his parties for years, had walked through the tent without pausing to find their tables. Instead, they had headed for the curb — and the parking valets. To get their cars. They had stopped by, Ben now realized grimly, but since he was no longer the head of a studio, they were not staying. They hadn't bothered to tell him; hadn't even said to him apologetically, as only a few had dared in past, that there was another event they could not miss.

Ben couldn't believe, in retrospect, that he hadn't seen this coming. He had watched it happen at Hollywood events — and done it himself — dropped by for cocktails before heading on for a more important dinner or just going home. Most people were only worth a drop-by.

But he had never experienced anything like this. He realized that when he was younger, his parties never included power players. Now, he had gotten so used to life as a studio head that he hadn't even considered this possibility. Certainly not at an evening for Nauman. Hollywood was too obsessed with art.

Ben looked around at the tables, many only partially filled. He checked Dianne's, where Nauman was already seated. The problem was clear. Some of the most important guests were to have sat there — the very people who had opted to leave. Of course, the two LACMA board members were at the table. But most of the Hollywood contingent was missing — probably in their cars by now.

There was a barren swath at the table — of the 12 seats, the six to the left of the guest of honor were empty.

Dianne would have usually dealt with this sort of problem, but she had her hands full on the other side of the circle. She was sitting between Nate and Gwen, with the Grossmans on the other side of Gwen. Dianne was talking with Nate as she tried to figure out what, if anything, was up with Fred.

"But he didn't even call," he could hear her say, "They've worked together for 25 years, and he can't even call."

Nate was denying anything was up. "Forget it," he was saying. "Sometime a cigar is just a cigar. Don't read anything into this.

Ben knew this was Dianne's most important conversation of the evening. But it meant no one was paying attention to Nauman, who looked forlorn.

Ben walked over to Evie, seated almost directly across the table from the artist. Unlike the guest of honor, she was surrounded by people and engrossed in conversation. As Ben took a step closer, he realized they were talking about Evie's favorite topic: Hermes. The women were weighing the assets of the Birkin bag versus the Kelly. Evie was saying that her robin's-egg blue ostrich Birkin got more compliments than any other handbag she owned — and she owned 17 Birkins in as many colors and skins. Gwen was in her element —

she began dissecting the merits of the different sizes and styles with Talmudic exactitude.

Ben walked over, putting his hands on Evie's shoulders. She looked up at him and smiled brightly as he bent down to talk into her ear.

"Evie," he said, "There's been a mix-up with this table and you can see that Nauman is virtually alone. Would you please go over and sit next to him? He is the most amazing guy and he needs someone to talk to."

Evie smiled up at him, sweetly, and leaned over to whisper in his ear. "I don't want to," she said in a patient tone. "I already know too many people. I don't want to meet anyone new." She beamed, proud of her answer. Ben knew it was from some movie, but he couldn't place which. She patted Ben's hand and turned back to Gwen, to continue dissecting crocodile versus ostrich.

Ben looked around to see how he could solve this problem. He had to get back to his own table. He needed to be there to make sure that the guests seated with him stayed. But he had to deal with this first.

He saw Milo's daughter standing near her father's table, where there was a seat waiting for her. She really did look like Claire, Ben thought.

Ben had liked Claire Sturges — though she had held herself apart from the Hollywood scene even while she lived here. He remembered how surprised he had been when Milo, then far from an A-list director, first showed up with this stunning model. Like so many others, he wondered what she saw in him. Throughout her years in L.A., she had remained close to her family and friends back East. A fancy sort of Boston family he recalled — all the things that didn't matter in Hollywood. The serious money had disappeared generations before, though.

But with her attention pulled back East, it was years before she realized that Milo had been screwing around, fucking actresses and extras during every shoot — if more blatantly when he was on location. He probably was a better actor than many people he directed. He cast movies with girls he wanted to fuck, girls he was currently fucking or girls he had fucked. Not just the walk-on parts — the principles.

So it was ironic that the woman Claire found out about was not one of the string of actresses, but Daphne Simmons, a young producer from London, who was, ostensibly, one of her few Hollywood friends. Things were difficult between Milo and Claire throughout pre-production, but then Claire figured out this incident wasn't unique. So she decided to pack up — and did. Ben always gave her that.

The sad thing, Ben knew, was that Milo hadn't really cared about Daphne. It was a reflexive itch. Yet he ended up marrying her — if briefly. He'd had to prove that his hook-up with Daphne was worth losing his marriage over.

This girl had some of Claire's petulant charm. He could tell she didn't want to be here. But, as far as he was concerned, she was made to order. She looked enough like Claire so that she was strikingly pretty, and her sulky manner registered as aloof — perfect for this.

He walked over and put his arm around the teenager. "You remind me so much of your mother," he said, "I was always crazy about Claire." The girl — what was her name? — looked at him, her eyes filling with tears. Damn, he was good. Even at this moment, he admired his own technique. He had sized her up instinctively — though he was a bit surprised by the effectiveness of his comment.

Something must be up with Claire, he decided.

"You having fun here?" Ben asked. He didn't remember that he had asked her this question earlier. In any case, he still didn't bother to wait for an answer. "Come and sit at this table for me." He kept his arm around the girl's slim shoulders as he guided her toward the open seats to Nauman's left. "I'd like you to sit next to Bruce Nauman, the artist. He doesn't know a lot of people either."

Ben could feel the girl stiffen, but ignored it. This seat had to be filled and she would be fine. "He loves young people," he said. He hoped it was true. At this point, he just needed a body. One who might actually talk to a civilian.

Ben sat her down. "Bruce, I have a huge admirer of your work here," he said to Nauman. "This is — Lulu." The name had come to him in a flash. He had to admire his own finesse.

The artist turned to the Lulu and smiled. "Hi," he said. "And who are you?"

Lulu felt the back of her neck getting hot. She could feel the flush spreading from her face to her throat and down to her chest. "I'm here on a sort of weekend pass." She pointed to Milo, seated a table away. "That's Milo Flintridge, the director," she said, "He won an Oscar for 'Splash Down.' He's my dad. I'm visiting from Boston for the summer."

Nauman smiled at her. "We're both here on a weekend pass," he confided, in a conspiratorial tone. "Are you having fun?"

"I hate it," Lulu said.

Chapter 1

RIGHT ON RED

"Lulu," Milo called up the stairs, "Pick up the phone. Your mother's on."

Lulu didn't move. She was in the hall just above, sitting on the short flight of steps leading to her room, her heron-like legs folded under her. She had been there, listening, since he started the phone conversation. Milo's voice carried. From where she sat she could hear everything. As long as she stayed completely still. Even in her anger at being out here in L.A., she'd figured this out.

"Lulu," he called again, "Come on. She's waiting."

Lulu had known when the phone started ringing that it was her mother. In fact, before the landline rang, Lulu had listened as mummy's distinct ringtone played three times on her cell — but she hadn't answered. Just hearing Milo's side of the conversation, though, Lulu would have known he was talking to her mother — there was an edge in his voice whenever he spoke to her. Even now, the air crackled as he called up the stairs.

It was the same each time they spoke. Lulu always hoped that, maybe this time, it would be different. A little piece of her believed her parents would one day remember they used to get along. Lulu knew it was unlikely. Yet some part of her continued to cling to that possibility. She needed to prove to herself, over and over, that they could not be put back together.

She had been on the step as the landline started ringing, and had heard the whole conversation. That was the way she could get the real news from home — even if one-sided.

"Hi. How is it going?" Milo had asked. "How are you feeling?"

There was a long pause. "I'm sorry to hear how tiring this is. How are you holding up though?"

Another pause, even longer. "Are they being helpful at least?"

Another long pause. Then he was saying, "No, she seems fine. Really. She's settling in."

"Lulu." he called again, "Get the phone. I can't wait for you right now."

Lulu missed her mother all the time. It was almost a physical ache. She longed to be home. But the only place she allowed herself to cry was in the shower. Lulu took an extra-long shower every day.

Even so, she did not stand up in response to Milo's words. She had been thinking about this call all day — planning what she wanted to say to her mother, rehearsing in her mind how she would say it. But now that mummy was on the phone, all Lulu felt was anger. It paralyzed her. Whenever her mother called, Lulu's unhappiness about being in Los Angeles boiled over. How could mummy have sentenced her to this?

Lulu was furious. But she also knew she would be furious with herself later — for wasting this time when all she wanted was to talk to her mother. Yet the anger swept over her.

Lulu had been in L.A. five days now — angry the entire time. She hated every minute. She hated the house — soulless and cold. It was decorated in what Granny would have dismissed as 'Early Trump.' She was angry about her bedroom, bigger and far grander than her own at home. What was she doing with a steam shower that had 10 nozzles?

She was angry at her father, whom she hadn't spent this much time with in years. She felt utterly disconnected from him. She was angry at Francesca, his latest wife, who cooed every time she spoke.

Since Lulu arrived in L.A. Saturday, she had felt uncomfortable around Francesca. At first, Lulu couldn't even look directly at her. She talked to a space just over her stepmother's shoulder. Now, if only because she heard Granny's voice drilling it in, Lulu looked Francesca in the eye when speaking to her.

Lulu could barely remember her other stepmother – she had been so young then and Milo's marriage to Daphne Simmons marriage had been so brief. But over the years she had met many of her father's girlfriends, if briefly. She'd never felt like this though.

And the feeling seemed mutual. Lulu could sense she made her stepmother uneasy. Francesca's nostrils seemed to flare whenever she talked to her – as if she were smelling something slightly unpleasant. Within two days, Lulu realized that Francesca never acknowledged her presence in a room unless Milo was there as well. She didn't bother to say hello, otherwise, and looked right past her.

Try as she might, Lulu could not fathom how a man, who had supposedly once loved mummy, could now be in love with someone like Francesca. Nothing about her seemed authentic. Lulu felt her stepmother never stopped acting.

Even as Lulu looked for similarities between her mother and Francesca, all she saw were differences. Francesca's accented purr was worlds apart from Claire's mid-Atlantic drawl – a tarantella versus a fugue. The silvery laugh and provocative looks through thick lashes were nothing like her mother's throaty chuckle and clear-eyed gaze.

Her mother was straightforward and serenely capable. Her stepmother, meanwhile, projected an aura of helplessness. Lulu had watched as men – everyone from studio executives to waiters – displayed an eagerness to laugh too hard at her jokes, or fetch her a drink too energetically. If she scraped her finger, men reacted as if she had dodged a bullet. But Lulu was sure there was a steely ruthlessness at the core of Francesca's yielding softness. It amazed her that her father couldn't see this.

It was not just Milo and his wife. Lulu was angry at all these people she had to meet – people who kept asking her if she was having fun here in L.A.

"No," she wanted to scream, "Of course not." But on the checklist of responses, that was not an option.

Most of all, however, Lulu was angry at her mother. It was irrational, but she felt abandoned. She was furious that her mother was not there for her; that she hadn't had the strength to resist this terrible sickness. Worse, that her mother had turned into this strange voice on the phone.

Some part of Lulu knew this was fear about her mother's illness and what the result might ultimately be. But hating everything about L.A., and resenting mummy for sending her here, would do — at least for a while.

It was a rotten decision. She knew her mother had cancer — she had sat Lulu down and explained the operation, the course of radiation required, the additional chemo. But Lulu could never have imagined this would mean that she would have to spend the summer in Los Angeles with Milo.

She hadn't spent this much time with her father since the divorce. At most, it had been a few days in Aspen before Christmas and then part of a week in late August. This was almost three months, and most of it in Los Angeles — a place all the Sturgeses talked about with disdain. She had tried to reason with her mother. But nothing would change her mind.

So here Lulu sat, brooding, at the top of the stairs, while Milo called up to her. Most people would not have picked up on the edge in Milo's voice when he spoke with Claire, a sort of clipped briskness.

She vividly remembered when she first heard this tone — those last months in the house on Camden. She had been so young, but she could tell his voice was different. She decided that by now it was probably ingrained — his default tone when talking to her mother.

Lulu was five the year of the divorce. It had felt to her like that entire year was one long fight — though the marriage unraveled in far less time. The long simmering silences, punctuated by bursts of accusations and slammed doors, took less than a few months to boil over. Lulu still felt like she carried a flipbook with photos of each minute of her last day at Camden. Mostly, though, she remembered crying.

But that was when her mother stopped crying. Claire had decided to pack up and leave. So she did. They got on a plane and went back East, to her family. She closed the door on Milo — and her life in Hollywood.

"Lulu, what are you doing?" She could hear Milo starting up the stairs. "Your mother is on the phone. You need to pick up."

"I have it," Lulu called down, as she stood up and went to the phone in a sitting room off the landing. She picked it up slowly and could barely bring herself to speak. "Hi," she said.

"Lulu," mummy's voice was almost a whisper. It felt like a caress through the phone line. Claire might have been reaching out to smooth her hair. "Hi, darling," she said in the strange husky voice that Lulu couldn't get used to. "I called on your cell but it went right to voicemail. There must be terrible reception at the house, since I can never get through. I remember how the canyons can be tricky. So I called the landline again. How is everything, darling?

"Fine," Lulu answered. She was already crying. She felt unable to say anything beyond a monosyllable. There was silence on the line.

"I know you want to be here, darling," her mother started again, "But, right now, it's better if you stay out there. And it's wonderful for you to spend time with your father. He's wanted this for so long, you know. He wants you to see his life there — where he grew up and what he does."

"It's okay," she heard herself saying. "I'm having fun." There was a long pause while Lulu searched for something to talk about. So much seemed off-limits. She also didn't want to tell her mother anything — withholding information felt good somehow. She could punish her mother by not telling her what was going on. Even though it only added to her own loneliness.

"Is Aunt Grace still there?"

Lulu didn't care if Aunt Grace was there. Yet Lulu had finally understood just how serious her mother's illness was only after she learned that her aunt was coming up to Boston instead of going to Toulon, where she taught an immersion French program for her Bryn Mawr students every summer.

Lulu really wanted to ask her mother how she was feeling, how the treatments were going. She wanted to tell her mother how inauthentic Francesca was — or "Chesca" as Milo called her; how lifeless the house felt

— like a Kardashian hostel; how horrible all of L.A. was. She wanted to tell her mother about how she sat next to an important artist at a big party, about the art world and the movie stars there. She wanted to tell her mother that if she was home, there would be no worries about whether she would be in the way. She wanted to insist, again, that she should be there with her mother.

Instead, she asked about Aunt Grace.

"Yes, she's still here" her mother's words sounded like a sigh. "It's so nice to have her. She's holding Web office hours, skyping with her Ph.D. students in France twice a week. Meanwhile, she's running interference for me here. You know how Granny and Pop-Pop can be. And I am so glad you're doing okay there." Her voice seemed to be drifting further away with each word.

There was another long silence. "How's Abby?" Her mother asked, "Is she having a good time in Italy with her parents?"

"I guess," Lulu said. She didn't want to tell her mother that she had been ignoring texts from Abby Spencer, her BFF. Of course she was following Abby's trip on Facebook and checking her Snapchat photos on the special account under her full name, Jane Abbot Spencer, that only her closest friends knew about. But every time she looked at Abby's Facebook page, to check in on her trip, that life felt more like an alternate universe.

Though Lulu was following several other friends as well, she had maintained radio silence with all of them — though not responding to Abby was the hardest — because she didn't want to talk about her mother's illness. She certainly didn't want to see words like cancer and radiation spelled out — even in a text to Abby.

That was the one good thing about being in L.A. Lulu had decided. It almost felt like she was on vacation from her real life — taking a hiatus from the overarching sadness she had been living with this entire year. Los Angeles, physically and emotionally, was light-years away from all her friends — and that aspect worked fine for Lulu right now. Not that she had stopped brooding about her mother's illness — but at least she didn't have to discuss it with anyone.

It was a relief to take this break from her friends' continual questions about mummy. Because they asked — since mummy was the one parent they confided in. Maybe it was because she was invariably amused rather than outraged or even shocked about what she called their "shenanigans." When they felt unsure or worried, she was always ready to help them figure out what was going on and what to do about it. After all, as a museum conservator, she was a professional at putting together puzzles of damaged or broken pieces of art.

Now Lulu now felt there was no one in her life she could rely on for this sort of help. Even her friends felt so distant. It was like she was looking at them through a scrim of sorrow. The terror she was confronting and the issues they were worrying about were exponentially different. She couldn't believe these were the sorts of problems that had once so upset her.

When Lulu landed in L.A. she realized how tired she was of telling her friends that, of course, her mother was doing fine. Of course, everything was going to be all right. She needed a break from having to be upbeat when they asked her how she was feeling – or when mummy's friends asked her how she was doing.

People out here didn't know what mummy was going through. So they didn't keep asking how her mother was doing – or how she was feeling about it. They just worried about where Los Angeles ranked on the fun meter.

There was another long pause. "Listen, darling," her mother breathed into the phone, "I'm feeling a bit tired. I just wanted to hear your voice. I'll call you again tomorrow. I love you so much."

She was gone.

Lulu slowly walked over to hang up the phone, flooded by all the things she had wanted to say. Her weeping turned to sobs. The tears lasted longer than the call.

Gradually, Lulu realized she could hear voices downstairs. She didn't want to be alone, thinking about what she should have said – which she did after all these calls. She splashed cold water on her face and headed downstairs.

Milo was in the library with Cesare. She would have known his voice anywhere, though she hadn't heard it in years. He spoke in a thick French rasp — almost a parody of a French accent. He was one old friend of Milo's whom Lulu did remember. When she was little, whenever he came to visit, he brought huge stuffed animals — two or even three times her size. One hulking gorilla terrified her for weeks.

Cesare was in the middle of a story as she paused at the threshold. Milo, on a sofa facing the door, motioned her to come in. "Lulu's here," he said to Cesare.

Cesare turned around, then got up when he saw her. He enveloped her in a bear hug. "Shit, is this Lulu!" His French accent was even more guttural than she remembered. Could he have gotten more French?

He kissed her on the forehead. "I would have known you anywhere. You look so much like your mother. We were all madly in love with her, you know. But you're so grown-up now! I can't believe it! How old are you? Sixteen?"

"Fifteen," Lulu answered.

He was still hugging her, but started to laugh as he released her. "Jailbait," he said. "So what are you up to? Are you having fun here?"

"Of course," she answered, on automatic pilot.

Cesare Rutani's friendship with Milo stretched back to their childhood. Abe, Milo's father, was friendly with Cesare's father, a leading Italian industrialist. He was a chemist whose fascination with metallurgy had built a chemical empire. They met one August, aboard Sam Spiegel's yacht, when the boys were both little. The boat was anchored just east of Antibes, near the Rutanis' villa. Antonio had come for cocktails the day before, and reciprocated by inviting Spiegel's entire party for lunch — which had evolved into a long, lubricated dinner. In the summers after, the families spent time together in the south of France. It went on like this until Milo's father lost his studio job — and the summer idylls stopped.

Milo and Cesare drifted apart as well. But they ran into each other on Ibiza a few years after college — or, rather, after Milo had graduated and Cesare finally decided that he was not going to try sophomore year at yet another school. Years later, they were still friends.

Cesare was intensely charming, a heavyset man who was light on his feet — whether in conversation or the dance floor. In another era, he would have been the classic playboy — driving fast cars, dating beautiful women, knowing the right wine, doing a mean rumba and probably dying young — or at least before his time — on that dangerous curve in Paris where both Porfirio Rubirosa and Aly Khan had spun out. In fact, Cesare did drive fast and date beautiful women. He was partial to the creamy minor royalty of Middle Europe, aristocrats from long-forgotten principalities that had once been incorporated into now equally forgotten Soviet bloc states behind the Iron Curtain. But he also operated, in the most off-handed manner, as an influential contemporary art consultant — buying just ahead of the curve and pulling his clients along with him.

"Sit down, Lulu," Milo said. "Cesare is just starting a story. He says it's all over London." He patted the sofa beside him.

"I'll clean it up — the PG-13 version," Cesare promised. "So Jim flew to London Thursday, to surprise Candace for her birthday."

Even Lulu knew he was talking about Jim Reynolds and Candace Tolkin, the current "It" couple. Candace had the soft golden glow of an iconic California blonde, though she had grown up on the Upper East Side of Manhattan. He had a mumblecore slacker's unkempt good looks. The ups and downs of their relationship had filled magazine covers for more than a year now. Lulu knew Tolkin was shooting a period romantic comedy in London, while Reynolds was doing a thriller in Hong Kong and Australia.

"He got the studio jet, and flew something like 16 hours to get there," Cesare continued. "He had a car meet him at the airport, to take him to her room at Claridge's. Candace's personal assistant was the only one there though. She acts flustered and says Candace is having dinner at The Ivy with the movie's director, Brian Thomas. He's an old friend of Jim's.

"So Jim drops off his bag and heads over to The Ivy. When he walks in, Candace jumps up and gives him a big kiss, saying how thrilled she is.

"But there's something weird going down. Even as Jim is standing there, Candace sits back down next to Brian and keeps leaning over to him, whispering in his ear. Her hand stays on his knee, their heads stay close together. Brian is looking a bit uncomfortable. Suddenly, Jim realizes that she is fu—sleeping with Brian. He sees that she is so caught up with it all — with starring in the movie and being with the director, with seeing herself as the toast of London and having the British tabs follow her every move — that she doesn't care if he knows it or not—"

"Boun giorno, darling," Francesca announced, flinging her arms wide as she walked into the room. Cesare broke off and stood up as Francesca threw her arms around him, cooing with delight. Lulu decided Francesca wasn't tall enough to pull off this grand gesture.

Francesca gave Milo a kiss, and he filled her in on the story as she bent to kiss Lulu hello. It was an air kiss. But Lulu still had to stop herself from wincing.

"Jim flies to London to see Candace and discovers she is sleeping with Brian Thomas," Milo said.

Francesca raised her eyes and was shaking her head as she sat down beside Cesare. "What a dope," she said. "Brian's not even a good director." Both men laughed. "From what I've heard, she not only needs a good director — she needs a great editor."

"Jim flew in to surprise Candace for her birthday and realized it as he sat at dinner with them," Cesare continued. "He sits there for one course, watching them share private jokes. Then he looks down at his phone, says "I have to take this," excuses himself and leaves the room. They think he's on a call. But it turns out he has left the restaurant, gotten into his car and had the driver take him back to the plane. He stops by her hotel on the way, to pick up his bag. He must have used that time to have his pilots get the jet ready. Cause it's set to go when he arrives. I don't know how the crew pulled it off, but he's on the ground in London less than four hours."

Milo is laughing. "How long did it take Candace and Brian to realize he was gone?" he asked.

"A while," said Cesare. "Maybe they thought he had also gone to the loo. Or the call was from the set. But after about 45 minutes, I heard, they asked the waiter and he told them Jim had left the restaurant. Right before the plane took off, Jim texted her that it was over. He asked where he should send her clothes. He said he wanted to get them out of his place, since she's clearly not serious about their relationship.

"Candace got hysterical," he continued, "They had to scramble to shoot around her scenes on Thursday and Friday. Now she's going around London, crying to everyone who will listen, about how broken-hearted she is that Jim walked out. That he is the love of her life, and that he had flown in, on her birthday, just to end it with her face to face. Not quite true — especially since he gave her the kiss-off by text!"

Milo and Francesca were both laughing with him at this point. "Who told you?" Milo asked.

"The DP's an old friend," Cesare said, "He knew about Candace and Brian — most of the crew did, of course. Brian told him this story at drinks. He's saying Candace's actions at dinner were a complete surprise. Jim was his friend, after all. He would never have mentioned it. But if she was going to play it that way, who was he to stop her? Her name is above the title."

Lulu was the only one not enjoying the story. Milo was laughing so hard that his eyes were tearing. She decided his story must remind him of his own close calls on sets. He didn't say anything, and Lulu had never heard any specifics, but she knew — more from what mummy hadn't said than what she had. All Lulu knew for sure is that he had been surprised by what he called Claire's "overreaction."

Milo moved his arm from the back of the sofa to pull Lulu closer — as if he could pull her into appreciating the joke. But she was not going to like it, even as she slid nearer. She was thinking about her mother and what life must have been like for her with Milo.

"How long are you in town?" Milo asked Cesare. "Why don't you come out to the beach with us for a movie Sunday. We're going to Fred and Hailey's in Malibu."

"I came in for a party on Monday," he answered. "I have meetings Monday and early Tuesday. But Sunday should be fine. Should I call them?"

"It'll be OK," Milo assured him, "I'll let them know. They'll be delighted to see you! Just tell that story."

Milo stood up. "I have to run a quick errand. Stay here and catch up with Chesca. She'd love to hear what's up in London. I'll be back soon." He turned to Lulu, "Why don't you come, Lulu?" he asked, "I can show you some things on the way." It sounded more like a demand than an invitation. But she didn't want to stay there with Francesca in any case.

"Lulu," Milo said, as they walked into the bright sunlight, "Let's take the Aston Martin. You haven't been in it yet." Her mother had always told her that Milo loved his toys, and this was obvious in the way he gestured toward the car. There was a large measure of self-satisfaction in his movement. The car was an icy blue-green, just slightly paler than his eyes. She wondered if this was why he had chosen that color. "We'll take Mulholland," he said, "so you can see the city."

He turned left on the canyon, heading up the hill. She could feel his eyes look toward her occasionally, a quick sideways glance, though he remained focused on the twists and turns of the road. He seemed to be tracing a pattern he knew by heart.

Milo drove fast. Passing one turn, he slowed almost imperceptibly, "I grew up on this street, Tower Road," he said. "Danny Kaye lived down the block. I remember how he and his wife, Sylvia Fine, had the greatest parties for kids. My father ended up selling the house when I was in high school. We moved over to Laurel Canyon. I'll take you by both houses later this summer."

They rode in silence for a while. Lulu looked out the window as the houses sped by. The clash of architecture was dizzying, just as her mother had described. There was an elegant French chateau, next to a sleek '50s post-and-beam, next to a stocky Spanish colonial with red tile roof, next to a serene Asian pavilion, next to a 60's Rat-Pack retreat. It was a jarring, jangly array.

"Crazy."

Milo turned. "What did you say, Lulu?" he asked.

She had been thinking this for days now, but had said nothing. "I said it's so crazy. All these different kinds of architecture jumbled together," she explained — and backtracked, "It's weird."

"It's very American, Lulu," he said, "Only more so — America on steroids.

"America is about reinvention, Lulu" he continued. "It's the American Dream, to head West and re-imagine yourself, recreating who you are. California was the apotheosis, Lulu. It's the end of the continent — the end of the line. People came here to escape their past, Lulu, looking for that fresh beginning. Especially in Hollywood."

She wondered why grown-ups never addressed the point. This was one thing Milo had in common with mummy. What did this have to do with houses? "So that's why these houses are so wacky?" she asked. She didn't bother to hide her sarcasm.

"Yes, Lulu," Milo answered, "it is. Think about it," he began again, in what she recognized was his instructor mode. It was his comfort zone. She heard it often when he talked with her stepmother about Hollywood.

"All these people, Lulu, came out here chasing the American Dream. In Los Angeles it meant, for one thing, they could have the house they'd always wanted.

"They didn't care what style was next door, Lulu, or down the block. You could have a New England clapboard next to a California craftsman bungalow. I grew up in a big Spanish colonial built by one of Goldwyn's first partners. And, Lulu, one regular at your grandfather's weekly poker game, just down the block, lived in a massive Regency pile."

Lulu realized this answer was about Milo, that he was trying to explain who he was. Didn't he see, she thought, it was too late? Saying her name every other sentence couldn't make up for the lifetime of not talking.

"On top of that, Lulu, this is Hollywood. Movie people had license to do whatever they wanted. They still do. They came here to escape rules. It's a frontier town — no veneer.

"Hollywood has always been about breaking rules, Lulu. The older parts of L.A. — Pasadena and Hancock Park — restricted movie people. That was where the Downtown powerbrokers lived — the bankers and lawyers and real estate developers. For them, 'Hollywood' was code for undesirables — it meant Jews, actors, gays, the "artistic" types with loose morals. People they considered marginal.

"So the movie colony built its own L.A. — in Beverly Hills and Los Feliz. And they were always testing the limits, Lulu" Milo continued, "They lived without putting on the brakes. During Prohibition, they drank and took drugs and partied on big gambling boats, anchored just outside city limits. The movie people ignored all sorts of laws — those applied to everyone else.

"Just think about the basics here," Milo persisted, "like red lights. You can turn on red most anywhere in America now. But when I grew up, you only could do it out West. I drove cross country one summer during college, and was surprised it wasn't allowed everywhere. But I shouldn't have been. Right on red is pure L.A.

"For some people in Hollywood, Lulu," he continued, "life is lived without ever stepping on the brakes. If they want to do something, Lulu, they do it. No one says, 'stop.'"

I don't get this metaphor, Lulu thought, it's dumb. "You stop at a stop sign," she pointed out.

"You know what I'm saying," he persisted, "The system in Hollywood encourages people to be out of control. I've seen it all my life. Even your grandfather. When he was at the top, he treated everyone miserably – including his family." Milo was silent for a moment, trapped in some memory.

"He was needlessly cruel to your grandmother – I saw it when I was younger than you." There was something in Milo's voice that Lulu couldn't remember hearing before. An underlying stillness. "He cultivated a lack of compassion. It's a great skill set for Hollywood. That's when I realized just how important compassion is." He paused, his eyes focused on the road ahead.

"People acting as if they are outside any limits happens over and over in Hollywood," his voice had returned to instruction mode, "Especially stars. Just watch, Lulu."

Milo seemed lost in his thoughts. Lulu turned to look out her window. "They don't have to take responsibility for their actions," Milo continued, almost as an afterthought, and she looked toward him again. "They have people to take care of that. Ronald Reagan was a total product of Hollywood. When he was president, and a big scandal broke, he announced: 'Mistakes were made.' You see, somehow, they were made. But no one was responsible."

He fell silent again, lost in memory. They turned onto Mulholland, and in certain places, between the houses, she could see the entire Valley spread out before her. It seemed to extend forever, refracting the dazzling light.

Milo had been gathering his thoughts. "You know, sweetie," he said, "I really like having you here, Lulu."

Lulu thought again about how often he said her name. She had read that using a person's name establishes intimacy — one reason politicians do it so often. She realized, suddenly, that most people she had met here in Los Angeles did it. Some said her name virtually every other sentence. But when Milo did this, it seemed to mean something more. As if he had been waiting for years to say her name — and now couldn't say it enough.

"I know this is hard for you, Lulu" Milo started again. "But your mother and I have been talking a long time about you spending more time in L.A. I've wanted you to visit like this for years."

Lulu was startled. This was news to her.

"Los Angeles and my life here are part of who you are," Milo said. His voice had a note of pleading. She was caught off guard. "You are more than just the Sturgeses and your mom's family back East.

"This is also you," he insisted. "Your grandfather started with nothing. He barely finished high school. But he worked his way up until he ran a big studio in the days when that was as important as it got here. And his father-in-law, my mother's father, was also a big deal — a powerful agent.

"So, Lulu, this is where I come from. You need to understand this part of your heritage. You need to know my life, Lulu. It's your life, too.

"Chesca has also been dying to spend some real time with you," he continued. He said this as if were an enticement. "I want you to know her. She's a wonderful, joyful woman. And she's helped me become a better person. Chesca knows how much I love you and care about you. How important you are to me."

Milo seemed to be considering each word. "I'm not sure you realize how much you mean to me, Lulu," he said softly. "I have missed having you in my life. I know I haven't been there for you — and I know I can't make up for all that lost time.

"But I want you to give me a chance, Lulu. I want this to change. I've wanted it to change for a while now. I want you — Chesca and I both want you — to be happy here — to have some fun this summer. Have some fun with us."

"The thing is, Lulu," his tone grew more serious, "your mother also needs you to do this now. You have to think of her as well. The treatment she has to go through is rough, and she needs to concentrate on getting better. She has to give that all her attention and energy. She can't worry about how you are doing out here.

"With you in Los Angeles, Lulu, she can focus on getting well. Her doctors talked with us, and we all decided that having you here with me would be best for her right now. "And it would be good for you, too. It's a win-win situation. So you need to try to make it work. You may be surprised by how much you like it, Lulu."

He paused for a moment, smiling down at her, before continuing in a cajoling tone. "You can have fun here, Lulu," he said, "without thinking you're betraying your mother.

Give it a shot. It will make it easier on everyone — especially you. And, Lulu, you're what I care about most. You should know that."

Milo waited for her to respond. He glanced over as she considered what he had said.

Lulu didn't think she could ever like Los Angeles. If nothing else, she had spent too many years hearing Granny and Pop-Pop talk about it with dismay, if not disdain. Her mother usually let their barbs pass without comment. For the first time, however, Lulu questioned whether that silence signaled agreement. Maybe mummy was just tired of arguing.

Lulu had sensed this ideological scuffle between mummy and her parents started years ago — long before she was born. Maybe part of it was that Miranda Thayer Sturges had never gotten over the fact that Claire, her youngest child, had decamped to Los Angeles and abandoned their East Coast life. Mummy had obviously been fascinated — if only for a time — by Hollywood's allure. It was so clearly a world apart from the one she grew up in. Yet Lulu now felt that some of it — the cosseted, stratified aspects — might have felt oddly familiar.

Lulu also couldn't help wonder why her mother never told her that Milo wanted her to spend time with him. Maybe, she thought, her mother felt she would get pulled into the life here and never want to go home. Stay in this weird, soulless life! With Francesca! As if.

But Lulu kept circling around the fact that Milo said he'd been talking for years about her visiting. It had to be true — since it was so easy to check. She had long wondered what had pulled her mother so far away from her family. And then pushed her back.

Lulu also realized she was tired of being angry — exhausted after less than a week. Yet she had tried to cling to her anger — to show these people that her life back East with her mother was what mattered. That this was like exile to some sort of cultural Siberia.

Now, after listening to Milo, Lulu could admit to herself that a part of her had long wanted to spend time with her father here in Los Angeles. It was void in her life she wanted to fill.

She didn't fully understand, but Milo, known for getting over rough ground as lightly as possible, was giving her an opportunity to soften her anger without feeling disloyal to her mother. She sensed what he was offering, though, and took it.

"Okay," she said, mumbling her acceptance. Then she smiled at Milo. "I'll give it a try. I don't want mummy to have to worry about me." She paused for more than a beat before adding, more quietly, in an almost offhand manner, "And I would like to spend more time with you."

"That's great to hear, Lulu" her father said. His smiled deepened — and relaxed. Lulu suddenly realized it had been tense before. He reached out to put his hand on hers. "You know, this is a great time for you to be here. I'm in the middle of prepping a movie, and that means I am in town. We start in North Carolina in late September, and we're setting up the locations now. So I can spend real time with you. This is gonna be terrific, Lulu! Just wait."

He began taking Mulholland's curves even more slowly. "We're going to Ted Welling's," Milo explained.

"You know, he's probably one of my oldest friends in L.A., Lulu — I've known him since we were kids. And I still work with him. How many people can say that?

"We met in high school, Lulu" he continued. "at Harvard-Westlake — it was just called Harvard then. His mother, like mine, was getting regular calls from the headmaster — so our parents got to know each other and eventually became friends.

"My parents were the first movie people that Ted's family ever invited to their home. And believe me, they knew that A.J. Flintridge had once been Abe Fleischman. They were the epitome of conservative Angelinos — the people who built L.A. That was the entire Los Angeles power structure then — Downtown. Movie people were pariahs — unclean. No mixing allowed.

"I had never met people like Ted's parents. They seemed so parochial — and intolerant. But they started having dinner with your grandfather and grandmother, and I heard from Ted how much they enjoyed my father's — your grandfather's — stories. They became real friends, Lulu. In fact, Ted's parents, especially his father, could be very funny. I decided they must have been bored out of their minds with their friends in the L.A. establishment. I know Ted was.

"And he's known you since you were a baby, Lulu. He started calling you 'contessa' when you were little. Remember? There's this movie called "The Barefoot Contessa," You were always barefoot. In fact, you were mostly running around naked as a little girl. And he would tease you about sitting up so straight — since you were very little. You took after your mother even then."

They turned off the road into a driveway, and stopped at a large gate. Milo buzzed the intercom. "We're just picking something up here," he explained to Lulu. "Then we're heading back."

A woman's voice came on the speaker, "Yes?"

"Hi," he said, "It's Milo."

"Hi, darlin'," the voice said, as the gate swung open.

When Lulu had visited Milo in the summers, she had seen Ted. But she had never been to his house in L.A. Milo turned down the long, steep drive. He seemed to drive on automatic pilot, oblivious to the lush bamboo curtain that rustled against the car, blocking the view ahead. Then they turned on a wide curve and the curtain of green parted. Lulu saw a massive French chateau with a large fountain out front. It looked digitally manipulated — an 18th century baroque villa with the city of L.A. spread out behind it.

She knew that Ted's grandfather and father had been developers and oil wildcatters — part of the oligarchy that built and controlled Los Angeles. But she was still stunned.

She sat back, absorbing the view. Milo turned to her, now that she had the full effect, and smiled. "Teddy's grandfather, Thaddeus Welling, bought this in the Loire valley, Lulu" he said, "right after World War I. When money was money." He smiled at her. "Thaddeus had it moved here. They took it apart and he shipped it across the Atlantic and then through the Panama Canal. He got the fountain there, too, Lulu.

"Re-assembling it took almost two years. And even though they had numbered each stone, after they finished it, they ended up with extra. So he built a little studio with them. Ted uses it as his office now."

Milo was still smiling as he pulled the car around the fountain. Water cascaded in the center, over three hefty bronze mermaids, and spouted from the sides to entwine the surrounding circlet of plump leaping dolphins. As they got out of the car, the front door opened and a young woman was standing there in a bikini, a sarong tied around her waist. She was the opposite of hefty.

"Hey Milo," she said, holding the door open. A shaft of light lit the room behind her, dark in contrast to the diamond-hard brightness outside.

Milo put his arm around Lulu as they walked toward the door. "This is Lulu," he said. "Lulu, this is Jennifer."

"Miles!" A man emerged out of the darkness behind Jennifer and waved them into the house. "And Contessa! How long you been here now, kiddo?"

"It's almost a week, Uncle Ted," she said, as she kissed him hello. "It's nice to be here with my Dad."

Ted gave her a close look as he took the cigarette out of his mouth and hugged her. He was speaking in a low voice, but that was his normal tone. He always seemed to be confiding the most delicious secret — each word wrapped up like a precious gift. "Your dad is so happy to have you here," he confided, "And I know your mom is going to be fine. You're beginning to look so much like her that I feel young again! She was a real heart-breaker, you know. But she only cared about your dad. She wouldn't give any of us a tumble. Believe me, we tried."

Lulu could feel herself blushing. Talking about herself always made her nervous. "That's so nice of you to say, Uncle Ted." She looked down at her feet as she mumbled a response. "But I really don't look like her. My eyes are too far apart, my chin is all wrong and my legs are like a stork. She's beautiful."

Ted tilted her head up and smiled at her. "Have you looked in the mirror recently, Contessa?"

Ted turned to hug Milo hello. The cigarette stayed in his mouth. He was wearing worn white jeans and a pale blue oxford shirt with the shirt-tails out. Lulu realized she had never seen him in anything else, no matter the occasion. This particular blue shirt was a coarse linen. "I thought we said 5 o'clock, Miles," he said. "You want a drink?"

"Water's fine," Milo said, "Lulu, you want anything?"

They walked into the house, where few lights were on in the wide front hall or the vast living room that spread out before her. But she could see arrangements of overstuffed sofas and armchairs as light poured in from a sweep of French doors along the opposite wall. Beyond, down a few steps, was a Grecian pool, as stately as the house, flanked by a large cabana.

The glare off the water made the contrast between inside and out even sharper. Lulu started — on the far side of the pool she could count at least seven young women on chaise lounges, wearing the smallest bikinis she had ever seen. But even that must have made them feel overdressed, for most wore just the bottoms. She had somehow thought only Ted and Jen were there.

"Jen," Ted said, "That lemonade in the fridge might be just the thing for Lulu."

"I'm fine," Lulu said, "I don't want anything."

But Jennifer was already heading into the darkness toward the kitchen. "This is a perfect day for lemonade," Ted said. "I'm mixing mine with gin, Lulu, but it's quite good without it. Or so I've been told

"It's ready, Miles, even though you're early," Ted continued, "Come on out to the patio." He headed for one of the French doors. Milo followed, Lulu in tow.

Three of the women waved to Milo as he walked into the sunlight. He waved back, then looked over at

Ted. "Two are friends of Jen's," Ted said, answering a question that hadn't been asked, "The others were with Stuart last night. I ran into him at Dan Tana's. They were all having dinner.

"I sat with them for a drink, or two, and must have said something, because they showed up about two hours ago. I know I've seen them around town, but I'm not sure who they are exactly." He shrugged. "Let me get you those pages, Miles."

As he headed off toward the small stone building just left of the cabana, he looked back over his shoulder, "Contessa, there are snacks on the table — if you're interested." She saw a large pitcher surrounded by tall drinking glasses on the table nearby, as well as many small bottles of water. And there was indeed an assortment of snacks, as Ted called them, though Lulu would have called it a feast — a fat disk of runny cheese next to a crusty loaf of bread on a wooden oval; guacamole and chips; pasta salad studded with olives and broccoli rabe, a big bowl of plums and apricots.

Lulu decided everyone must be on a strict diet, because most of the food looked untouched. She took a chip and loaded it with guacamole. Focusing on the food, Lulu felt less embarrassed about the women being virtually naked.

Two were headed their way — straight for Milo. Both were smiling brightly. "Hi, it's Samantha Roland," the taller one, a brunette, said as she kissed him hello.

She had a shingle bob and the taut, lean body of a Paul Manship sculpture. "I read for you on 'Hang Up.' For 'Girl in the Bar.'"

"Of course," Milo said, as if meeting a long-lost friend, "You were too adorable. What's up with you?"

"I'm in that Fincher film shooting downtown," she said, clearly delighted to tell him. "And you know Monique," she said as her friend, with cascading blonde hair and even less clothing, kissed Milo hello.

"This is my daughter, Lulu," Milo said. "Lulu, meet Samantha and Monique." Both women managed to take their eyes off Milo as they said hello, but immediately turned back to the director, as if they would miss something crucial if they looked away too long.

"We're going to St. Tropez next week," Samantha said. "There's some party on July 4th that we're all flying in for. Then we're probably going to hang there a few weeks. Are you going to be over there?"

"Sounds like I should be," Milo said. "But I have some work to do here in town. You'll just have to tell me all about it."

Lulu looked at her father, but his smile bore no trace of sarcasm.

"Oh, you should come," Monique said encouragingly, "Do your work there!" She had a distinct German accent.

Milo laughed. "I wish I could," he said.

Lulu turned to Monique. "Where are you from?" she asked. "France," Monique answered, her eyes locked on Milo.

"The northeast part? Like around the Saar?" Lulu asked, proud that she had remembered the name of that region. She had studied World War I in a history class this year. "No, not at all" answered Monique, her German accent more pronounced. "Paris."

"Where are you from originally?" Lulu tried again. "Where did you grow up?"

"Paris," said Monique. She finally looked directly at Lulu. Her green eyes managed to be both vacuous and disdainful. "I grew up in Paris."

Lulu wondered if there was a town named Paris somewhere in Germany — like the one in Texas.

As if on cue, Jen was walking down the steps, carrying a glass of lemonade. "Here you go, darlin'," she said, handing Lulu the glass. "What have you been doin'? You havin' fun here?"

"Of course," Lulu said.

Ted came up behind her, carrying pink typewritten pages in his hand. He handed them to Milo and then stood close to him as he discussed what he had written. Even then, Lulu saw that Milo had to lean in to hear.

"I solved your problem, Miles," Ted said, his voice even softer than usual. Lulu realized they must have had conversations like this for years. There seemed an intimate patois. She knew Ted had written some of her father's early movies, and was obviously still on call as script doctor.

"It works now," Ted confided, "I took out those opening lines, since they were doing the opposite of what you need. It didn't set up the beat, it slowed you down. Now, you get to the bit faster. Then I reworked George's speech. So you have a better idea of why he is doing this. The entire set up for the second act is cleaner. Her actions finally make sense.

"I also tweaked that speech we talked about," Ted continued in conspiratorial tones, "You were losing me, so I cut the kitchen sequence and reworked the hallway. You lose about 12 pages — and it saves you some money, too. You're going to need it. That's quite a gimmick you have planned."

The taller woman had edged closer as the two men talked. She was now almost looking over Milo's shoulder. The men looked up at her and smiled. Ted turned and started talking to her as Milo stepped away to focus on the pages. She had to stand close to hear Ted, though she kept glancing over at Milo.

After about a minute, he was chuckling. At one point, he laughed out loud. He soon turned back to Ted. "What a maestro," he said, clapping him on the back. "You did it! This works now."

"Don't sound so surprised," Ted said.

"Listen," Milo replied. "I've got to get back. Why don't you look at that other scene as well and I'll read it all through later tonight and give you a call. I've got to tell you about Ben's anyway. Have you heard?"

"You mean Fred not showing?"

"Much more than that. Ben must have felt like he'd been sucker-punched," Milo said. "But listen, we gotta go. Come on, Lulu" He kissed Jen goodbye and headed for the stairs. Lulu took a last gulp of lemonade before she put her glass down. Ted gave her a quick hug. "It's great you're here, Contessa," he whispered, "Things with your mother will all work out. You'll see."

Milo waved a casual goodbye to the others. "Bye, girls," he called. "Great to see all of you"

He turned back to Ted, "Thanks again, maestro," he said. "I'll check in with you tonight." Milo headed up the steps to the house, with Lulu just behind him.

As they turned onto Mulholland, Milo looked over at her. "You know, Lulu," he began, "my friendship with Ted is different from many others out here. In Hollywood, friendship is transactional.

"When you're making a picture, for example, you get close to the cast and crew," he explained. "You spend hours together, working toward a common goal — to finish that picture. It's like you're in the same battalion, or the same foxhole. You're all fighting as a team to make it over that hill. Battling the weather — or the studio.

"It's one reason why so many relationships develop on a set. Actresses spend so much time with their leading man, or their directors — " Milo broke off abruptly.

After a pause, he started again. "Though it's only for a time. Then you move on to the next picture — and a new set of friends. Literally. But Ted is part of my life, even when we're not working together — though, as you can see, I pull him in whenever I need help on a script. But it's the opposite of transactional. It's the real deal.

The car moved smoothly, slicing the curves. "You know, there's something else I've been thinking, Lulu," he paused. "Your grandfather kept a diary. I found it after he died, when I was going through his papers. I had no idea. He began keeping it in the late 1950s — sort of around the time he starting seeing my mother, your grandmother — and kept at it for about a decade. From what I understand, some other studio head had written a memoir and it made quite a splash. So he decided he was not going to be one-upped by that jerk!

"He heard from one screenwriter that the best way to write a memoir was to start keeping a diary. That way, the writer told him, when he sat down to write, he would have material to work from. So he did. I wouldn't have called him the most self-reflective person." He smiled at her, though it looked more like a grimace. "In fact, that's probably the last word I'd use to describe him.

"But you know the Sturges side of your family so well. You breathe it in every day. So Abe's world might be interesting, even fun, for you to read about. And it would be a window into what life was like in Hollywood then. Which honestly, Lulu, is not that different from Hollywood today. We've gone digital, it's the 21st century — but somehow it never seems to change."

He was silent for a moment.

When he started talking again, his voice was softer. "It was really tough for me to read," he continued "You'll see why. Abe is so —" he searched for the right word, "'unkind' to your grandmother. Cruel sometimes. Not that this wasn't also true with so many of the people he came in contact with.

"But it was —" He paused, again searching for a neutral word. "'unsettling.' And then, on top of that," he smiled at her as his voice took a step back, "I'm barely mentioned. Not until I'm about one, when an actress — I think Joan Crawford — tells him I'm cute.

"I haven't thought about this diary in years, Lulu. Frankly, I must have tried to forget it." His laugh was tense. "But I've been thinking about it a lot since you've arrived. It might help you know and understand your grandfather and his life. And it could help you understand me a bit more, too.

His voice took a step back again. "It will sure give you a taste of what Hollywood was like then." He paused again. "That is, Lulu, if you would like to read it. Would you?"

His voice had an unfamiliar tentative note. Though his tone was measured, Lulu could sense how much this mattered. His offer floated there, suspended. Milo kept his eyes on the road as they turned off Mulholland and headed back down the hill.

It was true, Lulu realized, she knew nothing about this side of her family. Granny Miranda Sturges and her younger sister, Great-Aunt Edith Phillips, had plied her with countless tales about growing up in Paris and then London, when Great-Grandpapa Edgar Thayer Jr. was at the U.S. embassies there. With their older sister, Constance, now a principessa who lived in Lugano, they were the celebrated Thayer Sisters, who scandalized European society of their day. Most of their escapades involved efforts to elude Great-Gandmama Lily Winslow Thayer's autocratic rules. At times, though, Lulu found it hard to associate these imperious doyennes, her grandmother and great aunt, with Mimi and Daisy, the madcap debs sneaking out to meet their latest beaus at a nightclub. Lulu decided their stories must have been wildly embroidered over the years — how could Granny have climbed down a trellis in a midnight blue satin cocktail dress, with the straps of her dancing slippers gripped between her teeth? As if! Mummy had told her years ago that if stories sound too good to be true — they usually are.

She had barely thought about her father's side of the family, actually. Yet there was a vitality here in Hollywood she had never experienced in her grandparents' house in Boston. She wanted to understand this place better. And, she decided, she really did want to know more about her father.

She turned to him. "Okay," she said, "Sure."

"That's great, Lulu!" His response had all the exuberance hers lacked. "You know, your 16th birthday is in August. That means you'll be old enough to drive. How about if I teach you? We can start this week! And we'll get you a car as a birthday present.

"Just stick with me, Lulu," Milo said, as they picked up speed going down the hill, "You're going to have fun here."

"I hope so," she said, and tried to sound like she meant it.

"I doubt it," she was thinking. Loyalty to her mother was not put aside so easily. But then Lulu remembered how much it mattered to her mother that she make it work here. She also could finally admit to herself that she wanted to spend this time with her father — and understand more about his life. Reading that diary would help.

She smiled back at him.

CHAPTER 1-A

DIARY ENTRY OF A.J. FLINTRIDGE

TUESDAY, FEBRUARY 15, 1958: *Started the morning with Bernie on casting. Jimmy Stewart said he would do "The Cross and the Rifle," but only if we get John Ford to direct. Timing looked impossible — though we tried various shooting schedules to see if we could make this work. Decided Stewart doesn't want to do it, and this is his way of refusing. But I'm taking him to lunch at Romanoff's Friday to sound him out. Meanwhile, looking into alternatives. Gary Cooper, Greg Peck, Randolph Scott, Bill Holden or Joel McCrea could do it. Bernie to begin checking availability.*

The girl we cast as the daughter in "The Restless Wind" came in yesterday for costume fittings. Last month we hired a sexy girl with a nice ass and now she shows up with a can so big two people should be carrying it. Maybe three. Bernie told her that unless she can lose the weight by the time production starts — three weeks — we need to replace her. We start going through some possibilities. Mentioned the girl I met at Ciro's. Bernie's going to call her in.

At the Executive Dining Room, we talked Russian threats and Sputnik.

Detoured to my office on way to the cutting room. Sara Steinhardt and Nancy had called. Hadn't heard from Nancy in months. Was about to return her call, when Arlene added King Vidor had called back.

He was my first call, and I start right in on the Tower Road house — as usual. I told him that I'd been driving by last week and the housekeeper had shown me through again. I lust after this Wallace Neff house that Vidor built — even more than I still think about Hedy. Which is a lot. I told him that I'd heard rumors it was coming on the market again. He said it's true. Made note to call my realtor & have her follow up. Maybe this will be the year!

Then called Nancy. Haven't talked to her since her trip down the aisle four months ago. We'd been fucking once a week — the last time was two days before the wedding. I never let her spend the night though. I asked her how it was going. She blurts out, "I married the worst fuck in Los Angeles." Made plans to get together Monday night.

Still thinking about this as I dialed Sara. She'd left word she was calling about dinner tomorrow — we'd talked about getting together. Turns out she's expecting me to eat with her family. She's hinted about this for more than five weeks now. I thought I had put her off.

Taking out the oldest daughter of a powerful agent like Arnie Steinhardt was not a bad career move. But this is getting too serious — for her. A family dinner with the Steinhardts was a place I didn't want to be. Especially on a Friday. Yet Arnie was too important for me to just dump her.

I said I had to work — for the entire weekend. As I was talking to her, I decided that I would see Caroline tomorrow night as well as tonight. She was too smart to get the wrong idea. And a good lay. Like Francie, who I was seeing Saturday. Both these girls knew when I wasn't in the mood to talk — an essential skill in a successful party girl. And something Sara couldn't figure out. As the daughter of a big-deal Hollywood player, though, she possessed other assets.

I said I would call next week. It was irritating that she sounded near tears. I decided to be nicer, since I didn't have to see her 'til Tuesday — at the earliest.

Went to cutting room to see rough assemblage of "The Hills of Rome." Charlie Feldman had wanted to demonstrate what a powerful agent he is, so he'd worked out a special deal. Under its terms — one of only two at the studio — the producer and director were allowed to have two previews and do their own edit before I could see the first cut.

But I had no time for this bullshit. I need to push the release date, so I'd demanded they run it for me now. Previews, as far as I am concerned, are a waste of time. Feldman, as expected, sided with the studio — not his client. The key thing for him is keeping us happy. Fuck the client.

As I watched this first edit, all I could think is: How did this idiot director have a career? There was no story flow and minimal coverage.

So few close-ups that we wouldn't have much latitude in cutting. I told him and the producer it was a total fucking mess. Unwatchable — and it's my job to watch movies! "This picture drives the audience out of the theaters," I told them, "People would be fighting to get out the door.

"Why are you making my life harder?" I was yelling now, "Your job is to make my life easier? Are you too much of a knucklehead to understand this?"

The director said nothing — he had been through this with me before. He knew the drill.

Went back to top and started going through reel by reel. Phil Lacy, my chief editor, sat with us and Helen was taking notes, as usual. The producer kept protesting, however, insisting he needed the previews. Finally told him that I was saving his piece-of-shit picture, that I was the best fucking editor in town and he would be a laughing stock if this pile of shit was ever seen by anyone — ever. It needed a major overhaul.

I cut six sequences. Buried under all this crap was a narrative that you could now at least follow. I decided it could work if we added a voice-over, to explain to the audience what the hell they were watching, and a strong score, to telegraph the emotion as well as parts of the plot.

I left them working on the footage. I said I'd be back after dinner, around 11:15 p.m., to see it put together.

I stopped by Projection Room 2-b to watch rushes from yesterday before heading over to Nunnally and Dorris Johnson's for cocktails.

✷ ✷ ✷ ✷

Nunnally and Dorris were having a welcoming cocktail party for Olivia de Havilland, in town from France to loop her new movie, "The Devil Makes Three." Downed Nunnally's usual lethal martinis with Richard and Sybil Burton, James and Pamela Mason, Joe and Rose Mankiewicz, among others.

Joe Mank was finishing his second double (Rose, was her usual three drinks ahead of him) and he started telling me that the movie business had short-circuited his real career. "What career was that?" I asked. After all, he had won Oscars for directing "All About Eve" and "Letter to Three Wives" and been nominated for "The Barefoot Contessa." What path did he stray from to get to the top of this profession?

He said he should have been a journalist and then a serious novelist. What planet is he from? He's never done anything else but movies. He had the briefest of reporting careers before following his brother Herman out to Hollywood to make pictures. He lucked out — as far as I'm concerned, he was not even the talented one in his family.

Nunnally joined our conversation about half-way through, and told me after that he's heard Mank tell his tale of woe before. Sometimes even when he hasn't been drinking. What this is about we have no idea.

I told Nunnally that Nancy had called today — and that I was seeing her Monday. I knew he'd appreciate it. He told me this same thing had happened to him more than a few times. We laughed about the curse of being good in bed.

* * * *

Went on to Arthur and Lenora Hornblow's for dinner. Guests had been invited for 7:00 — I showed up about 8:40, knowing they wouldn't have started dinner. I was right — it was 9:15 before we finally sat down. Typical!

One evening at Jimmy and DoDo Pendleton's I was so fed up by these endless rounds of cocktails before dinner that I walked out. Terrific Jack Woolf-designed house, but I don't wait that long for anyone. Certainly not for an interior decorator/antiques dealer. People like that wait for me.

Mary Pickford got so pickled she fell off one of Pendleton's antique shell-shaped grotto chairs — and was too drunk even to get up. Her husband Buddy Rogers took one arm and I took the other, we picked her up off the floor and sat her back down on the chair.

She was still so unsteady I wanted to take odds that she couldn't stay upright on that flimsy chair. But I couldn't collect on this because that's when I left. I don't like Mary even when she's sober — though I am not sure she ever is at this point. She's considered a mean drunk. But she was mean long before she was a drunk.

The Hornblows were giving the dinner for Bennett and Phyllis Cerf. The couples are close friends — Arthur and Bubbles were married at the Random House publisher's New York apartment. Arthur, ever the consummate producer, assembled a glittering cast for dinner: producers (Bill and Edie Goetz, Dore and Miriam Schary), directors (Billy and Audrey Wilder, Charlie and Doris Vidor) and an assortment of stars: Ty Power, Joan Crawford, George and Gracie Burns, Jane

Greer and her husband Eddy Lasker. With some added conversational sparkle supplied by Cobina Wright, the Hearst columnist, and Ruby Schinasi, Bubbles' mother.

Alfred and Jean Vanderbilt were swanning around. They're Arthur and Bubbles' horseracing friends — the Vanderbilts who'd controlled Pimlico (and the Preakness) and now run Belmont in New York. I doubt that any of Arthur's horses approached the same league as Vanderbilt's spectacular Native Dancer, though.

Right by the door, as I walked in, was a girl with a tray of daiquiris. I picked one up as I headed over to Bill and Edie Goetz — Nunnally had mentioned they just bought another Picasso. Bill almost throbbed with the thrill of conquest as he described the portrait — Marie-Thérèse Walter, at her most languorous and voluptuous. He went into such intimate detail you would have thought she was a tart he'd been pursuing for years — and finally fucked.

Not that Edie was worried about his obsession. She had the same tumescence of ownership. This couple is continually jazzed by each other. It's been 30 years, but they only seem to get happier. Some of this might still be their delight in proving Edie's father, Louis B. Mayer, so wrong. He'd predicted, to anyone who would listen, that it wouldn't last!

There was a Hollywood double vision to the party — a daughter of L.B. Mayer (Edie Goetz) standing next to a daughter of Harry Warner (Doris Vidor). It felt even stranger to see both Edie Goetz and Miriam Schary — two eras of Metro-Goldwyn-Mayer — in the same room. Dore took over after L.B. was fired. Complete changing of the guard. Now Schary is gone. Dore and Miriam's presence proved the Goetzes hadn't been friends only because Dore ran MGM while Arthur was a producer on the lot. Dore's been out of the front office for two years.

I was surprised Bill Wilder was there — Arthur had produced Billy's "Witness for the Prosecution," so I didn't think they would still be talking. Maybe Billy didn't torture him the way he has so many others. Audrey also seems to have weathered Billy's Marlene interludes. If not happy, than less maudlin.

Ty Powers looked tired. King had told me he was working with Ty on "Solomon and Sheba," — due to start shooting soon in Spain. Ty should get some rest — or start taking regular B-12 shots. Maybe two a day.

In any case, it matters to have a star, even an aging one, at dinners for out-of-towners. Though, for my money, Ty's ex-wife Linda Christian, is the one to invite. Aside from being drop-dead gorgeous, she may be the most charming woman in Hollywood. Too bad that's not an asset in the movie business. And too, too bad none of her knock-out charm ever shows up on film.

The daiquiris were deadly. By the time we finally sat down, I was almost as blurry as everyone else — if still a few drinks behind my dinner companions: Jane Greer, on my left, and Joan Crawford, on my right. When we changed to red wine at the table, they didn't slow down.

Jane talked about all the TV she's been doing. Seems the schedule is easier than shooting a film, and she's needed the flexibility ever since she had kids. But it's too bad since Jane has a face that belongs on the big screen — all planes and shadows. So sexy and mysterious you could get lost in it. Wasted on that little box.

Cobina was on the other side of Joan and we all had a great gossip — stories that couldn't make it into the paper. Any paper. Cobina can always be relied on to have the best details. We compared notes on Monty Clift.

Then Mrs. V. starts telling the entire table that foreign films present life "much more realistically." Why she decided to say this, I have no idea. Doesn't she understand she's a guest in Hollywood? Hollywood films, she insists, are nothing like real life. She went on like this for a while, and Mr. V. was starting to back her up.

No one was refuting her, or even cutting her off. They let her babble on.

She is just the sort of person I despise — her last name might get her a seat at this table, but she shouldn't be talking. Much less monopolizing the conversation. I couldn't take it — and didn't have to. "Were you in the Italian underground," I asked her, "fighting against the Nazis in occupied Rome?" "Of course not!" She started laughing, a metallic cascade. "Are you a poor Indian man who abandons his son when his young wife dies at childbirth in Calcutta?" "No."

"Are you an aging Swedish actress trying to woo back her former lover who has married a young girl?" Her laughter grew louder with each question.

"So how do you have any fucking idea how realistic those movies are? These aren't lives you know anything about. Madam, you have no clue what you're talking about."

I smiled as I said that last sentence. It usually fooled people into thinking they misunderstood my intention. But they hadn't. The thing here is we had two more courses to get through — and she was one of the guests of honor.

Not that I really cared about Hornblow at this point. His career was storied — but largely behind him.

As the dinner continued, both Joan and Cobina began showing the ill effects of those daiquiris.

It started with Cobina. She turned to her favorite complaint: How horrible her daughter, Cobina Jr., was to her. The most ungrateful, malicious child — especially after she (Cobina Sr.) had sacrificed everything for her. Cue the violins.

I'd heard this all before — I could probably recite it backwards in my sleep since Cobina starts in on this whenever she gets plastered.

It's always the same sob story: She left her wealthy stockbroker husband in Manhattan to make sure their daughter had all the advantages of European culture. Very "Dodsworth" — meeting only the right sorts of people in the chicest continental watering holes.

After years in glittering European capitals, they wound up in Hollywood during the war — more like sisters, Cobina says, than mother and daughter. Sure! But now that Cobina Jr. has a nice rich husband and three kids of her own, she only gives her mother resentment and rage.

Cobina Sr. is so in the moment here, that she must have gotten acting tips from Monty. Suddenly, she's weeping over all the sacrifices she made (I never understand how living in Venice or Paris is a sacrifice) and how she's now being repaid with viciousness.

Her weeping then shifts to dramatic sobbing. Quite effective. Cobina usually manages to work in mention of the career she could have had — and the day she met Sarah Bernhardt. (How did we miss out on this tonight?) She was a young opera singer in Europe when "The Divine Sarah" paid her the ultimate compliment. "You remind me quite a bit of me," she said. Maybe this is what inspired Cobina to such a passionate display of tears here.

But Crawford, on my other side, has no intention of yielding the field to Wright. Cobina had done a few small movie roles, but, compared to Crawford, is a rank amateur when it comes to displaying overwrought emotion. Crawford won't be upstaged — even at a dinner.

She starts in about her own children. Particularly her oldest daughter, Christina. Ungrateful, downright rotten! Before I know it, she's also sobbing. Crawford is drawing on a far deeper wellspring of tears. Cobina's like a circus pony going up against Sea Biscuit.

The entire table just looked at them. Then looked away. No one wanted to touch this. Even Greer, enveloped by the tears, knew instinctively to stay out of it. She, like the rest of the table, was busy pretending this was not happening. Unlike the others, though, she's such a remarkable talent that you believed her! I need to find a part for her!

Ruby was the one person at the table who actually acknowledging this crying scene. But only because she looked askance at anything that disrupted her daughter's dinner party.

I turned toward Ruby and started talking about the rough cut of "The Young Lions" I'd seen this week. We're thinking about using one of the actresses, so I needed to see it. I could feel the entire table almost start crying in relief about the change in subject. This topic could happily absorb everyone's attention.

"Brando is amazing," I said, "but Monty Clift is even better." Not only was the entire dinner party riveted, both girls stopped crying.

As we compared the two actor's acting techniques, the dinner party got back on track. Bubbles was so delighted she blew me a kiss. But I was still glad to leave early and head back to the studio. The one thing I regretted was missing out on the baba au rhum. I certainly had no interest in seeing the movie Arthur was screening — or hearing what that idiot, Jean Vanderbilt, thought about it.

The edit was ready for me when I got back to the studio. The flow was better, less confusing once we lost all that clutter. We went through reels 4, 5 and 6 again, slowly, then straight through to the end.

We're still going to have to reshoot the final chase — no amount of editing could make that work. But I decided they didn't have to go back to the location. This picture was already costing north of $800 thousand. Cheaper now to build the river bank here in town. This way, I can see dailies every morning. Since I clearly need to.

I'm going to look at it again in two days with a temp dub. We'll see how the music helps.

I called Caro right before I left the studio and told her I would meet her back at my house at 1:45. She was just what I needed to end the day.

CHAPTER 2

CLOSING THE DEAL: PART 1
(HOLLYWOOD HILLS)

B EN HAD BEEN WORKING ART MANNING, hard, for almost a week now.

They had done business together in past, since Manning was a powerful lawyer whose roster of A-list clients could set a deal in motion and often helped close it. He was regarded as a combative litigator, but also as a top-notch negotiator — something not always said about powerful entertainment attorneys.

When Manning came in to negotiate a deal, he never inadvertently killed it. He was not one of those lawyers whose art collections were more celebrated than their legal skills.

Ben knew that many industry lawyers were only too happy to have Manning in on a negotiation. It was one way of assuring that they would get the best possible pay-out for their client — as long as they were on the same side of the table as Manning.

Now Ben needed Manning's help for the new production company. But he was not sure how helpful Art would be. If he decided to come through, it would mean a lot for Ben around town. The nascent producer would be regarded as a real player making real pictures — not gleaning scraps thrown to him by the studio at his departure.

Ben had taken properties with him when he left Lucent. There was one in particular he had long believed could be a hit. But he needed a star like hip-hop artist Rick Howard to make that happen. And Manning was the gatekeeper.

There were other gatekeepers, of course. Many pilot fish were blocking the access to Rick Howard. Ben had been slow in realizing Manning was the key.

Robbins had wasted almost three days wooing Howard's manager, Mike Sorrento. He had even taken Sorrento to meet an influential art dealer. That was a mistake all around. The art dealer had told Ben that he had a special painting, so Ben took Mike in to see it. Ben knew, since he was giving Sorrento access to an important work, it would be a natural exchange for the manager to help secure Howard.

This art dealer was renowned for his iciness. He had a trick of only recognizing those he knew to be buyers — current or potential. Anyone else didn't exist. He was so practiced at this that there was not a flicker of acknowledgment when he looked at people not worth his attention. His strange pale eyes looked right through them without blinking, like a chameleon's. A membrane seemed to filter out all unnecessary people. Ben had always envied this attribute.

But the dealer had generated some warmth for Sorrento. He asked his assistant, another in the seemingly endless succession of beguiling hand maidens to art, to bring in something to drink. Then, responding to some secret signal, the young woman brought out an exquisite Monet canvas of Giverny. It was a misty dream in blues and greens, owned, the dealer explained, by the same family since the great-grandfather had purchased it directly from the artist.

But Bernie Madoff's Ponzi scheme had shaken the painting loose from the library walls of the family's secluded Swiss villa, then the collapse of the energy market had propelled it to his Beverly Hills gallery. It had never even been loaned for an exhibition, the dealer crowed, this was the first it had seen the light of day in public since the family acquired it more than a century before.

Ben felt in control, the feeling he most savored. It felt good that he still had enough clout to introduce Sorrento to such exclusive art. And Sorrento seemed impressed. He said immediately how much he admired, and liked, the painting.

Monet is so easy to like, Ben thought, not complicated or demanding, the way conceptual or contemporary art could be. It is a safe choice — like an Armani suit, the default uniform of Hollywood. This Monet had all the appropriate bells and whistles. As Impressionists go, Ben had to admit, it was breath-taking.

Indeed, Sorrento seemed drawn to the canvas. He stepped in close, bending down to examine it. "Look at this paint," he said, "It's piled on!" As if unable to resist, he reached out and touched a whorl of vivid green, blue and white with his fingertips. Ben saw the dealer lunge for Sorrento's arm, and literally hiss.

But Sorrento had already stepped back. His eyes, however, remained locked on the painting. "Amazing," Sorrento said in a soft voice. "But green just wouldn't work in my house. Do you have something more purple?"

The dealer gave Robbins a quick hard look while he motioned the young woman to remove the painting. There was no secret signal now. Ben felt the gallery's temperature plummet.

Ben and Sorrento moved on to Barneys, where they bonded over tropical-weight Italian cashmere, in various shades of gray, and Lucien skull crewnecks. Sorrento bought two jackets and three sweaters, working with Bernard, the salesman Ben had used for years.

It was at Barneys that Ben finally figured out Manning was the person to talk to about Howard. The lawyer exercised the real control here. Sorrento functioned more like the waiter, serving various projects. Manning was seated at the table.

Ben couldn't believe he had missed this. He decided he must be more anxious about setting up his new company than he realized. He wondered how obvious it would be if he just walked out of Barneys, leaving Sorrento with Bernard. He signaled Anita and she beeped him about an important call that had just come in. Ben excused himself and walked outside to call Manning. He set up drinks for the next day.

Over a series of drinks, Ben talked to Art about his nascent company. The news was not public yet, but Art was Hollywood's eminence grise, and Ben bet he already knew most of this anyway.

At the Tower Bar, Ben sought the lawyer's advice, and, in the process, laced admiration for Manning's long, successful career with just the right amount of envy and admiration. Then, he turned to the subject of Rick Howard.

Art Manning heard Ben out. As usual, Ben gleaned only a minimal read from him. Yet, a day later, Manning began orchestrating a meeting with Howard's brain trust. It was a complicated situation, though the whole town knew that Howard was looking for a career-changer. It had been a long time between hits. He had followed the biggest-selling record of all time with two duds.

Five years before, Howard had been the hottest recording star in the nation. His music videos were a cultural sensation. His concerts sold out online in less than 10 minutes. But the five years since Howard's last hit was almost two lifetimes in the music business. A generation had now grown up without seeing Howard on tour. They had not experienced his ferocious talent, seen how his electrifying stage presence belied his strange personal life.

For Howard's insulated life had taken a twisted turn. His lifelong anxiety about germs had escalated from an eccentricity into crippling wackiness. People used to joke about Howard's obsession with Howard Hughes – but he had long since jumped the shark. Over the last five years, Howard had turned his sprawling home at the top of Benedict into a series of interconnecting germ-free chambers. He insisted any tour would need a portable, germ-free safe chamber. For Howard, whose career depended on tours, standing on a stadium stage, surrounded by trillions of free-floating germs, was ever more difficult.

The controlled environment of a sound stage beckoned. And Ben was here to offer a solution that he knew was win-win. As always, he had worked out the odds — and there looked to be no downside.

Ben knew Howard's brain trust would assemble because they considered the singer a talent too big to fail. He had once held the world's affection, he could gain it again. Fans loved to lift someone up after a fall. So it was possible — if everyone could agree on the right path out of the wilderness.

Art set up a dinner at Sorrento's house, perched high above the Strip on one of the Bird Streets. The view was amazing, but Ben knew no one would be admiring it that night. Everyone was coming to address a big problem and Ben hoped they would realize — as so many had before — that he had the one good answer

Gil Skidmore, Howard's principle agent, was set to be there. Harry Preston, the head of Lucent Records, his record company, was also due. He was bringing the young company executive who worked most closely with Howard — and who, like the singer, was black. So this was one of those rare high-level meetings where Howard was not going to be the only African-American at the table.

Ben had invited Milo, since a director of his caliber would mean a lot in selling the project. Flintridge had not committed, but he had, nonetheless, agreed to help Ben pitch it. Ben realized this was a big withdrawal from the bank.

That made eight at the table. Any more would make it difficult to have one conversation. And Ben wanted no side chatter. He wanted the focus to be getting his film into production — clearly in everyone's interest. He wanted the whole town talking about his company — and he knew this could make that happen.

When the studio had sent out the press release about The Robbins Group, it announced the first three films. These were projects Ben had appropriated from the studio.

So the Howard movie would be Ben's first move after putting out his shingle. "Double or Nothing" was to be his calling card. It had all the right elements. He liked its attributes: highly commercial yet imaginative; a leading industry player presented in a startlingly new light, a gritty urban movie grafted onto a heartwarming story of redemption. Ben knew it could be a winner.

Before the dinner, Ben had checked in with Louis. Bringing in Howard, Robbins knew, would push this price tag higher than any discussed when setting up the company. Ben also needed to hear Louis agree this was a good idea.

Ben felt better after the call. Louis said extra funding could be found. Even in this economy, there was money sloshing around for movie investments. In harsh economic times, movies are one business that makes money — look at Hollywood during the Great Depression. In any case, many Wall Street investors yearned for a sexy investment like movies. The enticement of beautiful — and available — young women had lured East Coast money even before Jock Whitney financed "Gone With the Wind." Before William Randolph Hearst swooned over, and set up a company for, the former Ziegfeld Follies showgirl Marion Davies, or Joseph P. Kennedy obsessed about Gloria Swanson.

As Ben drove up to Sorrento's, he assessed the situation with his usual gimlet eye. He had to concede he felt queasy about the dinner. It had been set up before he formally left the studio. Sure, his move was announced when Howard's team agreed to meet with him, but he was still head of the studio — going to his office every day, tying up loose ends. Now that he was officially an independent producer, maybe some people set to be there would decide not to show.

Robbins didn't want to admit it, but he'd been unnerved by the Nauman party. He had never thought that roughly a third of his guests would leave. Was this something he needed to worry about now? Should he prepare for a life of slights? His name falling off an important agent's call list? Never making it to the top of the queue for a Gursky?

Ben cut off this unusual line of thought. It was a waste of time. He had built his many relationships over years of doing business. Relationships were what mattered in Hollywood. People would always take his calls.

Yet, Ben decided that he would need to move carefully. It was going to take longer than he had planned to assemble a deal. But he had the skills – and patience – required to win. And winning was all that mattered.

This picture was a good starting point. It would grab that attention of everyone in town. Over the years, many different directors and producers had tried to set up this script. But it had eluded, even stumped, them all.

Ben was certain that he had the key – Howard would make it work, and, despite everything, he was a superstar. Ben believed that Howard still possessed what had made him so thrilling to watch.

Now that Ben was thinking clearly, he realized he didn't have to worry about people not showing up tonight. This was Manning's invite, not his. He might lack social capital now, but Art was a man to be reckoned with in Hollywood. Ben was smiling as he got out of the car. People would not have recognized it, though, because it was the closest thing Robbins had to a real smile.

Sure enough, when he walked into Sorrento's home, just about everyone was already there. Even Howard had arrived, though, as usual, he was not speaking to anyone. He was at the other end of the room, playing with his pet squirrel.

The singer was notoriously shy, and had long ago adopted the protective habit of taking his squirrel everywhere – while he played with his pet, he did not have to speak to anyone. Ben remembered one night, about four years ago, when Rick came for dinner, and the squirrel had gotten lost. Ben had never been so close to a coronary as when he thought his dog would find that squirrel before he did.

Ben greeted Art with just the right degree of deference. As they shook hands, Ben clasped Art's upper arm warmly, displaying gratitude, affection and respect. He then slowly worked his way around the room — except for Howard. They were all in the living room near the picture windows, drinking Diet Coke or name-brand water and making small talk until Milo arrived.

Once Milo walked in, they moved to the dining room to get down to business. Howard put his squirrel in his pocket and joined them. As Ben had expected, no one had commented on the view — or the art.

At the table, Art opened the discussion, welcoming everyone. He said that Ben was offering Rick a terrific opportunity. "Ben could explain it best, of course," he stated and gave the floor to the newly minted independent producer. Ben started in talking about the movie he planned. He spoke about how powerful it was; he detailed the plot, explained who he wanted for the other parts. He talked about where it fit into the marketplace and who it would pull into the theaters. Which was just about every demographic. Ben felt it was as dazzling a pitch as he had ever heard.

He passed off to Milo, who gamely grabbed the baton, discussing how he wanted it to work. The others then joined in. Each talked about how to do it — not "if" but "when." Harry Preston thought Rick should have two songs ready as the movie came out — in addition to the soundtrack. The agency was focused on the tour ahead, and Gil also analyzed the videos to be shot.

Hearing them talk, Ben knew he had pulled it off. With Art's imprimatur, he realized he was about to put together his first independent project in more than 10 years. It felt good. The business had become meaner in the last decade, but he still knew how to get through the roughest riptides.

Rick, sitting in the middle of the group, had not joined the conversation. But this was not unexpected. All the men knew that Howard's default position was silence, even with those he knew well. He knew that when he weighed in, it would close the discussion.

The chef served the first course, heirloom tomato soup drizzled with ultra-virgin olive oil. Conversation did not flag, even as they started eating. Gil analyzed videos that Rick could then use in live performance. He described the full multimedia experience — Rick could "jump" onto the screen from the stage at key points, and the show would move onto film. Then, Rick could jump from the screen back to the stage.

Only Rick, Gil insisted, had the grace to pull off these seamless inter-media leaps in a live performance. Left unsaid was the fact that it meant Rick spent less time on stage. He would be offstage in his germ-free pod. But everyone knew.

Ben picked up on this use of film to talk more about the strength of his project and what it could mean for Rick. As Ben was speaking, Howard started to weep.

Now, most of the men in that room had sat with a star who was crying. This was not that unusual or even surprising. These men accepted that entertainers, especially actors, depended on their ability to be in the moment, fully present to their emotions. A spate of tears over losing a prized part, or a prized boyfriend, was not uncommon. Ben knew from experience that you handled big stars as you would a tearful baby, giving them something equally shiny — whether a different part or a possible hook up. The most passionate storm would pass.

But, even as he continued talking, Ben felt this was different. For one thing, Howard was not making a sound. He just sat there, at the center of the table, tears coursing down his face — a haunted silent movie in a world of sound. Howard seemed genuinely wretched — these were tears of despair. He was, Ben decided, like one of those Dickens orphans, overwhelmed by misery. The producer had never read Dickens, but he had seen enough movie versions so it felt like he had.

Ben faltered for a moment, worried that the deal was going south before he laid it out. But he decided to continue. So he did — acting as if he could not see that Rick was sitting there weeping. Ben was relieved as the others took their cue from him. They continued talking about the film, the related soundtrack album, the all-important concert tour. No one acknowledged that Howard was crying.

Suddenly, Howard put his head down on the table. He was crying soundlessly as his face went into the soup. It stayed submerged. Preston had been talking, and he was suddenly at a loss for words — but only momentarily. He finished his sentence.

Ben, who had been making every effort to focus on Harry as he spoke, was now riveted on Howard, unable to look away. Ben felt the fascination you have when watching a car crash — except it was his producing career going up in flames, like an old movie shot on combustible celluloid. He had a strange suspicion that the others were looking at him, not Howard. But he kept his eyes on Howard.

It felt like Howard was submerged in that soup for hours. But Art had stood up at the other end of the table, and was walking toward him. Sorrento stood up as well, still holding his napkin. They helped Howard up from the table. The star was still crying without a sound. The table was silent — as if a giant mute button had been pressed.

Sorrento, with what appeared to be genuine tenderness, gently wiped soup off the singer's face. One on either side of Howard, they walked him out. The table remained silent. Ben looked around, but the others didn't make eye contact. Most were too busy studying their own soup.

After a few minutes, Manning returned. "Rick is going to lie down for a while," he said. These were the first words spoken in the room since Preston had finished making his point. Art's voice sounded muffled, strangely hushed for a man who usually commanded attention when he spoke. "Mike is giving him something to make him feel more comfortable. Clearly, this was a trying conversation for him. But I know he's glad we're having it. He understands things can't go on like this."

Preston stood up. "Rick obviously needs some rest," he said, "This can't have been easy. Why don't we continue at some future date? We all need more time to think it through.

As he spoke, he was working his way around the table, shaking hands in goodbye. Ben wondered if he was only imagining that his handshake was more perfunctory than the others. On reaching Manning, Preston paused to pat him on the shoulder while shaking hands. Even now, he acknowledged Manning as elder statesman. "Art," he said, "thanks for setting this in motion. Why don't you have a long talk with Rick when he feels up to it? Then we'll take it from there."

Preston walked to the front door. Ben felt his deal was walking out with him. Short of tackling him, Ben realized, nothing he could do would stop Preston from leaving. Within a half-hour, if not less, Ben knew stories about this dinner would be all over town. He looked calm but his mind worked furiously: There had to be something he could do to salvage this.

"Thanks for coming, everyone" Ben started. "Thanks for accepting Art's invitation. This was always a long shot. But we have, all of us here, had a long and successful history with Rick. We all know how talented he is — and continues to be. I was hoping I could do something to acknowledge just how much we all owe him."

Ben knew it was not enough to save face. Saying that his movie project had really been about trying to help Rick through his time of trouble was not going to fool anyone in the room. It felt lame even as he said it. Everyone knew why they were there — and altruism had nothing to do with it. Like shame, Ben knew, altruism was MIA in Hollywood.

Milo stood up, looking to Manning. "Good luck, Art," he said. He reached over to give Ben's shoulder a quick pat. "Call me tomorrow," he said, "I have another angle."

He addressed the rest of the table before he headed to the door. "I owe my daughter Lulu a driving lesson." He said, "I promised we would start this week."

Chapter 3

THE SCREENING IN MALIBU

THAT WAS QUITE A DINNER the other night," Milo began.

He was driving Francesca and Lulu out to Malibu for a screening. They were on Pacific Coast Highway, heading north to Fred and Hailey's.

Lulu hadn't particularly wanted to go, but she had quickly figured out how much Milo wanted her there. He insisted that he didn't want her staying home without them, as if there weren't four in help at the house and she wasn't old enough to stay by herself.

He offered a slew of reasons why she had to come. There were going to be kids her age, whom she was sure to like. The movie, not due to open for a month, was worth seeing. He had read it, years before, when the script first made the rounds. The scenario had some interesting beats, he said, and he wanted to see how the director had handled it.

But most important, it seemed, Milo wanted her to spend time with his friends, people she barely knew. Lulu knew this was all part of his effort to pull her into his orbit. He seemed intent on proving that his life in Hollywood was better than her life with her mother back East. He was, she decided, engaged in some weird contest.

But she had also had her first driving lesson. Which was thrilling. So she got into the car as soon as he said it was time to leave for Malibu.

"What happened?" Francesca asked, and Lulu could hear the smile in her voice. "What have you been holding back?" She clearly enjoyed hearing Milo's stories of Hollywood. It was, Lulu decided, still an exotic landscape, to her, one she seemed eager to explore. And Milo had two generations worth of stories to tell, a rare facility in Hollywood, which was concerned only with "tomorrow."

"I never thought I would say this," Milo said, "but 'Poor Ben.' I agreed to go only because I felt sorry after his party last week. He didn't see any of it coming. He's in for a rough ride. He has no idea how much people hate him. But he's going to find out.

"Still, the dinner was really one for the record books," Milo continued, shaking his head as he laughed softly. "But you could also see how no one wants to help pick Ben up if – or maybe I should say when – he falls. He's been too vicious to too many people for too long.

"But, he was nice to your grandfather, years ago, Lulu," Milo's eyes met hers in the rear-view mirror. "This was at a time when not a whole lot of people were. And Ben was on the rise, so you wouldn't have expected anything. But he helped try to salvage a project for him. I don't think he even remembers. But I do.

"By the way, Lulu," he said, "What do you think of the diary?"

Lulu was startled. She knew Milo had seen her reading it, yet he had never brought it up before. Instead, Lulu thought, he had waited until they were riding in the car with Francesca – so any intimate conversation about it would be difficult. Though he had wanted her to read it, Lulu suddenly realized he somehow felt uncomfortable talking about it.

"Was he really like that?" she asked.

"Pretty much," he replied. "Enough so that the diary was painful for me to read."

"Why?"

"My father was smart and he could be funny. But mostly he was mean. I realize now, he was inconsolable. Never content with what he had. As his son, I thought it was only about me. But it was everything.

"No matter how delicious or wonderful something had appeared, it always tasted like ashes, like shit, in his mouth. I realized that only after years of therapy finally kicked in. I should have started it much earlier than I did. But I see it now."

"And Sara is your mother – my grandmother – right?"

"Yes," Milo said, his voice grew quieter. "She went from having a controlling, manipulative father to having a controlling, manipulative husband. She couldn't catch a break. I guess it was a dynamic that felt familiar to her. Maybe it was a relationship that made her feel comfortable on some level. She really loved him. But looking back, I can't imagine how hard it must have been for her – and I was there."

Francesca reached out to put her hand on his arm. "She died relatively young. He was decades older. But she died first.

"Anyway, getting back to Robbins," Milo seemed to shake it off. His voice strengthened. "I'd said I'd speak with Rick Howard's guys about a project that Ben loves," Milo explained. "I have no interest in doing it. But I agreed to help Ben sell it. I'm planning to pull out, since

I have too much on my plate. But I don't think it's even going to come to that.

"Art Manning was running the show. He organized this meeting of Howard's brain trust — manager, agent, executives from his record company — including Harry Preston, who's going to be there tonight.

"So we're sitting around the table," Milo continued, "and they bring out the soup. It's heirloom tomato. Everyone is talking about what Howard should do, and Rick starts to weep. The conversation continues, and he sits there, crying."

"No one says anything?" Francesca asked, sounding puzzled.

"No," Milo answered. "No one even acknowledges it. They all pretend it isn't happening. He just sits here, crying. Then it gets weird."

"It's already weird," said Francesca, "They all know him well. Yet no one consoles him?"

"That is not how it works here," Milo explained, "They call themselves his friends — but he's a big star. They all work with him. They all work *for* him.

"I've seen this dynamic before. I know Abe talks about it in his diary. But this felt different. The elephant is not just in the room, he's wearing a tutu, doing a tap dance, and no one can admit to seeing it. But then Howard put his head down on the table — right into the soup. Still, no one knew what to do." He paused, reflecting on what he had said.

"Rick is considered a talent too big to fail. For them, he is like one of those big Wall Street banks — he will get through this crisis. But maybe, Rick is starting to worry that he might be more like the biggest ship ever built, the one too big to go down — the Titanic."

Francesca interrupted him, and Lulu realized this was something her stepmother rarely did. "So his head is in the soup and no one says anything?" She sounded stunned. "How many people are at the table?"

Milo paused for a moment. "Eight," he answered. "It went on for — well, it felt like forever, but probably only a few seconds. Then Art gets up and the manager gets up, too. They both help Howard get up from the table and walk him into a bedroom, so he can lie down. I'm sure he was out for the night."

"That is a horrible story," Chesca declared.

"It's Hollywood," Milo shrugged. "There was a lot on the line for everyone at that table. Some are actually close to him. But no one knew how to deal with it."

He continued, on what seemed a different subject, though Lulu soon realized it wasn't. "I never confuse business and friendship," he said. "I figured this out early. It was when I was a kid — my father took me to a big star's birthday party. I must have been eight.

"He knew her but didn't work with her. He wanted to, though. It took me a while to realize, but he was the only person at that party who didn't work for her — who wasn't her agent, or manager, or hairdresser, or secretary, or assistant. Her best friend answered her fan mail. Everyone there was on her payroll — except her boyfriend — and my father and me."

Francesca gave Milo a questioning look. Lulu saw Milo look sideways at her. The car was silent for a while. Then he started talking again, with a brighter tone.

"My life is different," he said, "I've remembered that scene all my life, Lulu, and I've made sure that won't happen with me. I count these people tonight as real friends. And, since they are my friends, Lulu, we set this up so there will be some kids there for you.

"Fred made sure both his daughters were coming tonight. Zoe, the older one, is an actress. She's in her early 20s. But the younger daughter, Jasmine, is just your age. I think you'll have a lot in common. And she's bringing her friend, Emma Levinson. You met her parents, Nate and Gwen, the other night at the Robbinses. Nate is out of town right now — or else they'd be here. We're all going to be on the boat. But I know you'll get along with Emma — with all these girls."

"Just like I get along with Hailey," Francesca laughed.

"Come on," Milo said, "You do."

"Who's Hailey?" Lulu asked.

"Fred's wife, Hailey Hirshberg," Milo answered.

"You mean Hailey Morgan Hirshberg," teased Francesca.

"Chesca may be referring to the fact, Lulu," Milo volleyed back, "that Hailey, when she was Hailey Morgan, was a particularly celebrated Playmate of the Year. But it's been, what, 25 years? She's been running a successful nutrition business for the last dozen. Fully re-invented herself. Like so many people here."

"I don't think she fully reinvents herself until she stops with the Playmate card," said Francesca. "Tell me about it then. When she stops this 'Hailey Morgan Hirshberg' thing. She is a feminist manqué."

"Chesca!" Milo was chuckling. Lulu thought it sounded like part of a continuing conversation. "Hailey is being thoughtful here, doing something nice for Lulu. This is going to be a fantastic evening!" He stressed the second syllable of fantastic emphatically, as if to signal how much fun awaited.

"I want to see this movie," he continued. "It has some interesting beats. And everyone is talking about the girl, Maisie Anderson. The studio is thinking about her for Sonia. I'm not sure, based on what I've seen. So I want to see how she handles this."

Milo maneuvered the car to the center lane as he was speaking. Along the other side of PCH, Lulu saw a long white stucco wall and an austere white metal gate. Milo turned into the driveway.

He pressed a bronze button on the low white brick pillar near his car window. "Yes?" a woman's voice came over a speaker. "Hi," he said, "It's Milo Flintridge." "Come in," the voice answered, as the gate began to open.

They drove down a long lane, lines of clipped trees on either side. There was a big house off to the right and as they pulled up in front of it, Lulu could see through the first floor, out to the ocean beyond.

A trim Asian woman opened the door. "Hello, Elaine," Milo said as they walked in, "this is my daughter, Lulu."

"Nice to see you, Mr. Flintridge, Ms. Frateli," she said, "Nice to meet you, Lulu. Everyone's upstairs."

They walked up to a large room with a sweeping, arched ceiling, like the hull of a boat. A wall of sliding glass doors opened on to a wooden deck looking out on the ocean. Through the windows, in the gathering twilight, Lulu could see large birds, maybe pelicans, diving into the water.

A man was walking across the room toward them as they came up the stairs. He was tanned, almost as tall as Milo, heavy-set, but muscular. He reached the top of the stairs just as they did. "Milo," he said, as he hugged the director hello, "It's good to see you."

"Would never miss it," Milo said. "I brought Lulu. She's staying the entire summer. And you really missed it at Ben's on Tuesday — she had the seat of honor. Lulu, this is Fred Hirshberg."

Fred smiled as he shook her hand. "Hi, Lulu," he said. "I've heard so much about you." He looked her in the eyes, "I know your dad is so happy to have you here for the whole summer! You having fun?"

"Why yes," she said, on her automatic response. She got no farther, however, because a slight, desiccated man holding a tall drink had walked over. He and Milo exchanged quick, knowing smiles.

"Milo," he said, "That was quite an experience with Howard. But I gather I missed a show Tuesday. Cyd told me about it. But she was put on 'Nick patrol' early. So I need you to tell me what actually happened at Ben's."

"I saw Cyd briefly," Milo answered. "She had her work cut out for her. By the time I got there, Nick was doing 'Three Stooges' routines."

"Lulu," Milo said, "this is Harry Preston. He's runs the record division at Lucent."

Lulu smiled hello as her father continued talking. "Ben looked miserable. This mattered to him — that his party was a drop by.

"He forgot it's always about the job, not you." Milo's laugh had a bitter edge that Lulu was not sure the others heard. "He's spent his career in Hollywood, and still didn't realize Nauman was no insurance.

"I don't think that crowd he invited really cares about art. I've not even so sure Ben does. It's more about the chase for him — the get. I don't know how much genuine appreciation is involved. When I was a kid, I saw Edward G. Robinson crying over a painting. I don't think Ben has ever cried over his kids — much less that Rothko." Milo paused for a beat.

"Ben even had good food that night," he continued, "Worth staying for. He wanted it to be memorable. And it was. Just not the way he planned. Nauman's table was half-empty, and no one would sit next to him. Not even Ben or Dianne — they were both more concerned about you, Fred. Ben finally had Lulu sit next to Nauman." Milo put his arm tightly around Lulu, while the group laughed. She felt awkward, as she often did at parties — even when she wasn't being talked about. She knew she was reddening with embarrassment. She wondered when she could move away.

"The thing is," Milo continued, "he probably had a better conversation with her than he would have had with most of the people there. But he wouldn't know that.

"And Fred," Milo added, "I don't think anyone even noticed this psychodrama with Nauman. They were too busy talking about you. That's what they all cared about: Where the hell is Hirshberg!" Fred tried to look sheepish. Everyone else was chuckling.

Lulu was edging away when she heard Cesare's voice behind her. He was talking in rapid French, but she would have known his rasp anywhere. A woman's voice responded to his in the same rat-a-tat French.

Lulu turned and saw Cesare coming up the stairs behind them, with an elegant, dark-haired woman. She was so streamlined that she could have been a hood ornament on a 1920s roadster, her high cheekbones sculpted, her jaw line chiseled. She wore her hair slicked back in a tight chignon, like a ballet dancer. She was wearing cigarette jeans in soft brown leather and a black turtleneck so thin it looked gauzy. The contrast between her aerodynamic sleekness and Cesare's rolling bulk was striking.

The pair switched to English by the time they reached the top of the stairs. "Milo, mon ami," Cesare said as he drew near. Milo turned around, as did Francesca, who smiled up at him. "Darling," he said, as his arms enveloped her, "You're even more sexy today!" She cooed delightedly.

"Freddy," Cesare held his arms wide. "You look just the same! Tell me immediately how you do it! I hope it's okay that I brought Madeleine Devoise, a great friend of mine. Her family lives across the place from me in Paris. She's been on the catwalk for Karl at Chanel for two years now. And she just landed a part in the new Rob Tracey film."

"How do you do?" Madeleine said, in a plumy English accent. There was no hint she was French.

A strikingly beautiful woman joined the circle. She was exotic, with dark, curling hair, deep sea-green eyes and skin that had a pearlescent glow — like an Ingres odalisque or a Murillo Madonna. Then she spoke — her voice was high and chirpy, as if she'd just had a date with a helium tank. "Hi, honey," she said, reaching up to kiss Milo. "Whatcha been doin'?" She hugged Francesca, and then turned to Lulu.

"You must be Lulu," she chirped. "I'm Hailey, Hailey Morgan Hirshberg. Our girls are both here tonight to meet you. Come on over and say hi." She took Lulu's arm and led her across the room. "I hope you've been having fun here in L.A."

Lulu didn't need to answer because Hailey didn't pause. "I know it takes a while to feel settled," she burbled. "Just remember that everyone adores your father! He's fantastic." She chirruped the word. "So much fun!!"

"Jasmine — Jazzy is the one you want to meet. She's just your age. Sixteen, right? Well, she just turned 17, but we think you guys will hit it off. And her friend Emma is adorable. She starts college, at USC, this year, but they're never apart. My older daughter Zoe came too. But she's a little older, with different interests.

"Jazzy is the one you probably have most in common with. Jazzy and Emma. Your father was telling us how smart you are. Jazzy's hysterical. Such a free spirit! I get such a kick out of her."

Lulu looked longingly back at Milo. Walking with Hailey, Lulu felt more clumsy than usual. The woman moved with a careless grace. Lulu felt like a giraffe keeping pace with a cheetah — she could not match the older woman's luxuriant stride. They were heading toward two young women, standing near the sliding doors at the far corner of the room.

Both wore dark jeans, were roughly the same height and talked in a similarly animated fashion — but there the likeness ended. One was a younger, but blonde version of Hailey, so clearly her daughter. But this iteration looked highly maintained. While Hailey seemed completely natural — which Lulu was sure was not the case — nothing seemed casual about this girl.

Every surface looked buffed, polished and manicured — her soft blonde hair artfully arranged, her pearly skin glowing, her nails gleaming. Her dark jeans fit as if she had been sewn onto them; the skimpy baby pink camisole she wore was topped by a raspberry pink cardigan, tied around her shoulders. The night air was chilly at the beach, but her porcelain beauty seemed impervious. As Lulu got closer, she saw the girl wore heavy eye make-up, with lots of mascara. She looked familiar — and Lulu realized she'd been featured as the lead's snide best friend in a movie this spring.

The other girl was gesturing to make a point as Lulu and Hailey approached. Her features lacked the blonde's stunning symmetry, but there was a reprobate sparkle about her that caught your attention and held it. Lulu got the impression that if the other girl looked like Hailey, this one was closer in character — with that same languid sexiness.

She had wavy light brown hair long enough to skim her shoulder blades, and an unstudied air. Everything she was wearing seemed about to slip off — her ripped jeans fit, yet looked ready to slide down her slim hips; her T-shirt neckline was falling down one shoulder. Lulu wondered what was keeping it all up.

"Lulu," Hailey chirruped, putting her hand on the blonde woman's shoulder, "this is Zoe. And here," she put her arm around the other young woman's shoulders, "is Jazzy."

They both turned to her and smiled. "We've been hearing so much about you," Jazzy said. Lulu felt herself flush — as she did whenever she felt people looking at her. She smiled and said hello, then turned to thank Hailey. But the older woman was already gliding back across the room.

"You're here for the summer, right?" Jazzy said, "You're going to have fun."

"It's a big change," Lulu said, "But it's nice to be here with my dad — and Chesca," she remembered to say.

"I usually go to Maine with my mom and her family. But it seemed like a good idea for me to spend time with my dad. It's been years since I've been out here for such a long time — since they divorced actually. He wants me to see all the places he grew up — and his life now."

She got through it without a tremor. It helped that she had shifted the subject from her mom to Milo. But she did this for another reason — she had figured out Milo was all anyone here wanted to talk about with her.

"You'll probably go on a boat," Jazzy said, "Your dad and Chesca always spend most of August on a boat — usually somewhere on the Mediterranean."

A delicate-looking girl with long, straight dark brown hair joined them. She was wearing skinny white jeans and a long-sleeved white T-shirt with horizontal navy blue stripes — like a '20s French sailor shirt. That is, Lulu thought, if French sailors' navy stripes were made of blue sequins. She had on silver leather slippers, with a row of rhinestones marking the edge. One arm jangled with assorted chunky gold H-link toggle bracelets and silver ID bracelets. She handed Jazzy one of the two tumblers of soda.

"Lulu," Jazzy said, "this is Emma." Even as Emma said hi, her iPhone buzzed and she reached into her back pocket to pull out. She read it and quickly began texting. She was remarkably fast with one hand.

Zoe had been looking around the room and now stared over Lulu's shoulder. "Connor Ericson just walked in," she said. "I didn't know he was going to be here! He is so the real deal."

"Definitely," said Jazzy, sighing slightly. "They should all look like that!" She was now also focused on something over Lulu's left shoulder, with a measuring glance. Emma looked up briefly, nodded in agreement, then turned back to her cell.

Lulu waited for them to continue, but there was only silence. "What do you mean?" she asked.

"Most big stars aren't tall," Zoe said. "Connor is. Not that he's a real star yet — but they are all talking about him like he's going to be. Cyd told me the other night that she knows at least four directors who are talking about him for their next film."

"I think my father is," said Emma. Lulu remembered Milo had said her father was a producer.

Zoe took her eyes off Connor, focusing briefly on Lulu. "He looks like you'd expect a star to look. You don't realize this so much out here — you get used to the height of most guys." Her voice held a note of experience. As if she'd already been through three divorces and two trips to rehab.

"Until you see Connor," Zoe continued. "Then, POW. You realize how short most actors are — short with really big heads. That translates on screen. But when you see them in real life, stars are always shorter than you want them to be." She gave a dramatic sigh. Lulu thought she sounded like she should have been nursing a double old-fashioned on the rocks, instead of what looked to be plain water, no ice.

"Meanwhile, so many movie executives are short — especially agents. It's like an inverse ratio to power. My problem is not just that I'm tall; it's that I like guys who are tall. So it's nice when you see Connor. Aside from the fact that he's so adorable!"

Throughout the conversation, Emma's eyes had stayed on her cell, but she must have seen Lulu's sneakers out of the corner of her eye. "Those are super-cute," Emma said as she paused between texts. "That's such a fantastic blue. And the lemon yellow insets are perfect. Prada from last season, right? I can't believe I missed them!"

Lulu wanted to burst out laughing. She wondered if these girls even knew about the nation's economic woes. More than impervious, they seemed oblivious. "Prada!" she said, "Believe me, they're not Prada. Nothing I have is!"

All three girls stared blankly. Lulu wondered just how big a mistake it had been to admit this. They looked shocked that they were speaking with someone who owned nothing from Prada. She wondered if they would all now stop talking to her, turn abruptly and walk away — the way Brahmins in India used to treat an Untouchable.

Instead, Zoe reached over and patted her arm. "Go shopping with Chesca," she advised in a sincere tone, as if to a backward child. "I'm sure she'd love to get you a bag from Prada. And there is also a super-fabulous new Dior handbag that just came in. I saw it yesterday." She paused to consider what she had just said. "But, you know, Prada is better to have for every day. And that new chocolate brown satchel is yummy. Just go with Chesca."

"It's what stepmothers do," Emma added, "With my friends — their best handbags always come from their stepmothers! Emily's gave her an oversized red ostrich shoulder bag from Ralph Lauren. Gorgeous!"

"Girls," an older woman had been walking by, but now joined the conversation, "what did you just say about handbags?"

"We were saying," Zoe answered, without missing a beat, "what a fabulous Birkin you have, Evie. It's scrumptious! And Evie, I am not sure you've met Lulu Flintridge. Lulu, this is Evie Grossman, a total sweetheart!" Zoe bent to give the older woman a warm hug.

"I call this my froggie Birkin," Evie said, puffing up with pleasure. She was indeed older, but it was hard for Lulu to figure out how old. Her hair was a soft blonde and her face plump and smooth. She didn't dress her age either, with navy silk Capri trousers and an oversized grass green silk Indian blouse with intricate yellow beading at the cuffs and collar. She held up her handbag with pride.

"Doesn't this green ostrich look like a frog! It just might be my favorite." She giggled slightly, "My salute to Kermit!

"The thing is that every bag is my favorite when I carry it," she continued. "Isn't that how it always works! Maybe that's why I'm still with Ralph after all these years. I'm always at his side! I never let him go anywhere alone! And since I'm always at his side, he's always my favorite!!"

"You know, girls," Evie said, beaming, "It was a Hermes bag that first tipped me off that Harry Lefferts was leaving Janet. Ralph and I were so ahead of the curve on this!

"We were in Paris two years ago, and, of course, we stopped by the Hermes. It's on the way to most anywhere we go! And it helps to check out stores in different countries, to see what they carry.

"But anyways," she continued, "We were in the Hermes on the Rue de St. Honoré. They were checking to see if they had a small cream alligator bag I'd been looking for. While we're waiting, Harry walks in. Of all the Hermes in all the world, he walks into that one." She laughed at her own joke. "He's with a woman with jet-black hair and these incredible blue eyes — someone I've never seen before. He's telling her how much he wants to buy her a Birkin. He is so busy with her, he doesn't see us. But as she looks around the store, he spots us.

"He doesn't flinch. Instead, he walks right over, and introduces us all around. He says she an executive in distribution. They had a terrific year, he says, and he's buying her a Hermes bag for a bonus. That's how I met Tessa.

"But I will tell you, the tone of his voice when he spoke to her — I knew this was not about distribution. At least, not for movies! And there also was a certain look in her eyes! Now, I have seen that look on many, many women when they walk into Hermes. A sort of voraciousness — which is so understandable! But she had it when she looked at him. It was only about six months later that he left Janet. I'm surprised it took that long."

The three young women were listening intently. This was knowledge the others looked desperate to absorb, but Lulu was barely paying attention. Her focus had drifted past the group, out to the ocean.

It was dark and serene. Clouds scudded across the almost-full moon, hanging low over the horizon. Some trick of the late twilight made her think the moon was slyly winking. Maybe it was the passing clouds. A tapering silver beam radiated down, and the indigo waters sparkled where it sliced through. The deck was empty and inviting. Lulu wanted to go out — if only to get away from this conversation. She suddenly needed to be alone.

It always surprised her that people with houses on the beach in Malibu were never in the ocean — rarely even on the beach, from what she had seen. The wide swath of fine white sand behind the houses was invariably empty, except within the marked-off corridors in front of an access gate, where non-residents could sit — and usually did, jammed together — soaking up the California sun.

Whenever Lulu went with her father and Francesca to visit their friends in Malibu, they were invariably indoors. Along Maine's rocky shore — it was the shore back East, not the beach — despite that freezing water for most of the summer, seaside residents were invariably in the water — swimming and sailing, wading and playing. One of the first things Lulu usually did at Pop-Pop and Granny's sprawling summer cottage in Islesboro was to race down to the dock with her cousins and take the dinghy out to the boat. Then they would spend the rest of the afternoon sailing — the first of many such lazy afternoons. Lulu went out most often with Elinor, Dunham, Buff and Ned, the best sailor among them. There were usually more than enough of her cousins around to put together a reliable crew for the 46-foot wooden schooner.

In California, however, everyone was inside — adults watching movies, kids playing video games or texting. It was yet another piece of Los Angeles that Lulu could not understand.

She eased away from the conversation — they were critiquing some Chanel quilted low boots that had just come in — walked to the sliding door, opened it and stepped out onto the deck. Lulu couldn't see the beach below, only the expanse of ocean beyond.

Lulu slid the door closed behind her. She could hear the thrum of the ocean. Ribbons of frothy white shimmied across the inky surface, as the waves broke against the surf. A breeze off the water brought a chill, making her feel more alive than she had inside. The tangy saltiness evoked a memory of sitting with her mother on the beach in Maine.

She was suddenly swept away by a sensation of longing for her mother. She also wished she could talk to Abby, even for a minute. She knew how her best friend would have laughed about that Prada story. It was amazing how these girls saw Prada, when Converse was right in front of them. There was no one here that Lulu could tell this story. Surrounded by people, she felt alone.

But as she walked on the deck, Lulu sensed she was not alone. There was a flicker of movement off to her left. She had been looking up at the moon, so she couldn't see clearly in the dim light. She blinked her eyes to adjust. There, in the far corner, she realized someone had been leaning over the railing, cloaked in darkness. The figure had been so still it looked like part of the deck structure.

Lulu felt like an interloper. She paused before walking out to the railing directly ahead. She realized that the figure had straightened up with a slight sigh and was now moving toward her.

Connor Ericson appeared out of the darkness. At first, Lulu saw only his face. There was a brightness about him, as if he carried his own personal follow spot.

Lulu was sorry she had ever thought to walk out onto the deck. She would have given anything to just disappear. She had wanted to get away from those people — but not to interrupt someone else. And certainly not if that someone were Connor Ericson.

Her cheeks felt on fire. She looked back longingly at the party. She wondered if she could just casually turn around, pretend she didn't realize Ericson was there, and head back indoors.

She was about to do just this when she realized it would be even more awkward. He was almost next to her in any case. But he must have sensed her discomfort, for he suddenly held out his hand and spoke to her. "Hey," he said, "I'm Connor. Who are you. I know I haven't met you before, since I sure would've remembered."

Lulu was caught off guard by his accent. "You're English!" she said, "I had no idea!"

"That's the best compliment," he laughed, "Why thank you." His smile seemed to envelop her in his glow. "But you still haven't told me your name. Is it available only on a need-to-know basis?"

"I'm, Lulu," she said, "Lulu Flintridge." She explained about spending the summer in Los Angeles with her father.

"I'm glad there's someone at this party who knows even less people than I do. We need to stick together. Cause I know hardly anyone. But so many of them seem to know me. They sure talk to me like they do. And they all seem to expect that I know who they are. Mostly, I have no clue." His smile was infectious. She had heard this phrase but never experienced it.

"You'd be doing me a huge favor," he continued, "if you stay next to me the whole evening, and keep introducing yourself to anyone who walks by. Then they would tell you their name. And then I could find out who they bloody are."

His tone was so beguiling, Lulu decided that helping him navigate the party might be just about the best way to spend the evening. She felt there was nothing she would rather do than help him.

But as she reflected on this new feeling, Lulu began to feel awkward again. So she focused on something easier to talk about — his accent. "Your accent in that film was amazing! I mean, your acting was amazing, too, of course" Lulu began.

Watching him on screen, she had assumed he was American. But his speaking voice now reminded her of David Beckham or Michael Caine — a spikey cockney lilt that blurred around the edges. Lulu couldn't help thinking, however, that this cockney was pretend and it was his perfect Southern twang on film that was real.

"I was so sure you were from the South. But you grew up in England?"

"Yes," he smiled again. "You're right in a way. It was the South — South London."

Lulu knew he was teasing her and felt herself flushing again. "I didn't mean to—," she began. She recalibrated and started afresh. "My grandmother spent part of her childhood in London. Her father, my great-grandfather, was a diplomat and they lived there for a while. She adored it. I've heard so many stories. It sounded so wonderful."

"I don't think 'wonderful' is the word I'd use," Connor said ruefully. "And I'm almost certain a diplomat's daughter wouldn't have been familiar with the area I came from." He laughed at the thought. "Or, if she did, it would show you how much parts of London have changed. The opposite of gentrification, though." Lulu felt his teasing tone was directed more at himself than her questions. "Let's just say it was rough. Acting was a way out for me."

"But you enjoy acting, right?" she asked, "'Cause you sure seem to. It must mean a lot to you, right? That's most important isn't it?"

"You're right," he smiled. At the same time, though, his tone grew more serious. "It was something I could do that was my own. That's so important for a kid. For anyone actually."

"So did you always know you wanted to be an actor?" she asked. "I have no idea what I want to be."

"It was all by accident really," he said. "My mum was working long hours. She had two jobs to support the three of us — my younger brother, me and her. I guess I was a handful. I know now that she worried about me and wanted me occupied when she was at work. So she enrolled me in an acting class, when I was about eight. To keep me out of trouble more than anything. I was already up to quite a bit of mischief.

"It turned out I was good. Really took to it. I didn't realize how much I liked it, though, 'til I was about 11, I guess. I was starting football — the English kind." He smiled. "But I decided I didn't want to give up the acting. I won a scholarship to middle school. And then I got one to RADA — the Royal Academy of Dramatic Arts. I only stayed there for about two years though — well, nearly two years. I got a part so I left."

She heard something in his voice. "Do you regret leaving early?"

He gave her a measured look. "No one's ever asked me that here." He paused again. "I had a brill time at school. It was the first time I was with so many people serious about their craft and striving to do it better. An amazing experience. Everything I wanted and more. But I got the chance to play Mercutio in 'Romeo and Juliet' at the Old Vic. A dream role — you get to strut your stuff, all flash, and then you die." There was that smile again.

The door slid open behind her and Lulu heard Francesca's voice over her shoulder. "Lulu, darling," her stepmother said. "This is kismet! I had been telling Con about you! Just yesterday, I was telling him how happy Milo is," she paused and corrected herself, "how delighted we both are, Lulu, to have you here."

As Francesca spoke, she drew close enough to put her arms around Lulu. With "here," she kissed Lulu's cheek — a physical exclamation point. It was not her usual air kiss, yet Lulu felt it was somehow more artificial.

"The thing is, Lulu," Francesca cooed, one arm around her waist. "It's been almost two years since I moved here to be with Milo, and I haven't slowed down for a minute. This has been such a large change for me. But now I have some time to experience life here. Lulu, I want to do so many L.A. things with you — go shopping, go to the Hammer, maybe the Philharmonic — I've been hearing so much about this Gehry Concert Hall and I have never even been downtown. We can explore together. It is always so nice to go shopping with a friend — because that's what we must be, Lulu, real friends."

Francesca kept her arm around Lulu, but had turned slightly, so she was looking at Connor as she spoke. It was as if Francesca was acting out a scene for Connor — and had cast Lulu in a supporting character. Lulu smiled, since she knew this was her cue. "That will be nice."

"I've done so little in L.A.," Francesca continued, squeezing Lulu's waist again for emphasis before taking a step away. Lulu couldn't help noting that this had been her longest physical contact with her stepmother. "Making films has taken up such a big part of my life here, Lulu. Los Angeles has been so much about the movie business. My first was just a little film — that's when I met Connor. He stole that picture right out from over us!"

Francesca gave her megawatt laugh. "It was his first film here as well," she continued, "and we both had much to learn. Milo was my best adviser, of course! But it is good to have someone there, on the set, who understands what you are going through."

"You would have been fine without me," Connor insisted. "You were much more helpful to me. I wouldn't have felt safe enough to do the things I was trying without you there." Lulu was struck by the note of sincerity in his voice. What could have been idle flattery, she thought, sounded heartfelt.

"Exploring a city with someone can be so much fun," he said. "I've been working hard here. But some of my mates, not as lucky as me, who have had more time on their hands, have been exploring Los Angeles and are smitten. More so since they didn't expect to be. I've done some hiking though. I grew up surrounded by concrete. So nature is exotic — and zen for me. The trails here are brill. Hiking has saved my sanity when things get barmy here."

Connor seemed to be focusing so directly on her that the conversation felt deeply personal, even intimate.

"I've only been here a week," Lulu said, "We usually summer in Maine, so this has been sort of discombobulating. But I like hiking, I do it in Maine all the time — there's a walk we take along the cliffs there that has these ravishing ocean views. And in Idaho too, when I visit my Uncle Jimmy. I hike with my cousins all the time there — there's one mountain trail that we never get tired of. So I would love to try it here!"

Connor seemed so interested in what she was saying, and so interesting himself, that talking with him made her feel interesting, too. What she was saying seemed to matter to him. She felt he not only heard her but understood her. She had watched him talking with others tonight, and had seen how they had each seemed to brighten in his company, reflecting back the glow that surrounded him. He was definitely what Granny called one of "The Charmers."

"Those trails sound fabulous!" Francesca's laugh rippled through the night. She put her head close to Lulu's. It pulled Connor's attention back to her. "It would be such fun!"

She gave Lulu another affectionate squeeze, to punctuate "fun." With an exclamation point! Her stepmother, Lulu realized, had never been so physically demonstrative with her. She could not help wondering if it had something to do with Connor. Lulu also wondered if, back home in Italy, Francesca had ever hiked — or wanted to.

"And shopping together would be so much joy. I saw a bag that would be delicious for you! It's a green velvet Prada satchel — which would be lovely with your hair. I want to get it for you right now!" Francesca leaned over and kissed Lulu's cheek, to underline the sentence for emphasis. In doing this, she pulled Lulu around, so she was facing her, not Connor. "And there was a jacket there that I would love to see you in! This would be so fun for me!

"For weeks now, Milo has been talking to me about all the things he wants to show you, the places he wants to take you," she continued. "There is so much he wants to do with you. And so many places I want to go with you as well! We are both excited by this chance to spend time with you. We hope to have you here far more often." Her smile was dazzling as she closed the scene.

Lulu heard the sliding door again, and then Jazzy and Zoe were standing beside her. "Hi, Connor, Hi Chesca," Zoe said. "I am so excited to see this movie tonight! A friend of mine, Charlotte Enders, has a small part. The script was really good!" She turned to Connor, and her skin seemed to glow in the moonlight.

"Connor, I've been hearing so much about 'Chessmen,'" Zoe moved on to her Topic A. "Everybody is talking about it — and about you in it. They are saying it is an amazing performance. And I mean everybody! I know the industry screening is coming soon. But if you have a cast and crew, an early friends and family screening, I want you to consider me a friend, please! That's what I want to be, anyways!"

Jazzy was standing closest to Connor. Her chin was tilted down, even as her emerald eyes looked up at his, a position Lulu was sure had been artfully composed. Jazzy looked adoring and adorable. She reached over and took Connor's hand with her own, clasping his arm just above the wrist with the other. "What a cool watch, Connor," she said, as she lifted his arm for a better look. "Where did it come from? It's so unique!"

Jazzy had bent her head down to examine it. She then looked up — directly into his eyes. Lulu felt every move was choreographed. She wondered if others sensed this as well.

"Thanks, Jazzy" he said, meeting her smile with his own. There was a promise of complicity in it. "I found it at Maxfield's. It's '40s I think. I got it for myself as a present — instead of taking the trip I wanted. I'll have time for that later. Literally"

He was smiling even as he disengaged his hand, and turned toward Zoe. "I hope the movie works," he said. "We'll all know soon enough. But it's certainly made things more interesting."

"Dinner's ready," Hailey said. She was at the sliding door. "Ricky made Thai tonight. Come help yourselves please — we want to start the movie soon." Lulu was still startled to hear that Mickey-Mouse voice.

Zoe and Jazzy turned and the group headed inside. Lulu paused before following them. Her phone had vibrated with a special tone. So she needed to check the text. It was from her cousin, Elinor Curtis, Grace's oldest daughter: "Need to talk 2 you. Call."

Elly, a junior at Williams, was in India for the summer, building a library and public health clinic in a small village outside of Jodhpur. Lulu had been following her volunteer work on Facebook. She tried to remain calm as she called — but she could feel her heart racing. She was terrified that something was wrong with mummy.

"Elly," she said. Even that one word sounded slightly breathless. She took a gulp of air. "What's up? Is everything okay?" She wasn't sure she wanted to hear the answer.

"You tell me," Elly said. "I don't know what's going on with you, Lulu, but you need to check in with your mother. Regularly. That means at least every day. And call her — don't just text. This is such a rough time for her and you're so not helping. Mummy says she's frantic about not hearing from you. You've really need to get over yourself!

Lulu started to defend herself, but Elly cut her off. "There was a long text from mummy when I got up today, asking me to call you. You are so upsetting your mother. She's got enough stress right now. You shouldn't be adding to it. You're going to be sorry you're acting like this."

Lulu jumped in. "I am going to call her more often. I promise. But what do you mean I'm 'going to be sorry.' Is there something I haven't heard?" There was a catch in her voice that Lulu didn't bother to hide.

"No Goose, there's not." Elly's anger had banked, since she was using Lulu's family nickname. It had started when Elly's brother, Ned, was a baby, and had trouble with his L's. "I'm just surprised that Mummy needed me to talk to you. I guess she must be feeling overwhelmed at the house. And I am sure Granny isn't making it any easier.

"So why are you doing this? If you are still upset about being sent out to L.A. – get over it. Stop behaving like a brat."

"I am not," Lulu was stung. "You know how much I wanted to stay there and help. I could have been helping just like your mother. And I have started calling her. I did it today and I will from now on."

"Just keep it up," Elly advised. "It's better for everyone. Speaking of which, if I don't hang up right now and get into the shower, I will have missed my shot for the day. So I need to go. But I'll send you pictures later this morning, so you can see how it's coming.

"And don't forget to call her every day – at the very least."

Lulu stayed out on the deck, looking out on the breakers as she thought about her mother far away in Boston. She had sounded even more far off during the call today, disconnected from everything except her illness. After a few moments of watching the surf, Lulu felt calm enough to walk back into the house. There were more people now, probably close to 30, at the party. Many had already started eating, sitting at the long dining table or grouped around the coffee table, while others, their large yellow dinner plates filled with food, were figuring out where to settle. Lulu saw that the party had divided into male and female — with most of the men at the dinner table and most of the women around the coffee table, on the sofa and chairs or cross-legged on the floor.

She walked over to the food, laid out on large platters along the buffet. There were heaping bowls of curries, with meat and without, platters of green papaya salad with shrimp, piles of grilled vegetable skewers, platters of crab claws with ginger and chicken with lime and lemongrass, mounds of bok choy, large bowls of jasmine rice and sticky rice.

Francesca was just about finished going through the line, her plate filled with many small bites, and Jazzy was right behind her. Emma's plate was already filled, but she was standing with Jazzy as she went through the buffet. "Sophie wants to meet up later." Emma was reading texts. "She got in late last night. She says rehab was a total waste. Beyond stupid. And what we hear is true – Olivia just flew down and got her. She signed herself out and left. They started doing Jackie D. shots in the car on the way to the plane. We need to text her when we leave the house, and she'll tell us where they are."

Two men were standing nearby, already holding plates. But when they saw Lulu reach for silverware, the younger of the two smiled and motioned her to go ahead, handing her his plate. He was so handsome, Lulu thought. Of all the people there, she would have pegged him as the movie star. He was tall and slim, with classic features, short blonde hair and a beguiling smile. She didn't think she had had never seen him on screen though.

The older man, who was shorter and reminded Lulu of a bulldog, was now in front of her at the buffet, piling food on his plate. He did not pause even as he looked over. "I've never seen you here." His voice was an amiable growl. "So what brings you? And why don't I know you? Who are you?" She was taken aback. "I'm Lulu Flintridge, Milo's daughter," she said, "I'm here for the summer – from Boston."

"You're way too cute to be Milo's daughter!" he said, more loudly than he had too. "Milo," he called across the room, "This girl here says she's your daughter. You are shameless to bring her here with Chesca in the same room! I am shocked, shocked! I had thought those days were behind you!"

His voice cut through the laughter. "Milo, where have you been hiding this girl! You should always bring her. In fact, just send her with Francesca — you can stay home. Don't you know we would much rather have been looking at her face than yours all these years!"

Lulu felt herself blush as the room erupted in laughter. Francesca, who had finished at the buffet, paused to squeeze her arm, "Come sit with me," she said.

"Boston," said the absurdly handsome younger man, as he started filling his plate — though only with vegetables. "I'm from Boston! That's where I met Jake." He nodded his head toward the older man on her other side.

"I'm Mark," he continued. "Jake had been speaking at Harvard and he stayed an extra day."

"Oh!" Lulu smiled as him. It felt comforting to talk to someone from Boston. It made her feel a little less alone and off-kilter. "What were you studying?"

"Oh, I wasn't at college!" He shook his head, laughing at the idea. "I was Miss Bay State! Jake was in Cambridge because he was seeing the captain of the Harvard swim team. So he'd accepted an invite to speak at a house tea. He went to a party that night and a friend introduced us. That was it for M. Butterfly-stroke!"

"Wow," said Lulu, laughing with him, "I've never met a Miss Bay State! It's a thrill to meet someone chosen to represent my state!"

"I was Miss Marblehead before that," Mark said. "Now, that was a contest!"

Lulu had finished getting food. She said see you later to Mark and Jake with unfeigned regret, and went to join Francesca around the coffee table. As she walked by the dining table, she heard Milo talking about the problems created by some lawyer whenever he closed a deal. Milo paused to smile to her as she walked by. He looked happy that she was going to sit with Francesca. As she approached the coffee table group, Lulu could already hear the women dissecting the new Chanel boots. It looked like she was not going to escape discussing them.

By the time she figured out where to sit, however, the conversation had drifted to the environment. The women were comparing notes on various methods of composting. Then they moved on to the Jim and Candace saga. Madeleine, who had talked to some friends in London, added new details. The group was enthralled. "This is delicious," Evie said. She was not talking about the food.

"After the way she got that part," Zoe said, "It sounds like perfect karma." The group fell silent as all heads swiveled in her direction. She tried to look embarrassed. But Lulu could see she reveled in the attention — and was not a good enough actress to hide it.

"Well," she began, "I'm sure you all heard that script was actually developed by Amy Laurent, Candace's BFF.

She spent, you know, years on it. She went through, like, five different writers, and no one could get it right. I must have heard her talk about it for almost, like, four years. The third act just never worked. Amy kept at it, though. She knew the role was worth it. Finally, she's gets a version she's happy with — and the studio is high on it too. She has the writers do one last polish. And she comes into New York from L.A. for a meeting with Mel the next day. They messenger the final version to her apartment, so she can read it when she gets in.

"Well, Candace was staying at her apartment for a week or two. She was doing some work on her own apartment — I think the walls in her bedroom were getting some sort of mural hand-painted. Who knows? Amy had said, of course, stay at mine — they're super-best-bests after all.

"The script comes, and Candace sees it. She's heard Amy talk about it for years. So she reads it — and loves it! She calls Mel, saying she wants this part! It would be perfect! And you know how Mel adores her. But whatever, he gives it to her. She and Amy haven't talked since. Needless to say, she moved into a hotel til her apartment was ready."

"You know," Evie cleared her throat. Everyone is the group grew quiet. "Mel was never all that interested in having Amy do it. He says it is perfect for Candace — always was — and Amy could never have made that story work. He says that was always the plan."

"We're going to start the movie," Fred announced. "We can have dessert while we watch it."

They headed downstairs to what Lulu realized was the screening room. Overstuffed sofas and chairs and double-wide chaises lounges faced a movie screen that spanned one wall. Just past the doorway, Lulu stopped at a table that had large assortments of cookies, brownies, cupcakes and rice crispy treats, as well as bottles of water, sparkling and flat. A large cabinet nearby had shelf after shelf overflowing with an eye-popping array of candy and chocolates.

Lulu saw Francesca and Milo settle into one chaise, near Cesare and Madeleine. Jake and Mark sat on another. Jazzy and Emma lay on a chaise further back, near the door, while Zoe chose a chair closer to screen. Lulu was still looking over the candy selection. She filled a small glass bowl with dark chocolate-covered caramels and marshmallows, lemon drops and Mary Janes, Granny's favorites, and then picked up a water. Connor was sitting on a sofa, off to one side. She hesitated for a moment, and then went to sit next to him.

She offered him some of her candy. "Nice," he said, smiling at her in a conspiratorial way. Then, after he had studied the bowl carefully, he took two dark chocolate caramels.

She went back to their earlier conversation. "I couldn't quite figure out — were you saying you regretted leaving school early?"

"I did love RADA. But I needed to take a job." His voice was serious. "I was ready to work and I knew my mum could use the money. She was worried about costs, and I didn't want to add on to it. School was too expensive — even with the scholarship. I needed to stop taking money and start contributing. This way I could help her and my brother.

"And the part turned out to be the best possible introduction to the West End. I got offers for bigger parts, one after the other — and then Hollywood came calling." He was smiling again. "So now I can really support my mum instead of adding to her worries. I'm helping her buy a flat. That feels good."

"I understand what you're saying," Lulu said. "Mummy wanted me to come out here to spend the summer with my father. I wasn't sure about it. It's been years since I spent so much time with him. I was five when they split up and we moved back to Boston. But I'm glad I did — if only because it makes things easier for her. She not feeling so well right now and she needs to focus on getting better." She was surprised to hear herself talking about her mother. Yet Connor seemed so eager to listen to her that she felt comfortable discussing it. "And I'm enjoying it here."

She realized, suddenly, that this was true.

"It's exciting here," Connor noted. "I was fooled at first. People play really hard. But they work hard too."

He looked directly at her, nothing sidelong about it. "And look where it's got me: Sitting here at a party in Malibu, in the house of a studio head, talking to you." She felt herself flushing again. Yet that smile was hard to resist.

The lights were dimming, and he reached over for more candy. She saw the glint of gold at his wrist as he picked out two additional caramels. Lulu took a breath, and then reached over to clasp his hand with one of hers. She pulled it toward her as she leaned over to whisper in his ear, "So, tell me about this incredible watch?" She could feel his smile as she bent her head over his wrist and then looked up into his eyes.

He was laughing as the room darkened and the opening titles started to roll. It was several minutes, long after the opening credits had ended, before he slowly pulled his hand away, to reach for another chocolate.

CHAPTER 3-A

DIARY ENTRY OF A.J. FLINTRIDGE

THURSDAY, APRIL 10, 1958: *Scheduled 8:45am screening ahead of dailies — I needed to check the soundtrack of "The Hills of Rome" before looking at yesterday's footage. The producer and director have complained for almost a week about sound levels. We need to ship, but they were refusing to lock it. Listened to one reel and I knew those morons were right. The mix had flattened the soundtrack to a monotone — an amazing feat when you think about it. Nothing to do but approve a re-record of the entire film.*

I turned on Phil Lacy. "You work for me," I began, "Your job is to make my life easier. This is the opposite of what you're supposed to do." I told him to find out who on his team had somehow managed to do this this and then fire him. Then fire the nincompoop who approved it. I am surrounded by levels of stupidity!

We went through the first assemblage of "Scheherazade." I can't believe this is the script I approved. I should have stopped production when Cary Grant turned us down. Why I still go after him I don't know. Well, I do know: He would have made this work.

We did as much as we could to bring him aboard. We revised the opening bit, then the middle. We agreed to shoot on location in Spain. We switched co-stars and cut out one character that he said didn't work. We even added the subplot he asked for.

I'd brought in Ben Hecht to do a polish — he held us up for a shitload of money. But he'd written "Notorious" and Grant creams over him. It did get better, so he's at least worth the dough. I even hired that scumbag commie Donald Ogden Stewart, who'd written "Philadelphia Story" for Grant, to do additional dialogue. We didn't hire him exactly — since he's blacklisted. We had to pay him off the books through our London office — and shipped the pages from there.

All this to make it work for Cary. I took him to lunch four times, — twice at Romanoff's. Each meal, I thought we got closer. But he did the usual: Jerked us around — then walked away. He went for that crazy Hitchcock picture. Good luck! True, our script got better, its storyline finally made sense. But that can't explain why we ever thought Ray Milland could pull this off.

And certainly not if he looks like this. Is this really the best toupee we could find? We would have been better off taking all that money we spent on writers and bringing in Perc Westmore to do wigs. At least then our leading man would have hair. Or maybe just gone with Joe Cotton. He's got his own hair to start with.

Even the title stinks. What is this fucking film about? What the fuck does this name mean? "Scheherazade?" Audiences won't even be able to pronounce it! I said we need to change it.

Made it through five reels. A mess. At one point between reels, while waiting for Helen to catch up on the notes we had made, we started talking about the importance of tightening films. Charlie, who won the best editing Oscar three years ago, backed me up. "Every film can be cut," he said. "There is always some fat, slowing it down, that is better cut out."

He said he proved it to himself about 10 years ago. As an exercise, he got a print of "Citizen Kane." "I cut that sucker down to about an hour," he said. "It flew like the wind." I told him I'd like to see it if he still has it. You had to admire him for this — a man of conviction.

Went back to my office to return calls before lunch. Gloria, Caroline and Nancy had called. No word from Sara.

Called Gloria first, confirming Monday. I told her we could start the evening with champagne at Romanoff's and then hit Ciro's. The songwriter Jimmy McHugh was still doing his show there and I wanted to go. I didn't mention that the gossip columnist Louella Parsons was sure to be there — since she's seeing McHugh. We'd be in her column the next day. What I want right now.

Nancy said she could make it tonight or a week from tomorrow. I said tonight would be late, so we settled on Tuesday. Caro had called to see if Friday was still okay. She clearly had another invitation — so

I asked. She said there was a party out on a boat, but she would blow it off if she could blow me. One reason I like her.

As for Sara, she is probably still mad. Maybe it was over. Good. I was with Brenda last night and she ran into us at Romanoff's. She looked so bereft seeing me nuzzling that willowy red-head that you would think I had sucker-punched her. Where does she get off? That's one reason I am taking Gloria to Ciro's. Though taking her out is a waste of time — she's only interesting in bed. There she's a genius!

I like shtupping starlets and extras. More than like! Long-term for them is staying overnight. They come when you want and are grateful for the attention. Then they know to leave. And are okay with a taxi.

Sara, on every level, was more tsuris than she was worth. I had thought I was smart, figuring out this easy way to Arnie Steinhardt. I was a moron. I can usually work the percentages. But since dinner with her family, it's increasingly complicated. More trouble than I expected — or want.

Here she is — acting like the next step is marriage. I thought I had gotten her off that. Seeing her now every 10 days or so is more than enough, as far as I'm concerned. But she's only getting more proprietary. I still think she would be a good mother — but why does that mean I have to spend so much time with her?

Lunched in the Executive Dining Room. We talked Russians and Eisenhower. Not in that order. I stayed for four rounds of word game, then headed back to my office.

Lew Wasserman was waiting in my office. Lew had heard that Charlie Feldman of Famous Artists, the one talent agency MCA regards as real competition, had gotten me to agree to let filmmakers run previews before showing me their first cut. I explained that, even though Billy Wilder was one of the directors, I had screened his film before previews and then cut it — I don't need cards to tell me if a film is working or not. I'm the best fucking cutter in Hollywood. It didn't matter what was in the contract.

Wilder had gotten furious — panting with rage. He berated me, insisting that this was like a surgeon operating without looking at the x-rays. Or worse, not bothering to take x-rays. I told him when a broken bone is sticking out of your leg, you know what needs fixing. You know you have to operate on the shin, and not the arm. It was obvious to me that they had a broken bone sticking out of their leg — in two places. And I knew how to set it to turn it into a colossal hit.

When Wilder realized I was ignoring his argument, he switched to German. He knows yelling in German is more effective. I didn't care. I also knew Feldman would back me up. The studio was more important to him than any one client.

I made sure Lew understood all this — so that his client would, too. Lew assured me that he did. But he still asked me to include the clause — a face-saver, he said, for his agent-client relationship. 'If it would help,' I said, 'sure.'

But I told him I would never honor it and he had better not expect me to. He understood this too.

Sara had called during the meeting. She didn't mention last night when I called her back. I didn't bother hiding the coldness in my voice. Her excuse for calling was a big dinner for the governor — her father had a table and she wanted me to go with her. I told her I was busy *that night. Then I ignored her hurt tone. Hearing her sound so needy only irritated me more. I wanted to get off the phone. So I asked her to have dinner in three weeks. Then said I had to get back to my meeting. It would give me some breathing room to think about all this.*

I have been thinking it was time to get married — one reason I first asked Sara out. To be honest, it was more about having children. I know I'll never tire of shtupping girls like Brenda and Gloria — and there was an endless assortment of them available in Hollywood. But I also knew I didn't want this sort of girl to be the mother of my children. That woman had to be different. Someone, I had thought, like Sara.

She'd be a good mother, I felt — nurturing and warm. There's a sincerity about her. Since her family was in Beverly Hills, and her father a leader in the community, our children would be part of an extended, close family — a key asset in Hollywood. The fact that she's almost irritatingly close to her mother could be helpful — since her family could provide a solid support structure.

It would help, since I knew already that I wouldn't be there for her as much as she'd want. Her neediness is already a pain in the ass. And she's just the type who would try to interfere in the way I run my life. At 47 I'm too old to change. In fact, I'm not even sure how long I could stand her.

Arlene buzzed to remind me they were waiting in Projection Room 4-b to go through the last five reels of "Scheherazade." I wanted to get through them today, because this was one time I didn't want to come back to the studio for a late-night editing session. I put Sara out of my mind as I headed over.

I don't know how they managed to this, but it was an even bigger mess than the first half. The storyline was shapeless. Within 90 minutes, however, we hammered it out. Lacy said they would have an edit ready for me to look at by mid-day tomorrow. Then we ran through the first half again, to see how the cuts looked. It made sense now — even starring Milland.

Between reels, Phil told me that they were working full out on the re-record on "The Hills of Rome" and should have it ready in less than three days. He also needed me to take a look at a temp dub of "Walk This Way." Did that right before I left for cocktails.

He had thought the sound was hinky and he was right. All the gunshots in this Western sounded like they were fired using silencers. The shoot-outs were strangely muffled, with no reverb in the ricochet. What knucklehead had done this temp dub! We decided someone needed to go through and sweeten every gun shot. They have to reverberate down your spine. Not deadened so that they sounded faint and tinny.

Furious doesn't begin to describe how I felt. How do you fuck up the gunshots in a Western? I got up and turned to Phil, sitting two rows behind me. "What are you doing?" I said, "You're supposedly working for me. That means your job is to make my life easier. Not harder. Other people — the people who don't work for me — do that. People like L.B. Mayer or Jack Warner — they work at fucking up my day. That's their job. But your job is to do the opposite.

"Do you know what that means? That means you're not doing your job. Do you not want this job? Is that what you are telling me?

"The only thing I ask is loyalty. I have to come first. Always. There is no second place here. You should be spending every minute of every waking hour thinking about how you can make my life easier.

"So did you hire the nincompoop brother of some tart you're shtupping? Is that why this happened? Because only a fucking knucklehead, a total retard, could have pulled this one off. And you better not have been involved!"

He started explaining to me how this could have happened rather than profusely apologizing. Not the right move. I ripped his head off — and was sorry it wasn't literally. He stood up and backed away from me. I was still screaming as I pushed him up against the wall of the screening room. I leaned down, until I was about four inches from his face and grabbed a fistful of his shirt with each hand. As I jerked my hands back, it tore down the back — so I pulled it off him. All the seats in the projection room were bolted down. But there was one folding chair near the exit. As I walked out the door, I picked it up and hurled it at him. I missed.

I went to my office and changed my shirt. Just before I left the studio, I called Joyce and said we were on for tonight. She said she couldn't wait.

✳ ✳ ✳ ✳

Went for cocktails at David Selznick and Jennifer Jones's for Gene and Lucille Markey. Every time I see the Selznicks' house, I remember again how terrific a designer Paul Laszlo is — his signature jolts of color and chic, spare furniture. But though I admire it, I could never live in it. Billy Haines is the decorator that hits my sweet spot — lush and luxe. And perfect for the Wallace Neff house.

Good crowd: David and Hjordis Niven, Jules and Doris Stein, Arthur and Bubbles Hornblow, Cole Porter, Joe and Lenore Cotton, Eddy and Mildred Knopf, Joan Fontaine and Collie Young.

Gene looks terrific now that he has left his Hollywood producing and screenwriting behind and can indulge in horseracing full-time. He certainly enjoyed his life as a movie producer, marrying some of the most mouth-watering beauties — including Joan Bennett, Myrna Loy and Hedy Lamarr. But he's slap-happy since he married Lucille Parker Wright. It can't all be because she owns Calumet Farms, one of the nation's finest racing stables. True, he loves the horses, but she must be one incredible fuck.

And she's still his best audience. That was obvious since their earliest days together. He basks in her approval. I don't know how, but he's become an even better raconteur.

Gene was several drinks ahead of us — since he'd seen Duke Wayne before coming to the Selznicks. I've never understood how those two can be such good friends. Duke, of course, would like Gene — a decorated war hero and an admiral. But Gene's erudite and one of the best word-game players ever. I don't even want to think about Duke playing anagrams.

David and Hjordis Niven walked in just ahead me. Gene and David were so glad to see each other that I realized Gene must have used the fuck pad David and Douglas Fairbanks Jr. kept at Sunset Towers. I remember once a titled English broad, Dame Edith Sitwell, was in town for a speaking engagement and her literary group booked her into Sunset Towers. I think she may have been the only woman staying there who wasn't a tart or party girl. And boy, was she not a party girl.

I didn't realize that Jennifer had seen me with Sara recently, but she must have, because she asked about her — and clearly wanted to know how it's going. She started talking about how she knew that David was the one. She was living in Garden City, out on Long Island, she said, and she thought her dream of a film career was over. Her husband, Robert Walker Jr. was doing okay in radio but she felt trapped out on Long Island, no jobs in sight, taking care of their two little boys.

One blustery fall day, she recalled, she was in Manhattan, on an audition, and got on a double-decker bus on Riverside Drive. She was sitting on the top deck, though it was chilly, and they passed an older man, strolling along in a somewhat grand manner. He was wearing a luxurious topcoat with a big fur collar, and a bowler hat. She saw him for only a minute, but she remembers thinking: I want to meet someone just like that — a man who can take care of me.

Only a short time later, she was summoned to New York for an audition with David Selznick. When she walked into the room to meet him, it felt like she was meeting that man in the topcoat. Essentially, as she tells it, she never went back to Long Island. She still thinks it was the best thing she ever did. She does seem blissfully happy — if emotionally fragile as always.

I've always thought that Jennifer's vulnerability is one reason David's so smitten. She's the polar opposite of his first wife, Irene Mayer Selznick (Louis B. Mayer's daughter) — who could tackle virtually any problem head on. And win. Her successful career as a Broadway producer has proven this. Even I wouldn't have touched that original production of "Streetcar Named Desire." Marlon Bando and Elia Kazan are impossible separately — a nightmare together.

Jennifer is, of course, more beautiful on her worst day than Irene in her best possible iteration. Jennifer's like a peach — delicious and golden. And her personality is soft and yielding, like a soft little chick that needs to be taken care of. She's entirely scrumptious!

I'm not sure, though, if David's ever fully acknowledged his wife's emotional delicacy. So it felt strange when he started in on Vivian Leigh. He's surprised that she is being considered for "The Roman Spring of Mrs. Stone," the Tennessee Williams play about an aging actress and a gigolo. There's no doubt she'd be fabulous, he says, but he wonders if she's up to it. He says now that he could sense emotional problems back during "Gone With the Wind" — but that's bullshit, from everything I have ever heard.

Eddy and Mildred Knopf were brimming with their latest news — David Merrick, the Broadway impresario, is developing a musical based on "Lili," the moronic Leslie Caron movie that Eddy produced in 1953. That piece-of-shit story about the French orphan who travels with a flea-bit circus, working with its puppets — she talks to them like real people — had been a surprise hit. Eddy never lets you forget it was nominated for a bunch of Oscars and even won one. It shows the state of the industry that this crap just keeps on giving: Merrick is asking their screenwriter, Helen Deutch, to write the book. The sappy story was beyond stupid: The girl would have had to be retarded to be that simple. Or under the age of consent. Not my idea of a Broadway musical. I wonder what Cole would think about it!

Meanwhile, though, Jennifer Jones and Joe Cotton were able to cajole Cole into sitting down at the piano. Doris Stein joined in their pleas. Since that riding accident crushed his legs, Cole usually looks like he's in pain — except when he's at the piano. Yet he always seems reluctant.

You had to fight to get Gershwin away from the piano at party. If you had Harold Arlen and George there too — look out. Virtual fistfights over who could sit down at the piano first.

Cole was already on his third drink, so he gave in fairly quickly. I didn't want to leave, but I was already more than an hour late for the Goetzes.

The dinner at Bill and Edie's was star-studded, more so than their usual crowd. Claudette Colbert and Joel Pressman, Roz Russell and Freddie Brisson, Alan and Sue Ladd, Jimmy and Gloria Stewart, June Allyson and Dick Powell, Evie Johnson, Deborah Kerr and Tony Bartley, George and Gracie Burns, Jack and Mary Benny, Danny Kaye and Sylvia Fine Kaye, Loretta Young and Tom Lewis, and Arthur and Bubbles Hornblow. As well as the director Mervyn and Kitty LeRoy.

The Goetz house was designed by Billy Haines. As usual, I am struck by how perfect it is — luxurious yet cozy. There is nothing else like his interiors. Every detail is pleasing to me. Not to mention every painting. As I walked in, Bill pulled me aside to show me their new Picasso. It has all the bells and whistles. But my favorite is still their picture of Picasso's son, Paul, dressed as a harlequin. More even than their Degas bronze of the young ballet dancer. Why I like kids in art and not in real life I don't know.

I told Bill that Cole just told me Clifton Webb recently bought a John Singer Sargent in New York for $175, since the painter was so out of fashion. Bill's answer was that Sargent should be out of fashion. Even if you paid him twice that amount, Bill said, he wouldn't hang a Sargent in his house. "Frivolous and gaudy," he said.

We joined Danny Kaye back at the party and he and Bill were soon full of talk about "Me and the Colonel," — which Kaye is starring in and Bill producing. It's the Franz Werfel play: A Jewish refuge and an anti-Semitic Polish diplomat flee occupied France together.

I mentioned that Cole had been playing at David and Jennifer's. I'd forgotten one of Kaye's first big successes was Porter's "Let's Face It." Danny launches into the patter song from that show and Sylvia quickly sits down at the piano, to accompany him. Then he segues into one of his high-speed scat songs — to just about everyone's delight.

At the table, Dick Powell, George Burns, Gracie Allen, Jack Benny, Loretta Young and Tom Lewis all talked up their television work and argued that the small screen would complement the big screen, not fight it. TV would only add to the pie, they insisted, not destroy it.

Bill and I argued the other side. We were right — but they wouldn't admit it. Or even see it. It must be because they are all making so much money. It's phenomenal. Particularly since they can own their shows. Their template is Desilu — that new form of studio allows Desi Arnez and Lucille Ball essentially to print money.

After dinner, it was the usual Hollywood trick of the party dividing up into male and female — with the men talking shop. Then we settled in to watch a film. The Renoir in the Goetzes' living room flips up to reveal the projector.

They had "Gigi" — that story about French courtesans — due out in about a month. Another Leslie Caron film! And again she is playing a young girl. What is this! Audrey Hepburn got her start in the original play. I could see her in this part. Adorable, as always. But Caron!

Meanwhile, Chevalier is still doing the schtick he did in "Love Me Tonight," back in '32. And probably well before that. It continues to work. But the film doesn't.

I was glad to have a reason to leave. The screenwriters Albert and Francis Hackett were giving a big bash for Moss and Kitty Hart — guaranteed to be more fun — and I had said I would stop in. By the time I arrived, well after midnight, it had thinned out, but was still a good crowd: writers (Charlie and Ann Lederer, Henry and Phoebe Ephron, Edna Ferber, Alan Campbell, Nunnally and Dorris Johnson [a director, true, but always a writer at heart]); songwriters (Arthur Schwartz, Alan Lerner and Harry and Eileen Ruby); actors (Olivia de Havilland, James and Pamela Mason, Richard and Sybil Burton, Jane Greer Lasker, Harpo Marx and his current girl); producers (Jerry and Connie Wald, Charlie Brackett, Eddie Lasker, Dore and Miriam Schary); directors (Jean and Dusty Negulesco, Charlie and Doris Vidor) and, of course, Moss, a triple threat of writer, producer and director.

As I walked in, Arthur Schwartz was at the piano, playing four-handed stride with Harpo. Richard Burton, James and Pamela Mason, Doris Vidor, Eileen Ruby, Kitty Hart, Connie Wald and Alan Lerner were standing around the piano, singing. Harry Ruby was lurking nearby — clearly frustrated that he wasn't at the keyboard.

Charlie Brackett, Phoebe Ephron, Moss Hart and Jerry Wald were on the other end of the living room, playing bridge. Even from across the room, I could see that Phoebe was plastered — as usual. But I went over to kibitz, since I wanted to tell Jerry that I am already hearing fantastic things about the script for his newest Joan Crawford vehicle, "The Best of Everything."

Then Charlie and I talked about the transvestite movie that his former partner, Billy Wilder, was working on. Charlie was surprised that Billy wanted to work with Marilyn Monroe again — he had thoroughly despised her by the time they finished "Seven Year Itch." With that overarching hatred that was Billy's specialty. No matter how she was perfect for this role, Charlie predicted that shooting "Some Like It Hot" with her would prove a nightmare for Billy.

I got a Manhattan and joined Nunnally, Eddie Lasker and Charlie and Ann Lerderer over on the sofa. I continued talking "Some Like It Hot" with Charlie Lerderer, who had written the 1953 film adaptation of "Gentleman Prefer Blondes" that co-starred Monroe. She had exploded off that film — wiping Jane Russell off the screen. It had been a battle of the bombshells — with Monroe emerging triumphant.

Nunnally had worked with Monroe as well, in his 1953 hit, "How to Marry a Millionaire." He remembered the first time he saw rushes. She hadn't seemed to be doing anything, but on film she annihilated both Betty Bacall and Betty Grable. Even then, her skin radiated emotion. Bacall had the bigger role, but Monroe owned every scene she was in. He has now successfully transferred that movie into a TV show — though he's not as close to any of his three TV stars as he'd been to Monroe. At least from what I know.

As Nunnally started comparing the differences between producing a film and a TV show, I went to find a phone. I called Rhonda and told her I was leaving now. She should meet me at my house in about 40 minutes.

She was a good way to end the day.

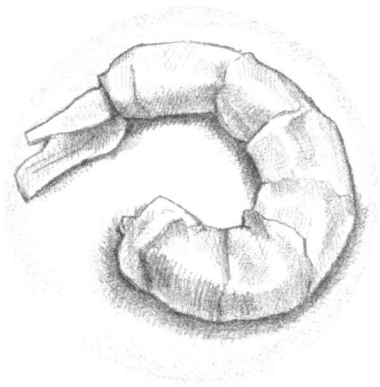

CHAPTER 4

CLOSING THE DEAL: PART 2 (BEL AIR)

BEN WAS SITTING AT HIS DESK, considering the best approach to take with Rob Tracey. Many in Hollywood had tackled this test. Few had passed.

Tracey was nothing if not elusive. He had been pursued for many projects over many years. Early on, he had learned always to say yes. So he did. The most seasoned veterans would heed his siren song. Even those who knew that "yes" was his fallback position could not resist. Having Tracey star in a movie was worth any amount of effort. Years were lost, sometimes the entire project, as filmmakers tried to get a script into the shape he wanted. He seemed far too young to have enticed so many pictures onto rocky shoals.

But getting him from that first "yes" to the first day of shooting could prove a treacherous, even deadly, task.

Tracey, was a serial enthusiast, warming up to an idea quickly, only to drop it without a backward glance. That's what lawyers are for. He was a master juggler — keeping projects in various stages of limbo, as directors or producers or studio executives or other bankable stars, waited for him to decide up or down on moving forward.

He was the Svengali of reworking. Subplots were changed, or added, or subtracted; supporting roles beefed up — unless they were cut, changed from men to women or women to men. Or he might want the location shifted to Europe, or China, or New York, with appropriate supporting roles and accents gained or lost; or moved from mountains to coastline or small town to megalopolis — or the reverse. He might need key plot points re-focused or details blurred. Or positive traits made provocative, or negative traits written out.

Many movies had improved during this process of trying to lure him in — emerging as better iterations. Some hadn't. Projects could be caught in the Tracey quagmire for years, only to be substantially overhauled for another actor or actress. But many other projects died waiting for him to commit.

Ben was still surprised that Milo had helped set up this dinner. But Ben knew that "Double or Nothing" could be retooled for Tracey. He was sure he would have realized this even if Milo hadn't suggested it. It was obvious. Ben still couldn't understand why he hadn't seen it himself.

Ben decided that the most effective approach tonight was straight ahead. This movie was what the evening was about. Small talk was a waste of time.

It was a terrific story and the lead, if played right, was Oscar-worthy. Ben was sure of it. He knew the entire movie was a winner. And the role of Harry was essential to every important beat. He would own the picture.

Ben knew that Rob was considering at least five projects seriously now, as well as a slew of lesser contenders. But another that had seemed about to go had just fallen out. Ben felt that "Double" could jump to the head of the pack.

It was a small dinner. Just Rob and Alexandra; Milo and Francesca, and Steve Loughlen, Rob's lawyer. Gil Skidmore, Steve's husband, had another dinner and could not make it.

Dianne had brought in Jeff from Cosmo's to handle the food and they had mapped out simple, classic courses. First was a cold cucumber-watercress soup with mint; then, grilled Santa Barbara shrimp with burrata, figs and beets over butterleaf lettuce and arugula. Then grilled wild salmon with fiddlehead ferns and roasted new potatoes with truffles, followed by flourless chocolate cake with homemade salt caramel ice cream.

There was no steak or lamb chops involved, since Rob didn't eat red meat. His intolerance to eggs ruled out pasta for the second course. And because he didn't like fruit sweets, he set the dessert agenda as well. But these were minor food issues in a town where the most outlandish food requests could be expected.

Gone were the days when lactose intolerance was as complicated as it got. Ben and Dianna had entertained through Atkins and neo-Atkins. The Scarsdale Diet had migrated south, to the Duke (N.C.) Diet, to the Palm Beach Diet, to the South Beach Diet, to the Argentine Diet, to the Paleo Diet. Food deliveries of entire meals, or just special protein shakes, went in and out of fashion. Meanwhile, gluten-free was now virtually pro forma. And Tracey had been ahead of the curve on the fruit ban — the latest digestive blip was no fruit of any kind after noon.

Dianne had long ago become expert at accommodating vegans. A piece of cake — as long as it was gluten-free, of course. Raw food habitués, however, were still tricky — even for her. Ben always wanted to use a variation of that Lubitsch line, "This is a restaurant, Madame. Not a meadow." But Dianna somehow always made it work.

Before each dinner party, the drill was for Anita to call the office of each guest, to go over food issues. This call was so crucial to any successful dinner that Ben always insisted his office do it — not Dianne's assistant. Even if guests had dined at the house many times before, Anita called — if only to make sure nothing had changed. Her assignment was not just to learn specific allergies but any new dietary requirements, even new likes and dislikes. This information was keyed onto the master list on his computer and set the menu parameters.

Dianna knew how much this dinner meant to him, however. So she had made all these calls herself. She had two pages of dietary notes by the time she was done.

Ben noted the time on his Dupre-Lafon desk clock and realized he still needed to double-check the wine before the guests arrived — to make sure nothing was off. But he went over the plan once again.

Milo had suggested this right after the Howard fiasco. He knew that the project Rob had been looking at most favorably was about to blow up and thought "Double or Nothing" could slide right in. It was ready to move, and those other projects would take too long to ramp up. Milo knew that Rob wanted something that would start mid-October. This could do it.

Milo knew about the sudden opening in Rob's schedule because he and the star were talking almost daily about vacation plans. Milo had invited Rob and Xan to come on the boat in August. They became close after Rob had passed on "Splash Down" and it went on to win three Oscars, including one for best director. The actor who ultimately took the role of Jack, the one Rob had passed on, had been nominated.

Milo and Nate Levinson were renting the Getty boat for the third year in a row. They planned on two weeks in mid-August, since Levinson was set to wrap production in late July. Shooting on Tracey's current film was due to end about the same time. Milo felt this group would work — not just because of timing. Chesca and Gwen Hedges, Nate's wife, got along, and Emma could be good company for Lulu.

Ben knew that Jake Harris, the media billionaire, was going as well — though Milo hadn't told him. And that there were more staterooms to be filled.

But Milo had told him that he and Rob had talked about this project and Rob displayed his usual enthusiasm. Milo said he had stoked it as much as possible.

Ben was still unclear why Milo was helping. It was even more mystifying, now that Ben had finally accepted that Milo had no intention of being in the director's chair for this one. So it wasn't self-interest, the industry's essential glue.

Ben was beginning to think Milo was paying back his long-ago efforts to help when Claire walked out. Maybe having Lulu here had reminded him of that difficult time

— and how Ben, as the new studio head, had been there for him. He asked Milo, but the director just smiled and shook his head.

"This is a good project," Milo had insisted, side-stepping the point. "I might just need a producing credit."

Ben heard the front gate buzzer. He adjusted the music level for the living room, then walked to the pantry to double-check the wine.

By the time he got to the living room, Milo and Francesca were there talking to Dianne. Steve was just walking in. Ben gave first Steve and then Milo a hug hello — and each received a strong pat on the back as well. Milo got a few extra.

Ben then walked over to Francesca. He grabbed her hands in both of his, then took a step back to admire her at arm's length as she stood to greet him. She was wearing a red dress that left nothing to the imagination.

"If you get any lovelier," Ben warned, "it will be illegal." Her laughter shimmered with delight. She tossed her hair back as she did so, and Ben could see teardrop ruby earrings glistening against her cascading dark curls. Ben wondered if they were JAR. Out of the corner of his eye, Ben could see that Milo, still standing, looked proud during the exchange — as if his taste were being validated.

They all sat down, since it would probably be at least another forty minutes before Rob and Xan showed up. The couple traveled on movie-star time.

Ben used the wait to unpack details of the project for Steve. Ben had always thought Gil, with whom he had more far contact, was the smart half of the couple. But Steve was quick – he grasped all the movie's varied beats, and saw immediately how it could fit into Tracey's body of work. The project could play on Tracey's persona while playing off it. Steve got it completely.

It was 50 minutes before the couple showed up. When they walked in, it was as if arc lights had turned on.

Alexandra Hobart walked in first, a diaphanous blonde so lovely, Ben always thought, that you had to fight the urge to marvel that she was could string words together coherently. A woman this beautiful didn't really need any other asset. Her large slate blue eyes were fringed with thick dark lashes. On anyone else, they would have been a powerful focal point. But on Hobart it was extraneous.

For every time Ben heard her speak, he knew that her voice – more than her beauty or even her relationship and marriage to Tracey – was what guaranteed the stardom Hobart had so avidly sought.

Her dark voluptuous voice played against all that luminous fragility – the timbre and tone of a luscious brunette issuing from this porcelain sylph. Beneath every sentence lurked a promise of something intoxicating ahead. A whisper of pleasure and excitement. Even when asking a question, she sounded provocatively knowing. For her many fans, this touch of abandon was only hinted at – but it was in every word she spoke.

Off-screen, she still had traces of her rural Tennessee accent – and more than a trace after a few drinks. Her language was X-rated – though her posture was perfect.

Hobart had been flown out to Los Angeles four years ago – specifically to meet Tracey. She had come in to read for a part in his new film. Hollywood had beckoned Hobart after she had starred in back-to-back Broadway hits. She had first emerged in a string of Off-Broadway successes, and established a glowing reputation in New York theater circles.

But she got on that plane as soon as Hollywood called. And never looked back. She landed the part in Tracey's film – and the star of the movie as well. The outsized, industrial-strength fame of movies was what she had sought. Unlike many other actors, she basked in the white-hot light of celebrity.

Broadway was too rarified for the level of success Hobart hungered for. She had come from nothing, a hollowed-out town in the Tennessee hills, so she still savored what celebrity offered. But she was already beginning not even to notice the small pluses – the way chefs could make whatever she asked the waiter about, whether or not it was on the menu; or that a bottle of Cristal was open and on ice whenever she walked into a restaurant.

In this, she was the polar opposite of her husband, who entered the room a step behind her. Some years ago, he had decided he wanted stardom expunged from his life. But this was impossible. He was an international sensation. He blazed in any room. It was uncanny.

Tracey was handsome in a clean-cut, all-American way, sandy haired and chiseled. Not tall, though. Ben wondered why the tabs always labeled him as over six feet. There was no way. There was also nothing brooding or mysterious about him. What he had, though, was a powerful punch of star appeal. Your eyes gravitated to him whenever he walked in a room. And stayed there.

Tracey had become a huge star before he was 20, and had lost none of his megawattage over the last 11 years. He not only came with his own spotlight, he seemed perfectly back-lit as well. Even in this room, his smile was incandescent.

It may have been partly due to his unstoppable enthusiasm. Rob always reveled in the moment—enjoying things 200 percent. No one, Ben thought whenever he saw Tracey, could be in such a great mood all the time.

It was this intensity that convinced an endless number of directors or producers or studio heads that Tracey really wanted to close a deal — and was not shining them on this one time. And they were all reading it correctly. Tracey was interested and eager — at the moment he was talking to them. Just as he had been equally sincere about a different project that morning, or a rewrite of a third project the day before — or would be about some other project tomorrow.

He usually had at least 15 projects in some stage of development at any given time. And those were only the films he was actively taking meetings for. Every project he was in discussions about would move along, sure it was the one he favored above all else. And it was — in that moment. He was in the moment every moment.

Rob presented this open and receptive attitude to the world. In a town where information was the most valuable, hoarded currency, he seemed profligate. Only up to a point, however. There was something opaque about him, Ben always thought, under all that hearty fellowship and high spirits. Maybe that's what made him a star, Ben decided. An essential elusiveness that seemed rooted at his core.

Xan asked for a bourbon almost as soon as she walked in. She declined the champagne that Francesca was drinking and the serious red wine that Ben and Dianne had started on. Milo had given him a head's up that she favored bourbon, so they had three kinds to offer. Ben was glad to see the cocktail was in her hand by the time she finished kissing everyone hello — giving Steve an extra hug in the process.

Rob put his arm around Xan as soon as they sat down on the sofa. As always, the couple sat knitted together. He stroked her arm, the fingers of his other hand entwined with hers.

Rob's shining adoration was tinged with awe. Looking at them, Ben saw Rob as a smitten teenager, thrilled that he had somehow landed the high school prom queen. Yet Ben would bet the star had never not gotten the girl. Even if every other teenager had gone through awkward stages, Ben was sure Rob had always been top athlete and stunningly popular.

It was irritating, Ben thought while looking at Rob. Usually these guys who peaked in high school were never heard from again — and here was Tracey, king of the Hollywood prom. Ben wondered if he himself could even rate a seat at the cool table at this point. He couldn't shake off the chill from the Nauman party.

Milo was just finishing a story about Lulu's near miss, during her second driving lesson. She was practicing parallel parking in Ted Welling's car court and had nearly side-swiped Alan Frankenthal's 1963 Havana brown Mercedes convertible. The director was a noted raconteur — probably one reason he could still keep setting up movies even after four bombs — but he could only moan as he watched the near miss between their Prius and his sedan. As she inched ever closer, Alan had gone white under his perennial tan.

Frankenthal managed to joke about it later, Milo said, but that look of horror said it all. Lulu had also been shaken up by her near-miss, Milo noted. But he had told her it was not important — her safely is what mattered.

Now the best part, Milo smiled, was that her driving had improved. She was now extra-careful when behind the wheel. So Milo had no need to tell her the cautionary tale of the silver Porsche 911 he had totaled when merging onto PCH at age 17.

"I don't know that story," Francesca pouted. "How have I missed it? We both need to hear that tomorrow."

Rob started describing his first accident, when he was a teenager. He hadn't seen a patch of black ice late one night and skidded right off I-95 right near a swamp. It had a sunny ending — like most of his stories. Two deer hunters with a grappling hook had stopped and pulled him back onto the road. Then they all went to a bar for shots with beer chasers.

Ben had stopped listening. He knew he should, but he was going over what he wanted to say about the movie. It took everything he had not to start right in on the plot. This is why Rob had come, after all, and Ben found it hard to focus on anything else. He didn't care about car crash stories.

Yet he knew he had to wait at least until the appetizer, if not the entrée. Anything earlier would hint at desperation. So he sat and waited, smiling and swirling his wine — until the second round of cocktails. Dianne could see what he was about to do. She reached over to touch his arm, trying to stop him from starting the narrative. But he was not to be deterred.

He could quickly tell that Rob liked the story. Beyond his usual enthusiasm, he was asking the sorts of questions actors bring up when they picture themselves in the role. Ben knew to discount the way he leaned forward intently, moving his hand from Xan's shoulders to her knee. At some point in the story, close to the fire, he stopped massaging it. Ben hoped that meant Tracey was actually engaged.

Ben was roughly a quarter into it when William came in to announce dinner. Milo broke in with, "To be continued." Dianne was the first to stand up. She walked over to Chesca and took her arm, chatting with her quietly as they walked into dinner. Ben wondered if they were talking about the ruby earrings.

Ben waited until they were all seated before continuing. The two waiters started pouring the wine, a spicy Corton-Charlemagne chardonnay. He had thought it would work with the minty, slightly garlicky soup. And it did. Not that Ben was eating. Rob's interest in the piece seemed palpable. He felt buoyed by the actor's response.

Ben was just winding up Act 3 when the waiters began bringing in the second course salad of burrata, figs and grilled shrimp over butterleaf lettuce and arugula. The design on each plate was architectural. Ben, who usually cared little for or about salad, smiled down the table to Dianne.

But when Xan saw her plate she tensed up and put her hand on Rob's shoulder. He turned to Dianne. "Xan can't eat shrimp," he said. "I thought we told you."

Dianne looked unpleasantly surprised. Her dinners were carefully orchestrated to run like clockwork. Not sputter out at the start. She had made the calls personally. She was sure Rob's office only mentioned his dietary issues. Alexandra had not even come up. Dianne wanted to demand why Rob's office hadn't told her. Instead, she looked toward Ben and began profusely apologizing.

"I am so very sorry," she said, keeping any hint of irritation out of her voice. "This is terrible! It should never have happened. I can't believe my assistant didn't get this straight.

"I knew about you and eggs," she said, gesturing toward Rob. "That's one reason we didn't have a pasta starter. You know, Jeff makes such delicious mushroom ravioli with truffles! But I somehow missed this about Alexandra and shrimp. I am so, so sorry!!"

"It's easily taken care of," Ben broke in. He wanted Dianne to stop talking. He knew he should have had Anita make the calls. This would never have happened if she had handled it. "Xan, we'll just give you this without the shrimp. It will probably taste even better!"

He motioned to one of the two waiters hovering near the table and then slowly repeated the gist of what he had just said — as if the waiter hadn't heard. The man spirited away Alexandra's salad.

She visibly relaxed now that the shrimp was no longer in front of her. As if, Ben thought, it was going to jump off the plate and burrow into her chest. "Please, everyone," Alexandra said with the beginnings of a smile. "Don't wait. Start eating. It's going to get cold!"

Dianne was still too intent on apologizing. "I am so, so sorry. We should have known," she insisted. "Allergies are so dangerous. We try to take care of this before — which is why that phone call is so important. You never know what people are going to be allergic to — or just don't like. You know, I keep a file on this, and cross reference it. For example, Rob, I certainly know about gluten!"

"Forget it, Dianne," Ben said, "Things happen." This was not offered as reassurance. He wanted her to move on. Now.

But it was as if a pause button had been pressed for the dinner. Ben tried to pick up the story where he had left off, but he could sense Rob was not listening. Then, sooner than he expected, Xan's new plate was brought out. Everyone started eating again.

Suddenly, Alexandra sat up straight — even straighter than usual. She was known for her perfect posture, but her long, graceful neck seemed elongated. Ben could have sworn she grew two inches. Her fork clattered onto her plate and its echo resonated in the sudden silence. Ben thought the reverberations got louder in the stillness. Xan's translucent skin was flushing pink across her cheeks. Her hand went to her throat as she took a deep breath.

Rob leaned over and put a hand on her shoulder. "You okay darling?" he asked. Again, everyone stopped eating. Milo put down his fork, which had been suspended halfway to his mouth. They all looked at Xan.

"My tongue feels strange," she said. Her voice was slightly raspy. She took a deep breath. "It's sort of tingling. The whole back of my mouth feels weird." she said. Then she shook her head slightly, and laughed. "But it's nothing," she said, "I didn't eat enough today. And it's probably some sort of nervous psychosomatic reaction, after seeing that shrimp on my plate."

Rob rubbed the back of her neck. "Well, it's all fine," he reassured her, as if speaking to a small child. "It's gone now." He leaned over and kissed her shoulder. Everyone returned to their salad. Ben tried to pick up his story.

He barely got through two more sentences before Xan put down her fork again. "I'm sorry, but my tongue does feel tingly," she insisted. No one was disagreeing.

"Something is wrong." Her cheeks were now a deep pink, and her neck and chest turning a soft rose.

"But there's no shrimp," Dianne seemed to be pleading, as she got up from her chair. Ben could see she was near tears. But all he could think was: Not another lost dinner.

He turned to the waiter, busy pouring more of the Pinot Grigio that Ben had chosen specifically for the shrimp. "Call 911. Now." Milo already had his phone out, but he motioned the waiter to do this immediately, too. When the waiter dashed out of the room, Milo hurried after him.

Dianne walked around the table and knelt down between Ben and Xan. "What can we do for you?" she asked.

Steve had also gotten up, and was hurrying around the table toward Xan. Her breathing seemed to grow more ragged, and she was groping for her husband's jacket pocket.

"She has to have her shot," Rob said. His voice was louder than normal, but he still sounded calmer than anyone else in the room. "I don't know what's up here. But she is having an allergic reaction. She needs it now." He grabbed her hand with one hand and reached into his pocket with the other.

"Here's your EpiPen," Rob said slowly and distinctly as he pulled a small slim object out of his pocket. "Do you want me to—"

She pulled it out of his hand.

That same moment, Jeff burst into the room. "We didn't change plates," he announced, as if this would fix the problem. "We gave her the new salad on the same plate. I am so sorry. So terribly, terribly sorry. I thought she didn't like it — not that she couldn't have —."

Ben cut him off. He didn't want to hear. He still couldn't believe his careful plans had led in this. "Just tell me you called 911," he said quietly. "I don't want anything else from you."

"Yes," Jeff said, "They're on the way."

He couldn't be sure whether Xan had heard any of this. The actress had grabbed the pen, pulled off the cap, hiked up her skirt and, with one swift motion, injected the epinephrine deep into her thigh.

Within seconds, her breathing seemed less labored. Ben thought the scariest part was seeing Alexandra Hobart slumped over.

Jeff decided he should try again. "I made a new salad for her — without the shrimp," he began. "I redesigned the dish and replated the course entirely. But we put it back on the same plate. I want to really apologize to Ms.

Hobart — everyone in the kitchen tonight wants to extend sincere apologies to —"

Ben wanted to stab him with the fish knife. But he didn't think it would go in deeply enough to cause real pain. "We have no interest in hearing you didn't mean to kill her," he said dismissively. "Not after you just gave it your best shot." This would have to do. "We have no time for your pathetic excuses. Just get her some water — Now."

Jeff limped out and Dianne hurried after him. It was going from disaster to calamity if Cosmo's decided never again to come to their house for small dinners.

Ben didn't care. He was just relieved to hear the wail of a siren as it neared the house.

Tears started to trickle down Xan's face. Rob gently pulled the EpiPen out of her hand. He began stroking her hair. Francesca, who had been sitting in shocked silence, had gotten up, walked around the table and was soon kneeling beside Xan, much as Dianne had before. She didn't know what else to do, so she stroked Xan's arm in a way she hoped was soothing.

Ben heard the front door open. He went out into the hallway — grateful to have a reason to leave that room. What a nightmare.

Two emergency medical technicians were striding down the hall toward him. Milo was leading the way and Dianne following behind.

"Good to see you," Ben said. "She's allergic to shrimp and she may have somehow eaten some."

The medical team walked into the dining room, pausing at the threshold to take in the scene. They went over to Hobart, still slumped at the table. Ben saw that her face was no longer severely flushed. She now had a waxy pallor. It still looked grim, Ben thought, but was probably an improvement. At least she wasn't going to die at his house, he thought, grasping for something positive.

Chesca yielded her spot as the men walked over. They clustered around the slight figure in the chair, while Rob talked quietly with them. As they began to work on her, the room fell silent.

"We're going to take you to the hospital," one said to Xan. He was speaking clearly and distinctly — the way Rob had just minutes before. "We're going to start you on an IV on the way. So you can start getting fluids even before you get there."

"We have a stretcher —"

"She can walk out with our help," Rob insisted. He helped Xan stand up. "That's better for us." Dianne came toward the now ashen-faced actress, to see if she could help. Xan's eyes snapped into focus as Dianne drew closer. She shrank back against her husband and started to sob.

"She's exhausted," Rob explained, as he continued walking her toward the door. Steve fell into step with Rob and asked if he wanted him to come in the ambulance. "Why don't you follow us in your car?" Rob asked. "That way we have one at the hospital."

Steve nodded. He quickly kissed Dianne goodbye and then shook Ben's hand. "We'll get back into this." He looked at Milo as he spoke, not Ben, "There is interest here." The lawyer gave Chesca a quick hug before hurrying to the front door, to catch up with Rob and Xan.

Chapter 5

THE SCREENING IN BRENTWOOD

THEY WERE LATE.

Milo had been on back-to-back phone calls, and lost track of the time. First, he'd gone over locations with his production designer, trying to figure out the right house. They finally nailed down the two strongest possibilities — each with an overlarge side porch.

Then Nate had called. They were both going to Tom Steadman and Sheila Adderman's for the screening that night, but he needed to talk before. There were things he didn't want to discuss within earshot of the others.

Particularly Sheila. And not because she blithely repeated comments she shouldn't have.

Nate was in the process of making an offer to Connor and he wanted to talk it through yet again. Milo had seen an early cut of Connor's movie with Francesca — including scenes that never made it to the final cut — and he had told Nate then that the young actor could deliver.

This offer was going to require finessing — given that Connor had committed to Sheila's project, and her film would then have to wait. Not to mention that Nate intended to talk about it with Connor tonight, since the actor was also due at the dinner. He had made Sheila and Tom's invite list largely because he was attached to her project.

"This kid has gotten a lot of heat off "Chessmen," Nate was saying yet again.

"You know Gil agreed with me," Milo broke in, "that this is the right next step for him. He's talked to him about it. And the agency is behind it. You're there.

"Gil and Steve are going to be at dinner." Milo continued. "So just talk to him there. He'll tell you again. It's the best move for this kid — and they know it. And you'll talk to Ericson tonight too. With luck, they close it tomorrow."

"Gil said he would deliver," Nate said, ruminating. "What is Connor, like 23? The way things are going, probably by the next film Gil will have his hands full. Thank god at this stage he still listens to his agent. So Gil can convince him, right?

"And he's also sure Sheila will wait until I've wrapped Ericson's scenes. It would only make her project hotter. At least he said that could be his selling point when he broke the news to her."

As they were winding up, Levinson had an idea. "If this deal closes," he said to Milo, "how 'bout having Connor on the boat for the second week? He gets along with Chesca, right? And it gives me time to talk with him about the film. He could join us at Corsica and stay through Sardinia."

"That should work," Milo said. "Ted confirmed yesterday that he'll only be in that cabin for the first week. Then he and Jen are going to Istanbul and the Turquoise Coast. Talk with Ericson about it tonight, if you want. It's not that far off. Nate, this deal is going to close!

"Also, I told Ben he could come for dinner while we were in Corsica," Milo added, almost as an afterthought.

"Ben Robbins?" Levinson didn't bother to mask his surprise.

"He wants to sit down with Rob again," Milo said, "so he's coming for dinner one night. He'll fly down from the Hotel du Cap. Rob knows. And so does Loughlen."

There was silence on the phone. "It will be fine, Nate," Milo said. "I'm helping him on this one project. I feel I owe him this. Then I'm done."

Milo didn't explain further — even if he was inclined. He'd suddenly realized the time. They were supposed to be there now. He didn't like being late.

Francesca, meanwhile, couldn't find the blouse she wanted. She had to go through her closet twice before she found the soft chiffon top — the one with small yellow flowers against a sea-blue background. The filmy fabric had been hidden by the folds of another blouse.

Lulu couldn't understand why her stepmother had been so intent on wearing it. She didn't think it was particularly flattering. Maybe on a blonde.

Lulu had texted Connor that they were running late. She had promised to keep him posted on their ETA.

Since the hike, they'd been texting regularly. He had started their quizzical banter as they waited for Francesca to catch up on the trail. His sly teasing had continued via text — a provocative tango of words just this side of flirtatious. Or maybe just the other side. Lulu wasn't sure. But she spent hours puzzling over it. Connor appeared to have loads of time for their rambling text conversations.

Lulu wished — as she had so many times this summer — that she could check in with Abby. She knew her best friend would be glad to spend hours analyzing what was going on here with Connor. And help her figure out what to do about it.

Lulu had played the same role for Abby all last fall, as she agonized over Jamie Fentress. Abby couldn't figure out whether he was into her. Jamie had been seeing Nina Travis for more than a year, so Abby couldn't believe he was even interested. Especially since Nina was one of the hottest girls at school — if not the hottest. She and Jamie were considered the coolest couple.

Lulu and Abby had spent weeks dissecting Jamie's texts and diagraming their various meet-ups — because Abby suddenly began running into him at so many random places. Lulu decided early on that these frequent appearances couldn't all be coincidences. But it was hard for Abby to believe Jamie might actually like her. She had long had a crush on him and had decided he was the one boy she wanted to be with, but she was had no idea if he felt anything approaching the same way. He might just want a break from Nina's high-maintenance demands. Maybe he just liked talking with her. But Lulu gradually got Abby to see the whole picture. Now she was happier than Lulu had ever seen her.

Lulu needed Abby to do the same for her right now. She wasn't sure why Connor spent so much time texting her. Yet Lulu felt unable to reach out to her best friend. Lulu had to admit to herself this time that it wasn't only her desire to avoid talking about her mother's illness.

It was at least partly because she didn't want to share the stunning secret of this growing flirtation with anyone — even her BFF. Lulu wanted to savor it all to herself just now.

Lulu was worried that Abby might simply discount the entire story. She had no experience of what Lulu's life had been like this summer. The very idea that Lulu had somehow become friends with Connor Ericson might sound preposterous to her. Abby might also think she was imagining all this — that it was a fantasy she created because of her crush on an actor. That was something Lulu did not want to hear.

"Emma is going to be there, Lulu," Milo was talking to her as they headed down the canyon toward Sunset. He was going through tonight's guest list.

"Nate finished shooting." Milo continued. "He got back to town yesterday. He and Gwen are coming and they're bringing Emma. We need you guys to share a cabin on the boat. I know it'll be fine, but it would help if you spend this time with her before.

"I know you'll like hanging with her. She's interesting. You know, she got into schools back East — I think Wesleyan was one. But she didn't want to leave L.A. Nate said Jazzy was coming too.

"Gil Skidmore, the agent, is going to be there with his husband, Steve Loughlen," Milo was also annotating the guests for Francesca. He still thought of her as fresh on the scene — since he continued to delight in her company.

"They collect art, Lulu, so that's something for you to talk to them about. They have an important collection — mostly large contemporary pieces. And their house is stunning. They had it designed for the art. Steve's a lawyer and Gil's Connor's agent.

"And Connor Ericson will also be there. He's invited since he's set for Sheila's new film. He's getting a lot of heat off 'Chessmen.' The word is he's amazing, Chesca." He reached over to stroke Francesca's knee. "But you always told me he was talented, right darling? You have an eye for talent!" He smiled at her. "Connor's clearly in his moment right now. So hot he's sizzling. It's irresistible to most people — sometimes it can be lethal."

Milo's eyes met Lulu's in the rear-view mirror. "Lulu, your grandfather used to call this 'The Forum of the 12 Caesars Moment.' That was the name of a fancy New York restaurant he would go to in the '50s and '60s— usually to close a deal in the showiest possible manner.

"His regular New York hangouts were Pavillon or 21." Milo filled in the back story for her — and probably also for Francesca. "But 21 was essentially a taproom and may have looked too scruffy for some people. And others just couldn't understand Pavillon. Sometimes a place like Forum of the 12 Caesars could be far more effective. It certainly was for me when I was a kid." Milo laughed. "He took me there a few times and I remember being so impressed. When I was eight or nine it was far more exciting than a boring joint like 21. Unbelievable, really.

"At The Forum of the 12 Caesars," Milo gave a dramatic pause, "every course could be served flaming. Not just the dessert, like Cherries Jubilee or Baked Alaska. And not just the entrée, like Steak Diane or Shish Kabob served on a rapier. No, every single course — appetizers, salads, side dishes, even cocktails and coffee. It was all flambéed. The place was ablaze."

Milo had turned onto Sunset and was speeding through the "S" curves, heading west to Brentwood. He took the turns too fast, but the Aston Martin stayed solid to the pavement.

"Right now Connor's life is sort of like that restaurant — incandescent. How he deals with it is what counts in the long run. His moment can flame out after a few months, or ignite and blaze throughout his body of work over a lifetime. We don't know yet. Most people can't keep it going. That's why there are so few real stars — stars that matter. Or people that matter, actually."

Milo was silent as he took the next few curves. When he started talking again, he returned to the guest list.

"If Art and Nancy Manning are back," he said, "they're going to be there. I'm sure you'll remember him from when you were little. He was a young lawyer back when my father was around, so I've known him basically my whole life. A hell of a nice guy.

"And she's terrific — runs their education foundation. She's also a serious rider. Keeps two horses down in Malibu. The others are out in Aspen, where they built a riding ring. She spends a lot of time there now — they both do. They were up there the last three weeks.

"And then Sheila's friend, Jocelyn Barnes, is going to be there, too. She's that college friend who's working with Tom — the one Nate was talking about. We'll see what's up with that.

"And this movie is supposed to be good. It's opening at the end of September, I think. The DP was the second cameraman on 'Splashdown.' Talented. I want to see how he handled this."

Milo broke off to shift into tour-guide mode. "We're almost in Brentwood now, Lulu. This house is going to be fun for you," he promised. "Not like Ted's. It's more of a piece with L.A.

"You had bohemians with money here, Lulu." He was warming up. "Not like back East. They were not looking to buy into an establishment. It was not about fitting in. People took chances. That's why so many important architects worked out here — Neutra, Schindler, Eames, Wright, Lazlo. It was all about private space.

"So everyone talks real estate here — has done it and will do it. There is chronic house-envy. Of epidemic proportions. And it's not just about modern houses or the case study houses. My dad lusted after a Wallace Neff house in Beverly Hills that had belonged to King Vidor. It must be in his diary, Lulu."

"I think it is!" Lulu said. "It's on Tower Road, right?"

"That's it!" Milo laughed, "He must have spent more time lusting after that house than any woman. Incredible piece of property. But his timing was always off. When it was available, he didn't have the dough. Taxes were insane then. And when he had the money, the owners wouldn't sell. But it seemed like every year he would have his realtor set up an appointment and he would go look at it. Then he'd spend weeks analyzing how he could pull it off. It's gone now. Some producer got his hands on it and ultimately destroyed it. Ripped the guts out and built crazy cantilevered decks that had no meaning. Then he tore it down.

"A friend of my father's coveted the Bing Crosby estate, four acres in Holmby Hills on Mapleton. It was a terrific '30s Gordon Kaufman house — also amazing grounds. It was torn down years ago by Aaron Spelling, so his wife, Candy, could have a house with a big enough footprint to include a room just for wrapping presents. Now the Formula One heiress bought it. She's overhauling it.

"I hear some of my friends talking about houses now, and it's like I'm transported back to my childhood, listening to my father and his friends talking about the houses they coveted.

"And Lulu," his tone grew measured, "I'm glad you are reading the diary. What do you think now?"

She had been thinking about her father a great deal as she read it, actually, wondering what sort of relationship a little boy could have had with a father like this. It had forced her to recalibrate her image of Milo. She felt like a car GPS – adjusting to accommodate for new, often conflicting, information.

Yet, she still felt awkward talking about it with him. And though he clearly wanted to discuss it with her, he only brought it up when others were around – as if he needed the presence of other people to muffle the emotions aroused when talking about his father.

Lulu felt it was even harder to talk honestly about the diary with Francesca right there. So she said the first thing that popped into her head. "Who was Jennifer Jones?"

"Jennifer Jones!" Milo smiled and shook his head. "What about Jennifer Jones? I haven't thought about her in years." Lulu thought he sounded almost relieved that she hadn't asked about his father.

"He's over at her house. And he actually seems to like her. Who was she?"

"An actress," he answered, "A beautiful actress. Luscious and adorable. It was hard not to fall for her. She was shy and sensitive. So vulnerable — but oh so sexy. Even when I was a teenager, sitting with her in my parents' dining room, over iced tea and poached salmon, you always felt you had a shot."

He looked over at Francesca and laughed. "She was my first real crush!"

His eyes met Lulu's again in the rear-view mirror. "Her husband — her third husband — was David O. Selznick. He was crazy about her — though that never stopped him from fooling around." He paused for a few seconds. Lulu wondered if he was thinking about his married life with her mother. "She starred in "Song of Bernadette" and "Portrait of Jenny," with Joe Cotton. Lyrical on film.

"But when I knew her, she was essentially retired and married to Norton Simon. You know the museum over in Pasadena? The one I should take you to since it has the best art collection west of the Mississippi?" He smiled. "That Norton Simon. He was also mad about her. Also intent on taking care of her. Not all that unusual, actually, when it came to Jennifer. I would have devoted my life to taking care of her.

"I got her to tell me once how she met him. And you know what, Lulu, it's about driving in L.A.!" He laughed. "Jennifer had been a widow for about five years when she met Simon at a dinner. I think he was instantly smitten — not hard where she was concerned.

"Soon after, there was a big party at Chasen's. They're both invited — so Simon had the host suggest to Jennifer that he pick her up and bring her there.

"It started out well. But Simon hadn't actually driven himself in a long time — he had a chauffeur. He couldn't handle left-hand turns. So they had to get from her house to Chasen's making only right turns. It took like an hour!

"When they finally reach the party, Jennifer, usually so shy and polite, gets out of the car, thanks him for the ride and tells him she'll get someone else to drive her home. He was dismissed! She was not going to spend another minute with someone who didn't know how to get around L.A.

"But during the party, he stays right at her elbow, and she begins to see how smart and funny he is. It's not enough, however, to wipe out the memory of that ride. So later that night, when he asks if he can see her for dinner, she gives him the brush-off. She has to leave town the next day, she tells him, to go to Paris for the Red Cross. I think she was on their board and had to be there for some meeting. He asks if he can see her when she returns — and she says she's not really sure when she's due back.

"That's it, as far as she is concerned. The next day she goes to Paris and checks into the hotel the Red Cross is putting her up in. It's a far cry for the Ritz, where she usually stays. She's never even heard of this dump.

"As she walks into the lobby, though, who does she see but Norton Simon. He looks startled and walks over. 'What are you doing here?' he asks.

'I'm in town for the Red Cross," she replies. 'This is where they booked me.'

"'What a coincidence,' he says, 'This is my favorite hotel in Paris. I always book the top floor!'"

"They got along so well, she said to me, that she stayed an extra week. By the end of those two weeks they were engaged. And every year, for their anniversary, he would book the entire top floor of that little hotel in Paris."

"Wow," Lulu laughed. "You know in the diary she tells Abe how she met Selznick."

"Amazing!" he said, "Synchronicity. I'm sure he was crazy about her. There was something about Jennifer that made you want to rescue her."

Milo barely braked as he turned right onto Rockingham. Only as they neared a long, jasmine-covered wall did he finally slow down. He rolled smoothly to the gate and stopped at the bell. "This is a Cliff May house from the 1930s," he explained to Lulu, "the template for the California ranch house. In the daylight you can see more clearly how the indoor and outdoor spaces flow together. And May sited it brilliantly. It's nestled in a grove of coral and pepper trees — more voluptuous, and far older, than the house. The exterior, Lulu, is a Platonic version of lush California design and landscape — down to the poppies that surround the house"

As they went down the driveway, Lulu saw a sprawling ranch house with so many sliding doors she had a hard time figuring out which was the main entrance. But if the exterior was Ur-California — Lulu felt teleported back East when she walked in. It was obsessively early American.

The house was crammed like a child's toy chest — with all styles and periods tossed together after a day of vigorous play. There was no order, or even coherence. It mixed urbane with rustic, mahogany with pine, sophisticated with naïve, baroque with austere.

The confusion was clear in the front hall. Four 17th century children's samplers were hanging opposite the front door. Lulu decided they must be important — since they were the first thing visitors saw. A burnished Chippendale chest, embellished with scrolls and shells, stood beneath them — yet managed to remain aloof. Its mahogany gleamed from almost three centuries of polishing, rallying against the simple maple picture frames. A delicate Hepplewhite pear wood candle stand was to the right. On the left sat a chaste pine spinning wheel. Lulu wondered if Sheila Adderman would be wearing colonial dress. Like a Williamsburg docent.

None of this furniture fit together. Lulu had always admired the early American furniture at her grandparents' home, or at Aunt Grace and Uncle Peter's, as serene and austere. There was a graceful spareness to it. Particularly the furniture that Granny and her sister, Great-Aunt Daisy, had inherited from their grandmother, Julia Appleton Winslow. They each had a few pieces from the Louis Appleton Collection – named in honor of Julia's older brother, a young aviator who had died during World War I. But the bulk of this important American furniture collection was on permanent loan to the Boston Museum of Fine Arts. Granny was on the board there, like her father before her.

But the early American furniture here was like a fun-house-mirror version – jittery and askew. Lulu could see into the living room from the foyer. It was even more confused. The sofas were Duncan Phyfe. The chairs around the room were a cacophony of tulipwood or mahogany Sheratons, pine ladder-backs and hickory comb-back Windsors. End tables were painted pine and the coffee table a decaled Dutch colonial blanket chest. All the upholstered furniture was covered in a clatter of stripes, in various shades of green. None had anything positive to say to the mustard yellow on the walls. The bottom third of the room, meanwhile, was beadboard, painted a crisp white.

There was a massive pie safe between the two tall windows on the opposite side of the room. The oversized piece looked like it had the original paint — a soft Shaker blue. But it might have worked better in a kitchen than a formal living room — which this aspired to. Through the screens on the cabinet doors, Lulu could see stacks of quilts.

A thin woman was striding toward them. She was so slight that at first Lulu had thought it was a girl her age. But as she drew nearer Lulu realized she was older. She was more gaunt than slim; her dirty blonde hair more dirty than blonde. "Milo," she said, with a welcoming smile, "and Chesca. Great to see you." She greeted each with a quick hug. Then she held out her hands to Lulu. "And Lulu! I'm Sheila, Sheila Adderman. So delighted you're here!"

Lulu took her hands, so thin they felt skeletal. No mob cap, Lulu noted. It would have been out of place, since Sheila's clothes were thoroughly up-to-date. She wore a boxy, short-sleeved, cream silk blouse capped by a gray cotton pique peter pan collar, over thin black leather leggings. But up close, her large China-blue eyes were as sunken as her cheeks. Her sallow skin had a deadened feel.

She kept one claw-like hand in Lulu's and put her other on Milo's shoulder as she walked them into the living room.

Guests were already there. Milo headed toward to an older man seated in a large arm chair in the middle of the room. He was deep in conversation with Nate

Levinson, who was leaning forward on the sofa. But as Milo approached the man stood to greet him. Lulu thought there was something different about him. It was more than the fact that he was the only man in the room not in jeans. He was wearing gray flannel trousers with a white, button-down oxford shirt and a navy cashmere cardigan tied around his shoulders — more Bar Harbor than Brentwood. Tasseled alligator loafers without socks sealed the deal. His thin, aquiline features were deeply tanned, and his smile animated his entire face.

"How's my boy?" he said, as he hugged Milo hello.

"Always better for seeing you," Milo answered. He turned to Lulu, who was standing a step behind him. "I don't think you've seen Lulu for a while. She seems to have gotten older — something you never do."

He pushed Lulu forward. "This is Art Manning," he said. "It's been years. But I seem to remember he used to do mock toasts with you, to get you to drink your milk."

"Young lady," Art's smile enveloped her as well, "You've gone and grown up on me. Do you realize you look so much like your mother that I feel I've walked into one of those '30s family sagas, like 'Come and Get It' — where Frances Farmer played the mother and the daughter. She was a great beauty, Lulu, but your mother could have given Frances a run for her money."

Levinson stood to join their conversation. "Hi, Lulu," he said. "I hear Emma really liked meeting you! We're all going to have some fun on the boat next month."

While Levinson was talking to Lulu, Milo leaned close to Manning. "Art, thanks again for your help with Howard," he said quietly. "I kept meaning to call you. We haven't had a real chance to talk since you left town. I'm assuming you know about that other dinner two weeks ago?" The lawyer responded with a slight crooked smile and a single raised eyebrow. "That felt like some other sort of movie. More like 'And Then There Were None.' I was in the Mischa Auer role!"

They both laughed, though Milo's was slightly ragged. "But I think I can get this one back on track. Then I'm done." Manning's pat on his arm offered support laced with consolation.

Milo turned to Levinson. "Nate," he said, as he reached out to hug him hello. "Doesn't look like those reshoots took too much out of you. And how's 'Dead Drop' looking?"

"Gil's over there with Tom," the producer answered. "They're opening another bottle of wine." It seemed like a non-responsive response, but Lulu saw Milo nod, as if it answered his query.

Lulu looked around for Emma and saw Francesca coming toward them, laughing, with Gwen. She was in a medley of geometric prints. Her pegged trousers were a bright blue and lemon yellow harlequin pattern, and her vest was kelly green-navy blue zig-zags. Her blouse had wide blue and yellow stripes. She was wearing a navy blue pork-pie hat tilted back off her face, its hatband a yellow and green fever chart. Lulu felt dizzy looking at her.

"Gwen is so funny," Francesca started in. "I was saying that there is such a lack of good material. And she totally understood — that she hasn't been able to find a flamingo pink silk taffeta faille for weeks now."

"We're both right," Gwen broke in. "She might be having a hard time finding a good script, but I definitely can't find that faille!" She turned to Lulu and smiled. "Hi Lulu. Emma and Jazzy are over there, getting something to drink. They're standing at the other side of the bar — Tom and Gil are blocking your view. Why don't you go over and the girls can get you a soda, too?"

Lulu skirted the adults, who were locked in conversation. The taller man, who had curly brown hair and boyish good looks, was talking. "The start day would be early March," he said. "We could maybe push to late March. Would that do it? And we'll give you the plane if it helps. When does it wrap?"

But before his questions were answered, he looked to Lulu. "You must be Lulu," he smiled, extending his hand. "I'm Tom, Tom Steadman. I'm glad you could come."

"Thanks so much for including me, Mr. Steadman," she answered, as she held out her hand. "Tom," he interjected.

"Tom," she repeated. "It's nice to be here. Your house makes me feel I'm home – like I'm back East. My grandmother treasures her early American furniture and just about her favorite thing to do is checking out other pieces. She'd be in her element." Now that she stood closer, she saw his face looked careworn and his eyes tired – as if he had seen too much.

"Nice to hear that, Lulu. We sure enjoy it. It's a passion of Sheila's in particular. This is Jocelyn Barnes," Steadman said, putting his arm around the woman standing beside him. His movement had a proprietary air, and so did his glance when he looked at her. "She works with me." The woman, who had masses of curly dark hair and wide-set eyes, smiled up at him before she turned to Lulu, holding out her hand.

"And this is Gil Skidmore," Steadman said, "He's worked with your dad a lot – and sometimes even with me!"

"I feel like I've already met you," Skidmore said, "I've heard so much about you from your dad." He had brown, slicked back hair and restless hazel eyes. His laugh sounded genuine as he reached for her outstretched hand and held it with both of his. But Lulu wasn't sure. He kept looking around the room even as he said this.

She followed his glance and saw Levinson nod to him imperceptibly. "How are those driving lessons going? Your father was telling us about that close call up at Teddy's house."

Lulu started at his question. "It's going fine," she said. "Much better since then." She felt her cheeks growing warm and knew she was blushing. It never seemed to get easier, she thought, as she looked for an escape.

It didn't really matter though, since Gil was not looking at her. He was looking down at his phone as he tapped out a message.

Lulu excused herself and walked around the U-shaped bar to Jazzy and Emma. Jazzy was wearing jeans and white T-shirt, again arranged precariously. The difference was this T-shirt had red bands on the hem and sleeves.

Emma had on skin-tight dark blue jeans, with zippers at the bottom, and a vintage yellow T-shirt, printed with a tattoo image — a large hand, palm up, holding a broken heart surrounded by a laurel wreath. As Lulu drew nearer, she saw that the heart was in matte red sequins and the wreath in matte green sequins. Emma's sequined slippers matched the red of the heart, but glittered. Her gold charm bracelet and tangle of vintage silver ID bracelets jangled every time she moved her hand. Which she did constantly, since she rarely stopped texting.

Jazzy was pouring diet Cokes and asked Lulu if she wanted one. Emma immediately noticed Lulu's shoes. "Hey, Lulu," she said. "So you went shopping with Chesca?" She clanked even more as she pointed to the tan suede driving moccasins. "Those Tod's are new, right?"

"I didn't really need anything," Lulu explained, "But she insisted that she wouldn't go home without getting me something." She didn't get into the strange dynamics of the shopping expedition with Francesca. "So I said yes to these. I thought they could go with just about everything."

"This isn't about need," Emma advised. "Not with a stepmother. Though, honestly, everyone needs at least one pair of Tod's. That's a basic. Now, what about that bag Zoe mentioned?" Lulu marveled that she remembered these details from three weeks ago.

"The Prada satchel," Emma must have seen the question in her eyes. "When it comes to clothes," she laughed. "I never forget. I take after my mother on this."

Lulu couldn't help thinking how different mummy was. It would have been the lyricism of an Emily Dickinson poem, not a Prada bag, that she remembered. Her mother had sounded even more tired than usual today. She had warned Lulu months ago that the treatment was going to take progressively more out of her each time. Lulu had thought she was prepared for this. She now knew she wasn't. But she quickly pushed aside these thoughts — she didn't want to start crying in the middle of the party. She would think about it later.

The three girls sat down on the Chippendale chairs grouped nearby. The upholstery rustled whenever Lulu shifted position, which was often since the chair was so uncomfortable. The cushion, she decided, must be the original horsehair.

Emma had been in Alexander McQueen on Melrose just the day before. She began describing — in intricate detail — the new jackets. Jazzy didn't have to pretend to be interested, she wanted to hear about every stitch and kept insisting she was obsessed with Sarah Burton — long before the designer had done Kate Middleton's wedding dress. Emma started showing pictures on her iPhone of skirts she had tried on. The two girls huddled over the phone, zooming in on fashion details.

Lulu wondered how she was going to get through two weeks of this on the boat. She began making a list of books to load into her Kindle. She was definitely bringing "Tender Is the Night" — mummy had said it was the perfect book to read on a yacht in the Mediterranean. She'd recommended Fitzgerald's short stories as well — especially the early ones. Lulu was considering reading through all of Fitzgerald. She had read "Great Gatsby" this year in English and loved it. And she was sure to be surrounded by "careless people" on the boat.

"What are you three up to?" Connor was leaning over the back of a nearby chair, lazily smiling down at them. His eyes had a mischievous glint.

"Hello, Connor," Jazzy turned the two words into an invitation. Lulu wasn't sure to what though. "What's up with you?" The invitation was more explicit. Lulu wondered how Jazzy was able to put a sexual topspin on every word — even "hello."

Connor raised an eyebrow, countering "What do you have in mind?" He was laughing as he said it. "And you're off topic. It's Question Time, and what I want to know is: What are you up to?"

"We were wondering when you were going to show," Emma said, "And what's up with 'Chessmen'? I heard the release date was pushed."

"I have no idea," Connor replied. "Why should they tell me? I'm just a little cog in the big machinery of Hollywood. I just shoot 'em, and then move on to the next." But he wasn't grumbling. His voice held a swirling undercurrent of laughter, inviting them to jump in and share his pleasure. "I've been too focused on a hike I heard about." His glance met Lulu's, flickering on hers like a bright pin light before moving on. "It sounds more fun right now. Getting out on that trail. Free-dom!" He pumped his hand in the air.

"My dad was talking about 'Chessmen,'" Emma persisted. "I think he saw some of it. It sounded so cool."

"I hope so! Maybe it'll hit. Meanwhile, are you three the 'style police'? Is that what's going on here? You getting ready to swoop down on whoever might set off the alarm at your posh checkpoints?

Jazzy laughed. "We're thinking more along the lines of 'stop and frisk,'" she said in her provocative tone. "Especially where you're concerned. Assume the position!"

He continued his riff. "So, who's naff?" he asked, "Who gets stopped at the checkpoints?" he asked. "You know, maybe this would be the one time African-Americans won't be the target — or even be the majority of people stopped. They create too many fashion trends. They'll breeze right through. It's the old white guys who'll get stopped — the ones whose pants are too high, right?

"And then what do you do with the chavs who can't pass? Banishment from L.A? To where? Vegas? Salt Lake City? Is that where I am headed — 'cause I certainly don't qualify as posh. Decidedly leaning toward chav. Just look at what I'm wearing — Levis, Hanes white T-shirt, Converse trainers. It all probably costs less than your T-shirt, Emma. I'd never make it through your checkpoint: Turned back for being 'Not Posh Enough.'"

Lulu was laughing as she grabbed Connor's hand and pulled him down into the chair he had been leaning over. "Excuse me, and what about my Levis?"

"That's easy," he laughed. "They're grandfathered in. Don't you know that rules never apply to the people in charge? Just us peons."

"Connor, I didn't know you were here." Francesca was walking toward them. "How could you ignore your favorite co-star?" She was pouting slightly, to match the mock reproach in her voice. She tossed her head as she pushed her thick hair back off her face.

Connor winked at Lulu, squeezing her hand before he let it go and turned around to Francesca. He gave her a quizzical smile as he stood to hug her hello. "I was going to get a drink, m'dear, when I decided I needed to find out what this gang was cooking up." He sat back down. "I finally figured it out: They're the style police, ready to set up a fashion checkpoint. And it looks like I won't make it through. 'Not posh enough.' But I was trying to jolly them along – so I could sneak past the barriers."

Francesca stood behind Lulu's chair. "Don't worry," she said. The irritation was gone from her voice, replaced by a studied amusement. "I can get you through this roadblock. I know the password." She placed her hands lightly on Lulu's shoulders. You could mistake it for affection, Lulu thought. "It's –," Francesca searched for an appropriate word she could offer.

"Adarp!" Lulu said. "That's Prada spelled backward! The week after it will be," she paused, "Roid"

They were all laughing now. "For Dior!" Emma said.

"Connor," Skidmore was walking toward them, "Can we talk for a minute?"

Lulu didn't think it sounded like a question. More like a command.

"Sure," Connor told him. "I'm on to you now," he continued teasing the girls as he stood up. "So don't think you're going get off so easily. I need to hear about all your checkpoint criteria and penalty plans. I'll be back!"

Skidmore opened a door opposite the bar and the two men walked into what Lulu could see was an office. The door closed with a click behind them.

Steadman poured another glass of wine for Jocelyn and himself and then carried the bottle to Francesca. She was no longer leaning over Lulu's chair.

"Francesca," he said, "This turns out to be a surprisingly good red wine I've opened. Can I offer you a glass?

"I could use a drink," Francesca cooed. They walked back to the bar, where Jocelyn was holding out a glass for her.

"Let me just finish up about the jackets," Emma picked up where she left off. "There's this amazing forest green velvet with chunky jewels on the collar and along the hem. It's also in this incredible, lush navy." Lulu's attention drifted. She started thinking again about mummy. But she tried to focus on Emma. The other was just too hard right now.

Lulu realized there was a little girl standing beside her. She couldn't have been more than five. She had Sheila's blonde hair and large china-blue eyes. But they were out of proportion on her face — she looked like an animated Keane painting. Lulu leaned down, until she and the girl were at eye level. "Hi," she said, "I'm Lulu. Who are you?" She held out her hand.

The little girl looked gravely back at her. "I'm Fiona," she said. "I like your hair." She reached past Lulu's outstretched hand, to touch the waves of her red hair. "It's pretty."

"I like your hair, Fiona" Lulu answered. "It's pretty, too."

"No, it's not," the little girl said. "Not as pretty as mommy's hair. And not pretty like yours."

"Of course it is," Lulu assured her, smiling, "It's prettier." Fiona gave her a measuring look, unsure whether to believe her. "Much, much prettier."

The little girl's eyes rejected this idea.

"We want to start the movie soon," Sheila had no trouble being heard over the party's din. "So we need to eat now. We got take-out Chinese tonight, from Mr.

Chow's. It's in the kitchen. Please go help yourselves. There's Chinese beer in case you want it with dinner. And wine, of course.

"And if that's Fiona Steadman I see, up past her bedtime, she had better high-tail it to bed. Otherwise there won't be any fortune cookie for her tomorrow."

Fiona ducked down, as if to hide behind Lulu's chair. But a large woman with an Irish accent, whom Lulu figured to be the nanny, suddenly appeared beside her, holding out her hand. Fiona refused it, now clinging to Lulu's arm as well as her hair. The little girl's voice started to rise. "Go away," she cried, "I want to stay here with my friend."

But when that argument failed her, she lowered her voice and nimbly negotiated her terms. If she went to bed now, it would mean a fortune cookie tonight as well as tomorrow. It was a deal she could accept. So she did.

"Wasn't Gil over here?" Nate Levinson was standing near Emma's chair. He was asking Steadman, who was still at the bar with Jocelyn and Francesca.

"Yeah," Tom said. "He went into the office with Connor."

"Thanks," Nate said, "I've been looking for him. There's something I need to ask. It's quick. I'm sure they won't mind if I interrupt. We're all about to have dinner now anyways."

He gave Emma's shoulder an affectionate squeeze as he walked past the girls, including all three in his smile. He knocked hesitantly on the office door, as if nervous about bothering anyone. Then, with one motion, he opened it, walked in and shut the door behind him.

"We really should start eating," Tom prompted everyone in his general vicinity — while looking only at Jocelyn. Lulu thought this must have been disconcerting for Francesca, who was used to being the center of attention. "This is a long movie tonight." He slid one hand to the small of Jocelyn's back and put the other on Francesca's shoulder blade to walk them toward the kitchen.

"Raf Simmons makes a really cool royal blue velvet jacket," Lulu heard Jazzy saying. They were still on jackets. "with these amazing flowers on it. Great with jeans."

Lulu wondered if you could make this sort of jacket seem about to slide off. She was sure Jazzy would figure it out. She didn't lack enterprise. Lulu decided that she didn't think about clothes strategically — the way these girls did. The notion was foreign to her. She often felt that she was navigating unfamiliar waters here. Not necessarily out of her depth, she kept reminding herself. But somehow treacherous.

Sheila walked over, "Come on, gals. There are no engraved invitations here. You'll like the film if we can ever get it started." Her skin was almost transparent, pulled tight against her skull. Her eyes glittered, and seemed to grow bigger as she spoke. Lulu could see the network of fine blue veins on either side of her temple and a larger one at her neck was pulsing slightly. Thicker dark violet veins protruded from the inside of her wrists. The three girls stood up and followed her into the kitchen. She pointed them toward the plates, without taking one herself.

The dark green granite kitchen counter was covered with platters of Chinese food. Minced squab with lettuce wraps, Beijing duck with all its accoutrements, crispy orange-peel beef, shrimp in lobster sauce, a steamed whole fish in ginger, baby bok choy, pea shoots with garlic. At one end were stacks of steamers holding delicate vegetable dumplings, at the other were two large serving bowls of rice.

Guests were working their way down the line. Lulu hung back, watching as Emma and Jazzy picked up plates and started to fill them. She noted that Emma took very little food. Like Francesca, she chose sparingly. Shelia, meanwhile, had yet to pick up a plate.

"You okay, Lulu?" Her father put his arm around her, pulling her close. "I'm so glad to see you and Emma getting along. I knew you would like her if you gave it half a chance.

They took a few steps away from the counter. "Thanks for reminding me about Jennifer Jones. I'd forgotten how much Abe had liked her."

"There don't seem to be a lot of people that your father felt that way about."

"Abe's your grandfather, Lulu." He gave the semblance of a smile. "Not just my father. You're connected here, too."

She could now see the sadness behind his eyes. "Was it hard?" she asked quietly.

"What?" he started, "To live with him? I don't really remember him as part of the household. He was so rarely there. It felt like he was looking for any excuse to be out of the house."

Lulu was surprised she had missed this sadness before. "To be his son?" she asked softly.

"He thought of me as a screw-up," he said. But then he stopped and started again. "He was not an easy guy. You could say that he had high expectations — virtually impossible to meet — for himself as well as others. Certainly as a boy and a young man I could never even get close to meeting them. Maybe part of it was because I knew he didn't think I could. Or maybe I just reminded him too much of Sara — boys are usually like their mothers. But it was most probably a little of both."

He paused again. "It was probably harder to be his wife.

"I finally learned about the dynamics in play there during a college course. Pure Psyche 101: He couldn't respect Sara because she had loved him enough to marry him. Something clearly had to be wrong with her. Classic madonna/whore. Abe was like so many men of his generation here in L.A. They married the 'good' girl but only enjoyed the 'bad.' The girls he liked, felt most comfortable with, were starlets — especially the ones who were never going to be stars. There was a desperation there that he seemed to need.

"I was just a little boy when I realized how cruel he could be — how mean he was to my mother and to the people who worked for him. They never worked 'with' him." His laugh sounded almost harsh. "I watched what he did and what he said. And I've always tried to do just the opposite.

"Sometimes — and I know this is strange Lulu — I think I couldn't be who I am as long as he was alive. I was too busy fulfilling his idea of who I was. Maybe that was one way I could win some validation from him." He smiled somewhat lopsidedly. "It was complicated. He was complicated. I might be throwing too much at you too quickly."

Lulu could see that, though it pained her father to talk about this, he wanted to have the conversation. It was as if he'd been waiting a long time to talk about this with her — just like he'd been waiting a long time to say her name.

"You know, I think Granny felt something like that about her own mother," Lulu said. "I don't think Lily

Thayer could ever have been as nasty as Abe. But from what I hear she definitely was caustic. Granny still talks about how her mother was never happy with anything she did — even the way she poured tea wasn't right. Granny can sometimes be a little like that too, of course." She gave a half-smile just thinking about it.

He pulled her another step away from the buffet line. "Listen, Lulu, we need to talk about something else. I realize this is a difficult time for you," he said, with an underlying tone of reassurance. "But things are going to be fine with your mom. I know she's been sounding a little ragged lately, and she's working at the Fogg just two days a week right now, but the test results have been extremely positive." His voice changed as he switched subjects. "And it's wonderful for me to have you here. Just looking at you makes me feel proud. I don't what to miss any more time with you."

He gave her shoulder a squeeze and then his voice took on a lighter note. "But that doesn't mean you need to hang with me any more tonight, Lulu. Go sit with Emma and Jazzy." He kissed her forehead before he let her go.

Lulu was glad she didn't have to sit with Francesca. Once she filled her plate she joined Emma and Jazzy, down at the far end of the long mahogany dining table, which had seriously carved and gilded lion's paw feet.

Jazzy and Emma had finally moved on from jackets. They were analyzing Zoe's latest beau. The topics were related, though, since he owned a big sportswear company.

"I like his vintage Mercedes," Emma seemed to be going down a check list. "He's a good driver. He dresses kinda cool for an old guy. Plus she can use his account at Maxfield's anytime she wants. And also the one at Fred Segal. The dinners and parties he takes her to are awesome. He's always fine about taking her friends out for dinner with them and lets her take friends out for meals without him. He's even kinda funny." She started laughing, "With all that, yeah, I'd do him."

"Ick," Jazzy shrieked, "How could you say that! He's fat! I told her unless he agrees to start seeing a trainer regularly, she should dump him. It might help if he did a cleanse. Maybe even a liquid diet for a month. Or two. It's fine that he takes her friends out to dinner all the time. But he shouldn't be eating himself while he's doing it!"

Emma's cell gave a trilling hum. She looked down. "Sophie and Olivia are going to a party on Oriole, at the top of the Bird streets. It's not starting til late so Sophie says we should come after the movie. She'll text me the address after she gets it."

Sheila was at the other end of the table, leaning forward in an animated fashion as she talked across the table to Art Manning. They were both laughing, as was Gwen and the woman sitting beside Art, whom Lulu assumed was Nancy, his wife. She looked like a rider,

Lulu thought. Slim and fit, her dark blonde hair pulled back in a tight bun at the nape of her neck. Her elbows stayed tight to her body even at the table.

The man sitting beside Sheila was also laughing. Lulu decided it must be Steve Loughlen, Gil's partner. Emma confirmed it. Loughlen was a bald version of Gil, similarly tanned and wiry, with the same long, tapered fingers. He was wearing an indigo-blue work shirt. But Lulu could tell from here that it was linen, not denim.

Milo and Francesca were beside Steve, but weren't paying much attention to what Sheila was burbling. They were focused instead on Tom and Jocelyn, still locked in conversation. Tom was talking intently to Jocelyn, the way he had at the bar — as if he wanted to consume her. The food in front of him couldn't begin to slake this hunger. Their heads were even closer together. Lulu couldn't understand why no one else seemed to notice.

Milo certainly had. He kept his eyes on them as he sat talking to Francesca. They were both laughing softly. Then Milo looked up suddenly — Nate had just walked in from the kitchen. He put his plate down next to Francesca, then headed back to the kitchen.

"I'm getting another bottle of red wine," Nate announced to the table. "Do you want me to bring white, too?" He patted Milo on the back as he walked past, and nodded his head once.

"Would you please bring me another beer," Francesca called after him.

"Maria will take care of it," Shelia said, somewhat imperiously. She pressed a buzzer next to her table setting.

"So how bout this?" Connor was sitting down in the seat next to Lulu. She had been so focused on Tom and Jocelyn that she hadn't seen him enter the room. "It looks like I am going to be able to sneak through your posh checkpoint after all. If, that is, you go back to the original meaning of 'posh.' The wealthiest toffs, when they sailed from Britain, would always travel 'port out, starboard home.' I'm going on the boat with you for a week!"

His smile was so potent she couldn't help but smile back. "Great," Lulu said. "That will be so much fun!"

She was almost startled as she realized how happy she was to hear this. It was far more than knowing that Connor would make bearable the long days on the boat with Emma — not to mention Francesca. She had to admit to herself — if to no one else — how excited she was that he was going to be there.

Lulu gave him a congratulatory hug. "I'm really so glad you're coming."

Lulu thought of something else. "If you are going to travel with us, can't you stop in London on the way over or the way back to see your mother and brother? I know how you've missed her."

"How did you know I was just thinking about that!" His smile took on added warmth.

"Synchronicity!" Lulu laughed. "I'm getting another Coke," she announced as she stood up. She hoped that she captured some of Jazzy's inflection as she smiled at him. "Can I get you anything?"

She brought him back the beer he asked for. And quickly started laughing over one of his stories.

CHAPTER 5-A

DIARY ENTRY OF A.J. FLINTRIDGE

THURSDAY, SEPTEMBER 25, 1958: *When I got to the office I went over the preview cards from last night again. I had already cut two sequences after the screening, but that wasn't enough. The preview audience had confirmed this film was still 20 minutes too long. Which meant 30. I've been saying this to the producer for two weeks now. I told Bob to have the second reel queued up for me within a half-hour. We'd start looking for cuts from there.*

Detoured to casting on the way to the projection room. Gary Cooper's wife, Rocky, and his agent had told Bernie they don't think Cooper's fans want to see him play a character so morally ambiguous.

The only correct response is: 'Screw you, I don't give a fuck what you think.' This film won't work unless viewers are unsure which way Cooper's character will jump.

I know Coop's newfound Catholic guilt over leaving Rocky so publicly for Patricia Neal when shooting "The Fountainhead" — and then shtupping Anita Ekberg even after he went back to his family — is giving his wife the upper hand here. But no matter how right Cooper is for this role, this is too high a price so Coop can keep putting his cock wherever he wants.

I have no interest on backing down. Coop's dick may control his life — but not my studio. Bernie and I discussed who else is available. He's checking Randolph Scott, Fred MacMurray, Glenn Ford, Robert Mitchum, John Wayne, Bill Holden. If we need to, we'll recast the girl once we figure out who we have in the lead. We need to nail this down by the end of this week. It's already taken too long.

Also gave Bernie the name and number of that girl I danced with at the Coconut Grove on Tuesday. She's got a look I like, so I had told her we'd be in touch. Told Bernie he should call her in for the singer at the juke joint. He already brought in that girl from Don the Beachcomber — he agreed with me that we should try her as the hotel front-desk receptionist. He also confirmed that the girl I met at Perino's is now set for the new James Mason film. As I walked to the 4-b projection room, I made a note to call her tomorrow.

We got through four reels before lunch. Cut three sequences entirely. The director fought over every frame. "You are making my life harder," I warned him. "That is not the fucking job I hired you for. Your job here is to make my life easier. Not to deliver a piece-of-

shit movie that drives audiences out of the theater. Your job here is to keep the asses in the seats." Finally got so fed up that I kicked him out of the room.

Took a break for lunch. Word gamed through it. I won three rounds out of five.

Finished cuts in afternoon. I allowed King to come back — as long as he didn't say a word. So he sat there — royally pissed off. I told Eddy I wanted to see the finished cut with a temp dub tomorrow at 3 p.m. And I wanted two scorers from the music department to sit through it with us then. The music would matter and I wanted to talk them through the movie — I was fucking tired of solving these problems after the fact. I told him to check in with Helen once he finished the cut.

Moved on to watch the first assemblage of "Restless Wind." Just first half, but much better than expected. It was kismet that our original choice for the daughter had turned into a fat pig, with an ass as wide as the Grand Canyon. Even if she'd been able to lose those final 10 pounds, that girl would never have been as hot as this trick we hired to replace her. From her first entrance at the soda fountain, this girl had the look that demanded, "Fuck me. I want it now!" You wanted to sweep aside those sundaes and root beer floats, throw her on the drug store counter and mount her right there.

Her whole attitude, but especially those eyes, beg for it. It didn't matter what the dialogue says. Once we saw her first footage, the scene where she's walking home from school and meets the new boy in town, we pumped up her part.

She was going to explode off this movie. There was nothing gamine or innocent — nothing like Leslie Caron. Bernie had already set her next three roles. Meanwhile, I sat there, trying to figure out if there were any more scenes we could add. For her, we reshoot.

I have a date with her Sunday night. The first of many, I hope.

Headed off for cocktails at Sam and Francis Goldwyn's to celebrate their return from Europe. Good crowd: Bill and Edie Goetz, Otto and Mary Preminger, Jean Simmons and Stewart Granger, Dinah Shore and George Montgomery, Jack and Mary Benny, Eddy and Jane Greer Lasker and screenwriter Lenore Coffee.

I told Jean Simmons the word on her new Wyler picture is terrific. She told me she had a terrific time making it. She talked about how good it was to work with Greg Peck. I decided to add him to our list as a possible Cooper replacement.

Jean was talking with Sam and me about how much she liked musicals. To prove it she did a verse from "If I Were a Bell" — the song she sang as Sister Sarah in Goldwyn's "Guys and Dolls." She said this was something she wished she had more opportunities to do. While she was singing, Sam beamed with pride.

Had to leave all too soon for a dinner at Jerry and Connie Wald's. Star studded, as expected, with Humphrey Bogart and Betty Bacall, David and Hjordis Niven, Joe and Lenore Cotton, Joan Fontaine and Collie Young. Also Mervyn and Kitty LeRoy and Eddy and Mildred Knopf. Virginia Robinson (of the department stores). Sam Taylor was there and another writer, Cliff Odets, was expected.

Jerry was near the door when I walked in. I said hello, but barely paused. He was talking with Eddy and Mildred Knopf, and if I had to hear another story about adapting the "Lili" screenplay for Broadway I would have ripped his throat out.

I got a gimlet and headed over to Sam Taylor, who had written Hitchcock's recent movie, "Vertigo." As we caught up I realized we hadn't had a lengthy conversation since he'd worked on "Sabrina" with Billy Wilder and Ernie Lehman, four years ago. He reminded me how difficult that shoot had been. It was only Lehman's second picture — his first had been with Charlie Brackett, Billy's former partner. So he was unprepared for the nightmare that was picture-making with Billy.

Lehman got so rattled by Wilder's method of starting production without a finished script that he essentially had a breakdown — he started crying on the set one day and couldn't stop. Taylor told me that even as Lehman was headed home — where Billy's doctor was going to meet him and give him a shot to calm him — he had to drop off the next day's pages at Julius Epstein's house. Someone needed to work on them so Billy would have dialogue to shoot. Sam worked with Epstein for the next four days of shooting.

But Sam insisted that "Sabrina" shoot was a piece of cake compared to "Vertigo." He started talking quietly so Bogart wouldn't hear. Humphrey might have thought that Billy and Bill Holden and Audrey Hepburn were in league against him on "Sabrina," Sam said, but Wilder was a prince compared to what Hitchcock did to Kim Novak on the "Vertigo" set. Taylor was speechless about Hitch, which is saying a lot. "Fucking insane," was all he could mutter.

It was the first time he'd worked with Hitch and he promised it would be his last. He shook his head in near disbelief when he added that Ernie was now working on a script for Hitchcock — the Cary Grant film. Good luck with that!

Clifford Odets finally arrived right before we sat down to dinner. He's with the model Nancy Mills — and he's not only old enough to be her father, he looks it. His skin now has an ashy pallor, especially next to her creamy complexion. Quite a dish. After that long fallow period, Odets regained some of his luster last year with that stunning rewrite of Ernie Lehman's scenario for "Sweet Smell of Success." My favorite line is still "a cookie full of arsenic." But Odets gleams darkly now — his "Golden Boy" glow is long gone.

Jerry is producing Cliff's next screenplay — and letting him direct. It must be great, since Jerry's too experienced to do something like this otherwise. He knows letting a writer direct can be a train wreck waiting to happen. Odets is going to need a seasoned DP — a shooter like James Wong Howe, say. He'll also need a top-notch editor on it from Day One — to make sure there's enough coverage. First-time directors usually have their head up their ass when it comes to shooting sides. They're so obsessed about finally getting control over their precious fucking dialogue that they don't even think about what the assembled footage will look like. Or won't look like. Schmendrick assholes.

Wald must have a lot of confidence in this project, since he was moving forward with it, though he already had three other movies due to shoot next year. He and Odets have lined up Rita Hayworth to star. Odets told me proudly that his screenplay, "The Story on Page One," would do for Hayworth what "Gilda" had: Put her back at the top of the Hollywood firmament, where she belonged.

Rita was also due for dinner — this night was, after all, a Jerry Wald production. She was coming with Jim Hill, her husband of about six months. Hill already sounded like yet another mistake in her long road to connubial bliss.

Prince Aly Khan had fucked her over. The word is she got out of that marriage with nothing to show for it — except her daughter, of course, who she's mad about. But Aly Khan, who tosses rubies as tips to Paris Ritz cigarette girls and I happen to know kept at least three other women in hot and cold-running sable the whole time he was with Hayworth, tried to give the actress nothing when she walked. And since Rita had broken her Columbia contract to marry Aly, that prick Harry Cohn made sure she crawled before he would take her back. Then Dick Haymes, talentless shit that he is, used her as a meal ticket. She put up with it until he slugged her in public.

Now she's married to James Hill, a writer who essentially lucked into a partnership at Burt Lancaster's production company. Hecht-Lancaster had a solid body of work — both commercial and artistic successes. Harold Hecht, Lancaster's friend and producing partner, had brought Hill aboard as a writer. The company became Hecht-Hill-Lancaster or H-H-L. I am not the only one who wonders why.

We waited an extra half-hour for Rita and Jim, before we finally sat down to dinner. We had waited two hours — which is Connie's limit. As it was, the beef Wellington was badly charred and potatoes Anna hard as a rock.

Rita and James came as the entrée was being served. So they missed the shrimp cocktail. But they had clearly downed more than a few cocktails of their own before they arrived. Rita took the seat next to me, with Jim on the other side of her at the end of the table. Jerry, ever the producer, had placed them directly across from Odets and Mills.

Rita was at the giddy stage — when everything seems hilarious. Each sentence Cliff said to her evoked peals of laughter. Her effervescent mood was infectious. She always did have that sparkling laugh. The table fizzed and the room suddenly felt carbonated.

The only person immune was her husband. Hill sat there at the end of the table, brooding and cantankerous. I'd heard he is mean drunk and he seemed intent on proving it.

It started when she tipped over her wine glass. He was lacerating. "You stupid cow," he said, "Can't you even sit down at a table without making a fucking mess? You idiot! It's embarrassing for me to go anywhere with you. You're worse than a cow — you're a clumsy ox. Always doing something moronic like this. Fool!"

Ordinarily, it might have been entertaining — but here was this pischer slapping around Rita Hayworth. Aside from the insanity of his onslaught against a real movie star, Rita herself is so shy and nervous that it's like blinding a puppy.

"It's nothing," Odets broke in. "Forget about it. These things happen all the time." He spilled over his own wineglass. Hayworth shot him a wordless thank you, and a hint of a smile. As she smiled, Odets reached his hand out to her, jerked his elbow sharply back and knocked over Nancy Mills's wineglass. "Oops," he said, "Now how did I do that?" He smiled back at her.

Hill was having none of it. "Idiot!" he said, still focusing on his wife. "Look what people have to do to make you feel better. You should be in a drunk tank — not a Beverly Hills dinner party. When we leave, I'm going to take you there. Then you can dry out — finally. I'll pick you up in a month. But in your case it might take two or three."

Odets looked directly to me, shaking his head. He put the palms of both hands on the table. I could see he was getting ready to stand

and address the situation. He looked down the table and locked eyes for a few seconds with Wald. Hayworth was already in tears. This was taking too long.

I turned to Hill. "Who the fuck are you?" I said, "Really, who THE FUCK are you? Because I know who she is. She's Rita Hayworth. She's a MOVIE STAR. She's sold more tickets, put more asses in seats, than you'll ever dream of. Her pin-ups helped win the fucking war.

I stood up. "So what have you fucking done? Latched on to Burt Lancaster and Harold Hecht? Big fucking deal. I worked with Burt before he ever knew your name, and I'll work with Burt when he forgets it. Because, believe me, he will. No one will remember it. They won't even remember what a piece of shit you are. I'll never even remember talking to you tonight. You're nothing. You don't exist."

I swatted him away. "So why don't you leave? No one wants you here. You wouldn't be at this table except for Rita. You're her driver — she needs you to get her here and take her home. And I can do that tonight. In fact, I'm due at a party after this and I'd be delighted to escort her — before I drive her home. If she decides she wants to go."

The entire table was silent. There was no movement — except Connie, who had put her hand to her forehead, her elbow propping it up on the table. She couldn't bear to see what was happening to her carefully orchestrated dinner party. Jerry reached across the table to clasp her arm, trying to console her.

"What are you waiting for? Get the fuck out." I took a step toward Hill. He stood up and began backing away from the table. When I took another step, he turned and walked toward the door. He tried to stalk out, making an exit statement — but it looked more like scurrying.

Connie had already motioned to two of the maids even before I sat down. They appeared, one on either side of Rita, to blot up the wine spills on the tablecloth and cover them with a new napkin. Then they brought both Odets and Hayworth new glasses of wine and whisked away the place setting where Hill had been sitting. There was no sign he had been there — except for the pall over the entire party.

Odets picked up his new glass, and stood up to make a toast, "Rita, after 'Story on Page 1,' 'Gilda' will be considered your second best movie. And no one with even remember 'Separate Tables.' So look out!"

"Hear, hear," Connie chimed. Then she also stood up. "If anyone besides me is having trouble digesting this sorry excuse for beef Wellington, I have some Perino's chicken à la king in my ice box. We can heat it up in a jiffy. Can I assume that everyone at the table wants it? Because I sure do!

"And we're going to change to white wine. We have a delicious Corton-Charlemagne iced and ready. We're also opening more champagne if anyone wants it."

Trust Connie to know how to defuse the situation. We sat at the table, drinking, until the food came out. It did the trick. And that Perino's dish is fail-safe — perfect Hollywood comfort food. The dessert, a trifle smothered in freshly whipped cream, was being served when I finally stood up.

"I'd told Jerry and Connie," I began, "that I would have to leave early to get to Ray and Fran Stark's anniversary celebration. They're giving a party at Romanoff's and I promised to go. I know how much *they would like to see Rita. So I thought we can stop there before I take her home."*

Odets got up as well. He was not going to lose his future star so early in the evening. "We're going as well," he said to the table, but looked directly at Jerry. "I know Jerry and Connie will understand." He walked around the table to help Rita up from her chair. Nancy Mills followed behind them — and I put my arm around her as we walked out the door. "I'll drive Nancy," I said.

I love Jerry and Connie, but was glad to leave that dinner. The one thing I regretted was that they were going to show "A Night to Remember," a new British film about the Titanic, that is supposed to be good. But I could catch up with it another time.

The anniversary fete was in full swing when we got to Romanoff's: Kirk and Anne Douglas, Fernando Lamas and Arlene Dahl, Ray and Mal Milland, Joseph and Lenore Cotton, Gary and Rocky Cooper. As well as many directors: Jean and Dusty Negulesco, Henry and Skip Hathaway, Nunnally and Dorris Johnson, John Huston; and producers: Charlie Brackett escorting Clare Boothe Luce, the Sol Siegels. Also David and Hope Hearst and his columnist, Cobina Wright. Old friends of Fanny Brice — Fran Stark's mother — were also there to celebrate — Garson Kanin and Ruth Gordon, Spencer Tracey and Katherine Hepburn and Moss and Kitty Hart.

By the time Nancy and I got to Romanoff's — we had taken a slight detour, stopping up on secluded curve I know on Mulholland for about 15 minutes — Cliff and Rita were already dancing. As usual, when Rita hit the floor, it was like she brought her own personal follow-spot. She shimmered in a golden glow, radiant and exultant.

Even in that crowd, other dancers backed away to give her room to move.

There was almost no connection between the crumpled woman crying at the dinner table and this lithe dancer, rumba-ing with sexiness and grace. She had dazzling muscle memory. Though she was dancing with Cliff, he was not even in the same frame. Odets was excluded from her personal spotlight, his shuffling steps awkward and clumsy. But he was having the time of his life dancing with this movie goddess. Because now that Hayworth was one with the music, she lived up to her star billing. She was a name above the title.

When Nancy and I walked in, we walked right into Arnie Steinhardt, who was standing near the door with his wife, Millie and their two daughters Sara and Ida. There was no way I could have avoided them.

It had been almost a month since I had spoken to Sara. I said I would call her and hadn't. There was nothing I wanted to say. She had been standing, laughing with her sister, when I walked in. But once she saw me she grew pale and silent.

With one glance, I could see Arnie's jaw set and his chin jutting out more than usual. A vein in his forehead throbbed. His wife's eyes began to blink very fast and her red skin got redder. The time is now, I realized — I had to shit or get off the pot.

I leaned over to whisper a few words in Nancy's ear and then walked over to Steinhardt.

"Hi Arnie," I said. "It's been way too long!" I gave him a hearty handshake and then kissed Millie on the cheek. She pulled away but

I ignored it. I turned to Sara. "I've missed you," I said simply, and swung her out onto the dance floor. I knew she would have refused if I asked — so I didn't. But her stiffness was more a show of resistance than the real thing.

"I've been thinking about you a lot," I began. That, at least, was true. Not much else I said was. I told her I cared about her and wanted to be with her. That I had resisted this but knew in my heart it was the one true choice I could make. That only with her by my side could I see my life in Hollywood ever being happy. I said other things that I don't remember — and don't want to. Sara had a sort of dazed, happy expression — like a contented cow.

At the end of the dance, I kissed her and told her that I would call her tomorrow, so we could have a long discussion. I told her I respected her too much to expect any sort of response right then. I said I knew she would want to think about this overnight. And, of course, talk about it with her father and mother.

I walked her back to her family, said goodnight to Arnie and Millie and left. I knew I had sealed my fate which her — too bad I don't even like her at this point. She has none of her father's spunk or smarts. But she would be a good mother. And I am only marrying her, I don't have to spend all my time with her.

My car was still near the front door. Nancy was in it, waiting. We drove back to my house. She took a taxi home later.

Chapter 6

CLOSING THE DEAL: PART 3
(CORSICA)

B EN AND DIANNE were the only people on deck. Dinner was supposed to start in less than an hour. Ben had already finished more than half his glass of rosé as he sat looking out on the yachts and fishing boats moored in the picturesque port of Ajaccio. He had to slow down, he reminded himself, rosé could be deceptive. And he needed a clear head. Dianne hadn't even touched her Lillet. She was too busy looking at the furniture in the salon.

Some of the lights of the Corsican capital were beginning to go on – though it was not even close to twilight. The boat was anchored outside the harbor — it was too big to come in any closer. It towered over everything — not just the other boats, but all the buildings that lined the port.

On the whole, Ben decided the trip hadn't been so bad. His jet had landed in Corsica just over an hour ago. The car, as arranged, had been waiting at the jetport to take them directly to the port, where a Zodiac was ready to ferry them out to the boat.

The traffic from the Hotel du Cap to Cannes had been a nightmare, of course. But no different than any other August day in the south of France. Taking the mountain route instead of the coastal highway, Robbins now decided, hadn't made much difference. All the roads on the Côte d'Azur were insane this time of year.

It had been good, though, that Ericson was early. Anita had texted the actor several times to warn that the drive from St. Tropez to Cannes would take far longer than expected. Anita had advised him to allot at least three hours for the trip — which proved realistic.

Milo had said this was Ericson's first visit to the Riviera, and Ben didn't want his inexperience to screw up the plans. After Milo asked Ben to give Ericson a ride from the south of France to Corsica, the producer had decided to take the jet from Cannes instead of Nice, since it was between Cap d'Antibes and St. Tropez — if far closer to Antibes.

The take-off slot at the Cannes Airport had been difficult to arrange. If Ericson had missed it, they might have had to wait almost two hours for another opening. Dinner would have been long over by the time they arrived.

It looked to Ben like Connor hadn't slept the night before. He wasn't surprised. It must have been wild for this kid in St. Tropez, after "Chessman" hit. He'd seen photos of Ericson celebrating at Cinquante-Cinq and Voile Rouge when the movie grossed $100 million after four days. The shot from Voile Rouge had him brandishing a magnum of Cristal while girls danced on a table nearby. Ben had already heard many stories about Ericson's sexual exploits in Hollywood — so it didn't seem out of character. The kid was clearly quite a swordsman. Though the Tessa story sounded highly unlikely.

The actor looked spent when he walked onto the plane. He had paused at the central table, where Ben and Dianne were sitting, to say hello and thank you. But then added how tired he was and immediately headed for one of the two large chairs at the back of the plane. They leaned back and he could stretch out. He slept straight through the flight.

It was going to be the earliest dinner of the trip, Milo had explained. Ted and Jennifer were due to leave that night for Istanbul. So they needed to eat early — 7 p.m. instead of 9 — since the couple's jet had to take off before 10. And Ben himself planned to leave by 10:30 if it all worked out.

Milo and Ted Welling walked into the saloon roughly half an hour before dinner was due to begin. Ted was laughing as they walked out onto the deck.

"He really is amazing," Ted was saying.

"Hey Ben," Milo broke in. "I hear you landed on time. I'm glad this all worked out." He hugged him hello. "Quite a view, isn't it?"

"Quite a boat is more like it," Ben replied, as Ted shook his hand. The steward who had given Ben and Dianne their drinks reappeared, right on cue, carrying a tray with two more glasses of rosé and a small bowl of olives. Off to the side, on a small bar, Ben now saw a platter with prosciutto and melon so juicy that the tray was dripping.

Ben suddenly felt overdressed in his navy blue silk blazer and gray linen trousers. He should have realized that this group would be uber-casual. Both men were in jeans — Milo's a faded blue and Ted's, white. Ted wore a pale blue oxford shirt with the shirttails out, Milo had a white T-shirt under his thin navy cashmere crewneck. Ben was irritated that he had encouraged Dianne to wear her ruffled pink Nina Ricci dress.

"I was telling Miles that I just got a call from Jason," Ted said, bringing Ben up to speed. Ted was speaking so softly that Ben took a step closer to hear him. "I've decided that guy is a talented actor. Too bad it never shows up on screen."

"He can grunt in four languages," Milo broke in, sounding less than interested in anything having to do with the muscle-ripped action star. "But acting is more than being able to beat people to a pulp and torture them — onscreen and off."

"He has talent, Miles," Ted insisted. "Just listen. He called me from Mexico. He's shooting outside Zihuatanejo for about six weeks. And Uri is there, as usual." He turns to Ben to explain, "You know, Uri — his old friend, driver, secretary, bodyguard, procurer.

"It's about two weeks into the shoot and Jason's getting bored. So Tuesday, while he's stuck out on the set, Uri begins pulling a party together. He walks along the beach, telling every pretty girl that there is going to be a party in Jason's suite that night and she should come 'party with Jason' — that he would really like to be with her.'

"Uri's getting a good response. It looks like it will be quite a gathering. But what he doesn't know is that, right after he flirts with one particularly cute girl, she picks up her phone and calls Carrie."

"What?" Milo has started laughing. "She calls his wife! She's a journalist?"

"Even more unlucky," Ted continues, "It turns out, by sheer chance, she's an old friend who just happens to be vacationing down there! So she calls Carrie and tells her what this guy just said to her. It's not hard for

Carrie to figure out it was Uri. So she immediately calls Jason, furious!"

"When do we get to the talented actor part?" Milo asked.

Francesca appeared on deck, wearing white linen palazzo pants so thin they were almost sheer, and a red chiffon halter top with a wide red satin sash that ended with a dramatically oversized bow. Ben was relieved to see her outfit. Dianne would be fine. "Are you talking about me?" she said, striking a pose.

"No, the opposite of you," Milo replied. "We're talking about Jason. Talent free." He greeted her with a kiss that was more than perfunctory. "You look lovely, darling," he added, almost under his breath.

Ben noticed again how Milo brightened when Chesca appeared. This marriage was clearly happy — and was so good for both of them. Milo seemed almost grateful that he had found the woman he could finally settle down for.

She trilled a laugh as she kissed Ben hello. He reached out to give her a hug but she was already looking around for Dianne. He settled for a squeezing her upper arm and few pats on her back. "I see Dianne's already spotted those faux Ruhlmann armchairs." Francesca laughed. "I'll go say hello."

There was a flash of red in her thick dark hair. 'Shit,' Ben thought. 'Not those fucking rubies again.' Dianne had talked about those earrings for two full days after that dinner. She couldn't seem to help herself — though she must have realized that every time she mentioned anything related to that unmitigated disaster it felt like whipcords of acid lashing his skin.

Robbins felt sure that, once they got back to the Hotel du Cap, he would finally have to call JAR. And there was no way he could get a deal out of Joel Rosenthal on a pair of ruby earrings. This was going to be one expensive trip — it had better be worth it.

"So this is where Jason's a real master," Ted said, picking up his story. "He convinces Carrie that he knew nothing about it! That Uri was using his name to get girls. He was working hard on the set all day, and Uri was up to his usual stunts. It was so clearly untrue: She knows how wiped he is after a long day of shooting. How could he possibly have time to party?

"Of course, Carrie wants to believe this. How else could she have been able to look the other way all these years? So she gets furious at Uri. She tells Jason that she doesn't want him around. Ever again.

"Jason handles this perfectly: He insists he is even more furious at Uri than she is! Here the guy was, using his longtime friend — and employer — as bait to lure girls. Who knows how long this has been going on! He tells Carrie he is going to fire Uri today. Swears it."

Ben is chuckling, shaking his head in wonderment. But Milo is laughing. Hard.

"Jason texted me a few hours ago," Ted said. "I just got off the phone with him. He wants me to take Uri on for six months. He said he's keeping him on the payroll, but wants him stowed safely out of Carrie's sightline. He figures it will take about that long to convince her to let him come back. And he doesn't really want him to take vacation — cause he needs him around and available."

"You said yes," Milo stated.

"He's a compadre," Ted smiled.

Lulu had come up to the deck and was listening as she slowly put some melon and prosciutto on a plate. She had to strain to hear Ted, but she got most of it. She knew Ted could always get Milo to laugh — they were such old friends, they seemed to have secret passwords. But this was peals of laughter. Lulu didn't even smile. She couldn't help wondering if her father had ever used this sort of tactic with Claire.

It must have been things like this that had scarred her mother. Lulu had always wondered why mummy refused to marry Jeb Lawrence, though Lulu was sure she loved him. He had been crazy about her — yet she would never let him in. Lulu had realized this — though she was only 13 when that relationship finally dissolved. It had to be something tied to her mother's life with Milo, Lulu had decided. Living in Los Angeles this summer, Lulu was beginning to understand what had been in play.

It was close to 7 when Jake and Mark appeared on deck. Ben noted that Harris wore his uniform of faded black Levis and white T-shirt. A chunky charcoal gray cashmere cardigan protected him against the chill night air. Mark was wearing a thick sweater patterned like French sailor T-shirt, dark blue bands on a white background. As they walked toward Ben, the steward reappeared, right on cue, with another two glasses of rosé, and an iced tea for Lulu.

After both men greeted Ben, Mark, who had picked up the iced tea as well as his own glass, walked over to Lulu. Ben saw they were soon laughing together. But Jake stayed near Ben, and pulled him aside.

Harris didn't bother with small talk, Ben noted. He was so rich he didn't have to. "I was just talking to Art," Harris said. "Have you talked with Irv since the divorce?"

Harris was referring to the older producer Irv Fraudlich and his much younger, and now former, wife, Monica Frappo. Fraudlich had a housekeeping deal on the lot.

The way Harris said it alerted Ben that this was no idle question. Maybe, like everyone else who had any dealings with Irv, Jake had developed an intense loathing of Monica.

"No," Ben responded. "But I was happy when he told me he was getting rid of that cow. I was so tired of hearing her tell Irv — and everyone else she talked to — how they should do their job. As if she knew anything — except how to fuck.

"He met her in Vegas," he continued, glad to be able to show off his knowledge on this to Harris. "They say she was a showgirl, but I never thought she had any discernible talent — even as minimal as that. Except in bed — though not on her back. She's too old.

"If it wasn't incredible sex, I have no idea why Irv married her. They say 'force of habit.' But did he need a — was it fifth wife?"

"You know," Harris said with a taut smile, "she once told me what a gay man would think about something." Ben did a double take — and he wasn't faking.

"Yeah, she did!" Jake said. Ben reflected on the stupidity involved.

Harris's smile was more like a grimace. But he circled back to Irv. "You know he's living in a two-bedroom rental in Santa Monica?"

"Say what?" Harris had Robbins's full attention.

"Yeah," Jake elaborated. "She got the house in Bel Air, the apartment at 15 Central Park West, the horse farm in North Salem and the ranch in Aspen. He's renting in Santa Monica, 15 blocks from the beach."

"She must be on the ride of her life," Ben said. "Shit! What does she have on him?" He was so stunned that he said this aloud.

"I was thinking you might know," Harris said. "There's no way I can stay in touch on this boat. I hate being out of the loop." He almost growled his frustration.

Ben tried to look inscrutable, as his brain churned, searching for some insight. He needed to be in the know tonight — about everything.

"He's connected in Vegas," Ben began, thinking fast. "It's no secret that a good chunk of his financing comes from there. Monica must have figured something out about the money. That's really all she thinks about."

A beautiful younger woman joined their conversation. She put her arm around Welling and snuggled close. "You know Jennifer," Welling said to Ben. No last name. A professional girlfriend, Robbins decided. He didn't bother trying to make conversation. He smiled his hello — she didn't even rate a spoken word.

"We're all packed, darlin'," she said to Ted. "Jesse has all the bags and they're putting them on the launch. The stateroom's being cleaned now. Connor's taking a shower in the back cabin, but ours should be ready for him by the time we finish dinner."

The Levinsons emerged just after 7. Nate, who had clearly gotten the memo, Ben decided, was in jeans and a pale yellow linen shirt, with the cuffs rolled up. Gwen wore teal raw silk palazzo pants and a filmy green, pink and blue silk peasant shirt, loosely tied at the wrists and neckline. It wafted around her, like a mini-caftan. She had a silk chiffon scarf in the same shades of green, pink and blue tied around her head. Its long ends trailed over her shoulder as she walked. The look was Elizabeth Taylor at her most faux bohemian, Ben decided. Gwen could easily have played a bit part in "The Sandpiper."

Emma was a step behind them. Lulu, as usual, immediately felt underdressed. She had put on her navy pique skirt and lacy white blouse from J. Crew, with a vintage navy cashmere cardigan. But it was school-girl boring next to Emma's leather aqua V-neck peplum top over vividly patterned Mary Katrantzou trousers in a glittering banknote design. The trousers sat low on her hips and the V-neck was plunging.

It was 7:40 when Ben pulled Milo aside. "I've got the air controller staying late for us," Ben said, "but I don't think we can't push it too far. Ted is set to leave first, so I can stay here and go through some details — if it works. But we both have to be wheels up by 10:45."

"I've already told Russell to knock on their door," Milo said. "This is one night we can't wait for Rob and Xan. We've already gone through five bottles of Domaine Ott. Cesare Rutani always runs late, and he's been here almost 15 minutes."

"We're going to sit down for dinner," Milo announced to the group. "We need to start since Ted and Jen can't be late for their take-off slot."

Everyone moved toward the dinning saloon. Except Ben. He paused to make a note to himself to call Irv the next day. If his price was right, maybe Irv would finally give up "Home Team." Ben had made several forays to try and convince Irv he should let this project go. And, maybe if he lingered, Ben hoped, he might be able to greet Rob and Xan in private — away from the group.

By the time Ben entered the dining saloon, Milo had almost finished with the seating. He motioned to Ben that he was next to Dianne, who was already seated, at the very end of the table. There were two empty chairs facing them — which Ben assumed were for Rob and Alexandra. Milo had set up a sort of demarcation zone, so that Ben and Rob could hold what amounted to a separate conversation. Milo was next to Ben and Lulu was opposite him. They could serve as a buffer.

Mark and Ben were seated on the other side of Lulu. Francesca was next to Milo, opposite Mark. This looked fine, Ben decided.

He was just sitting down as Rob and Xan entered the room — almost an hour late. Ben felt a flash of something close to satisfaction. On the movie star clock, they were essentially on time. Rob had to be interested in his project.

Xan looked meltingly lovely, Ben thought. He decided he should be thinking of a project for her as well. She was wearing cream-colored moleskin riding breeches which redefined the notion of skin-tight, a thin cream silk camisole and a slate blue Chinese jacket, embroidered with iridescent cranes, butterflies and bats.

However, instead of striding in slightly ahead of Rob, their usual formation, Xan was almost a step behind her husband, holding onto his arm with both hands. She looked slightly unsteady, a hesitancy that could have been brought on by the rolling motion of the sea. Except there was no rolling motion.

Ben had gotten up when he saw them enter the room, but Rob shook his head, signaling he should remain seated. As they walked toward the table, Xan seemed to grow paler — her perfect complexion looking less like luscious thick cream and more like skim milk. But Ben wasn't sure if he was imagining it.

The actress acknowledged him with only a glancing smile, and made no eye contact whatsoever with Dianne, barely looking in her direction. Rob covered her hands protectively with his as they got near. Right before they reached the table, Xan pulled Rob closer, then released his arm to step behind him — so Rob could take the seat opposite Dianne. She sat down beside him, next to Lulu, kissing the teenager on the head as she did. "Happy pre-birthday," she said brightly.

'Thanks, Xan, " Lulu answered, with a quick smile, coloring slightly.

Ben relaxed and smiled at the teenager — or rather relaxed as much as he could. There was nothing unusual in Xan's actions, he told himself. He needed to stop thinking everything was keyed to memories of that terrible dinner. To stop imagining trouble, and stick to the matter at hand — getting Rob to yes tonight. Milo was here to help it along. It was going to happen.

Ben partially stood up so he could reach across the table to shake hands with Rob. "So great to see you," he said, a bit too loudly, trying to grab Xan's attention as well. He took Rob's hand with both his own, emphasizing his delight.

Dianne echoed his sentiment. "So lovely to see you," she added. "And lovely to be here."

Xan had been picking up the glass of rosé at her place setting, and, as Dianne spoke, her hand jerked back. Though the glass was less than half full, Xan's sudden movement sloshed the pale pink liquid over the rim. It hadn't looked like that much wine, but it splashed across Lulu's white shirt as well as Xan's trousers. The ghost of a frown crossed Xan's cameo face, as she bent to mop it up.

"Don't worry about it," Lulu said immediately. She would have been more comfortable if Xan ignored it. It always made her self-conscious when people fussed about her in public. Lulu felt her cheeks getting hot. She was sure her face was already pinker than the wine stain.

So she tried to deflect the actress. "Is anything wrong?" she asked, "Are you ok?"

Xan smiled at her, "Of course, honey." Her voice held steady, but her smile quivered slightly. "It's just that... the last time I sat at a table with... Ben — and Dianne —" She had hesitated almost imperceptibly before saying "Ben" and had to force out the last two words — "I had this terrible allergic attack. It was a no fun —"

"Let's not even think about it," Ben smiled as he interrupted her. He could see Alexandra was tense. Her anxiety felt palpable. Rob reached out protectively, putting his arm around her, but it didn't help. She couldn't seem to relax. Ben started thinking this entire trip might have been for nothing. Well, not nothing — those earrings were going to cost him plenty.

"You know," Rob began, talking directly to Ben and Dianne. "Xan was a little nervous about sitting down to eat with you tonight. That meal we had was a bit traumatic for her. She was actually saying she wanted to eat in the cabin. But I convinced her that this was going to be fine. She knows how excited I am about this project."

Xan kept her head bent down as her husband spoke. Ben decided he'd been right all along — she had yet to even look at Dianne. She seemed obsessed with getting out the wine stains.

If only she had stayed in the cabin, Ben thought. Maybe then he'd have had a chance. He'd been right to dwell on the worst-case scenario. Now it was going to be even worse than worst-case — since he would have to call JAR tomorrow. No getting out of that. He could write off the cost of the plane, the car, even the Hotel du Cap. But not those earrings.

Lulu could see Xan was nervously twisting her fingers, even as she pretended to sop up the stains. "My gosh," Lulu began again, "What happened—"

"We don't need to discuss it," Ben cut her off. He smiled directly at Lulu "Let's forget it." His voice was soft, but it cut through the air like a knife. "It's over."

Dianne put her hand on his arm. She could sense he was coiled and ready. She knew the signs. But most of the table wasn't listening — because Connor was making a star-worthy late entrance.

"Sorry I took so long." He paused at the threshold, apologizing to the room. "I needed to clean up before I could think of sitting down with all of you."

"Hey, Connor," Milo smiled, and motioned him to the empty chair one seat over, between Francesca and Nate. A steward filled the wine glass while Connor walked around the table to his seat. Levinson stood up, to give his new star a special welcoming hug.

"How's my guy," Nate said. It wasn't a question, but Ericson answered. "All good." He gave Francesca a quick kiss hello as he was sitting down, and then reached across her to shake Milo's hand. "Thanks again for having me along," he said.

Connor then addressed the entire table. He gave a cocky grin. "This has been one hell of a summer."

The entire table seemed jazzed by the young star's success. Jake, who was seated directly opposite Connor, offered a toast, "Welcome aboard and congratulations What's past is prologue, babe. Just you wait." His laugh was a growl. "To the best looking Elijah we've ever seen. L'chaim!" The table filled with laughter as everyone raised their glasses. "L'chaim!"

Connor held his rosé aloft in turn, "I see that I'm finally going to have some fun this summer. It's about time!"

Milo put his arm around Chesca as he leaned over her to talk to Connor and Nate.

When Xan reached out for her glass, Lulu saw that her hand was still shaking. She realized that the actress avoided even looking toward Dianne, instead keeping her eyes focused down the other end of the table. When talking to Lulu, Xan turned her entire body, not just her head — essentially sitting sideways on her seat. Lulu had an odd impression that Xan's gaze was clinging to her, as if she were some sort of psychic life preserver.

"What happened?" Lulu asked. "I know allergies can be so scary. You know my Aunt Gr––"

"Was I unclear?" Ben said more quietly. He smiled at Lulu as he spoke. "No one's ever accused me of that." Dianne's hand was clutching his arm. But he didn't care.

"It's just my Aunt Grace had this terrible al-"

"I thought you were going to be quiet." Ben's voice was quieter still. "So do it. Look how upset you're making

Xan. Shut up." His tone was curt, as if talking to a dog. But his smile deepened.

Ben realized, so sharply that it felt like a stunning blow, that his deal was lost. The odds may have been slim, he now saw, since he had not reckoned on Alexandra presenting such a problem. But it was really this girl and her questions, he decided, that had made it impossible. She had ruined his deal. He wanted her never to speak again.

It was the smile that fooled Lulu. "I was just saying," she began, "that my Aunt Grace has a terrible allergic reaction to peanuts. One time she —"

Ben could not believe this teenager was still talking. He could almost see palpable waves of anxiety crashing over Xan. She seemed about to flee the table. Any small remaining hope he had for his deal would walk out with her.

Yet the girl kept talking. Every word she spoke twisted the knife deeper into his project. The damage was probably irreparable. Yet nothing he said seemed to stop her from babbling.

"What are you doing here anyway?" Ben's voice was no more than a whisper — but precise as a shiv. "Isn't your mother dying of cancer? Shouldn't you be with her during the chemo?" The girl seemed to gasp for breath and her cheeks flamed redder than her hair. "Chemo is really rough you know. What if she dies and you're not there? How would you feel, knowing that she died as you're sitting here on a yacht off Corsica half-way around the world?"

Lulu was too stunned by Ben's words to offer any defense. Not that she could have — he was a master at this art form. Hard-bitten men had quailed before him — and few had come close to causing him the trouble that he felt she had. This teenager had taken down his entire project — and forced him to watch as she did it. He was now looking grimly at a picture with a start date — and no star.

He couldn't have stopped himself even if he wanted to — though Dianne's hand was now digging into his arm like a claw.

The girl's cheeks were crimson — as if he had slapped her several times. Hard. Tears welled up and spilled down her cheeks, diamonds against the deep red.

"Crying won't help your mother at a time like this." Lulu flinched. "If you feel guilty about leaving her when she's in the fight of her life against cancer — good. You should be."

Lulu was trapped in a horrifying nightmare — Robbins smiled serenely as his steady torrent of soft words engulfed her in acid and bile. She felt powerless even to look away. At some point, she realized, Xan had put her arm around her. The actress had been standing up to leave the table, but as Ben words spewed out, she sat down to put a protective arm around Lulu. Yet she was unable to shield her.

"Lulu!" The girl's head snapped back as Connor said her name.

Connor and Nate had been listening to Milo, who was leaning over his wife to tell them the story of Chesca's first Hollywood screen test. She'd been on holiday when her agent had called, so she'd shot her test on her own iPhone. It was a video selfie. They were all laughing, Chesca the hardest. Jake had heard it before, but he and Mark were laughing as well. Milo knew how to tell a story.

Connor, looking at Milo, had caught sight of Lulu's face out of the corner of his eye. Milo, seeing Connor's startled expression, turned just in time to hear Ben's last sentence.

"Lulu!" Connor repeated, intent on drawing her focus away from that end of the table. "I need a martini to celebrate. Come with me while I make one — and fill me in on the trip."

He couldn't quite break this terrible spell for Lulu. "My mother is not dying," she gasped, willing as much vehemence as she could muster.

Milo had been surprised when Connor interrupted his story. But then he heard Ben's words and his daughter's reply. He saw that Rob and Xan looked shell-shocked as they rose from the table, almost bloodied from the conversation. The actress's arm gripped tightly around

Lulu, pulling her up as well. A French breakfast radish, even a beet, would have looked pale in comparison to his daughter's face.

"You're absolutely right, Lulu," Milo said assertively, "Your mother's going to be just fine."

Lulu saw that Connor was standing up as well.

"What's wrong with you, Ben?" Rob said. "Slime is too nice a word. People warned me. They call you the 'Smiling Mamba' you know? I ignored them. But I shouldn't have. I was wrong."

The smile still played on Ben's face. Milo turned to him. "Get out. Now. You need to get off the boat."

Xan's skin looked even more ashen once she stood up. She seemed unsteady on her feet, though she still sought to shelter the teenager, cradling her in both arms. But Lulu pulled away. She turned her back on the table and covered her face with her hands, seeking some vestige of privacy. On top of everything else, she felt horribly embarrassed to be the center of attention.

Connor was standing beside her. "Come on," he said softly. His accent was pronounced. "You need to show me where the bar is. And I'll make you a rum and Coca-Cola. Maybe even with the rum. It tends to work better that way." She couldn't look at him. He put his hand around her shoulders, bending like a willow against a fierce wind, and gently guided her to the door.

Rob and Xan were only steps behind them. Though the actress's gait had seemed unsteady when she moved away from the table, her step grew longer and surer as she crossed the room and approached the door. Walking out onto the deck, Xan was again slightly ahead of Rob, settling into her celebrated smooth stride.

Ben, however, hadn't yet moved. Dianne, too, seemed frozen. Her hand was still on his arm, though her fierce grip had gone unheeded. He couldn't even feel it. She seemed unable to lift her eyes from the table. Ben could tell she was trying to pretend she wasn't on the boat — certainly not in that room. But she was. If not for long.

"It's over, Ben," Milo began again, since Robbins hadn't moved, "I've been trying to help on this because you were kind to my father once. You didn't know how much it meant to him. I did though. But now we're done.

"You can take the hacker back to the port. It's ready now. Russ will call your pilots to let them know you're on the way." Milo was getting up as he spoke and headed for the door. "Get off the boat, Ben. Now. Good night, Dianne."

Ben could feel the entire group watching him. Their eyes were cold, displaying only a remote curiosity. These same people, who had greeted him warmly just an hour ago, now regarded him as if they were immune system antibodies and he some sort of foreign matter that needed to be expelled from the bloodstream. He could hear Gwen whispering to Theodore Welling at the other end of the table, asking him what exactly had been said. She was too far away to have heard anything.

He was a bug on their windshield. Something to be flicked off. Dianne had yet to look up. She was deeply absorbed by the pattern on the plate in front of her.

Ben knew the mood at the table was going to get ugly. The others probably felt they were growing ever more tainted as they were forced to breathe the same air. He needed to get out of that room and off that boat. But he realized, almost with pride, he had no regrets about what he had said. That girl deserved it and more for the trouble she had instigated. She had no right to have a seat at the table, much less to talk while sitting there. Even his youngest child, as a toddler, would have known better than to chatter like that — going off-topic with a star when a deal is in motion.

He could feel a growing miasma of disdain. He sensed their collective attitude hardening into contempt — the typical Hollywood attitude toward interlopers.

Ben knew he had to make a clean exit. He at least had to control that act. He stood up with as much dignity as he could muster. He had placed one hand under Dianne's elbow, so she got up with him. It was like pulling up dead weight. She seemed shocked into virtual paralysis since the incident. He didn't want to have to drag her out the door. So he paused to regroup before moving away from the table.

He looked out over the group. "It's always such a treat to spend time with all of you," he began. "Dianne and I didn't mean to interrupt your holiday, but this issue was pressing and I needed to consult Rob about it. I should admit as well that Dianne had always wanted to see this boat — we've both heard so much about it — so I'm glad we had this opportunity."

The room was quiet. He felt they were all just waiting for him to leave.

"But now that my conversation with Rob is over," Ben's smile broadened, with no hint of irony, "We need to get back to the Hotel du Cap. I am sorry to leave before this delightful dinner is over, but it seems we must. Not just time and tide, but air traffic controllers wait for no man — or woman."

At the last two words, he put his arm tightly around Dianne, pulling her close. He figured that the only way he was going to get her out the door was by propelling her. So they moved together, in a kind of shuffling lockstep. It was not the most graceful exit, Robbins had to admit. But it was an exit. And that's what mattered.

The hacker was indeed waiting when they got on deck. Dianne didn't begin to cry until they were in the car, heading for the jetport. She still hadn't said a word.

* * * *

When Lulu reached the bar with Connor she was crying so hard she had trouble catching her breath. Her tears came between gasps. He produced a rum and Coke in what may have been record speed. All the while, he kept up a soft, beguiling patter about his time as a bartender. Once the drink was ready, he leaned over the bar, pulled one of her hands away from her face and gently wrapped her fingers around the icy glass. "Drink it slowly," he said, "That Coke should help your hiccups too."

She turned away from him, and began to drink. He came around and stood close beside her, continuing his patter about his adventures tending bar, and then began gently massaging her shoulders. It felt good. She hadn't even realized how tense she had become. Her entire body was one clenched knot.

"That guy is an asshole," he said softly into her ear. "You need to forget every word he said. Every syllable of every word — every consonant and every vowel."

His hands moved in a slow deliberate fashion on her shoulders. She began to slowly relax, her body responding to the pressure of his hands. His movements were steady and sure. She could feel his breath on her cheek. It was all so calming.

His movements seemed to change subtly. There was something insistent in them that made her slightly breathless and tingly. His fingers went deeper and moved more slowly, his massage strokes lengthened. She willed herself to ignore it, as she stood there, drinking the cocktail — her first. And trying to wipe clean everything that Robbins had said.

"Lulu, darling," Milo was walking toward the bar. "I am so, so sorry. You can't know how sorry I am."

She felt the storm of tears return as she spun around. "Daddy," was all she could say, as she put down her glass and rushed to his arms. His warm hug enveloped her. She couldn't remember running to him like this since she was a little girl. But this was no skinned knee that a hug could make better.

"It's my fault," he said, his tone both reassuring and comforting. "I blame myself entirely. I should have realized this could happen. If his deal didn't work — you were his ideal target.

"He's got that reptilian brain — a lizard-like response that operates on pure instinct. So if he was going to strike out, it would have to be on the person he thought was the least important at the table. That's how it works. And you were right there, Lulu, within reach. I am so terribly sorry.

"It might not make you feel much better, Lulu, but you should know it had nothing to do with you. He knows nothing real about your mother's medical records. He might know some basic facts — like she's ill. But that's it.

His one real skill is sensing where you are most vulnerable — then going for it. And he doesn't stop. He once made one of his executives pass out. He has no "off" switch — far too mean for that.

Connor had walked behind the bar as Milo was talking. "I'm mixing martinis," he announced. "You want one, Milo?"

"I could use a couple," Milo responded. He turned back to Lulu. "You have to forget everything he said."

"That's just what I told her," Connor said.

"He knows nothing about your mother, Lulu," Milo spoke slowly, emphasizing every word. "Nothing personal or private. Remember that. Nothing.

"So you have to forget about it. Don't let the terrorists win, right?" She knew he was trying to joke, but she couldn't bring herself to smile. She felt she didn't really deserve to be comforted. Not with her mother so ill and so far away.

Milo tried a different approach.

"Besides, you have to forget about it since you need to focus on your birthday," Milo paused for effect. "I'm no fortune teller. But where you're concerned, I can see something coming in to focus. It's getting clearer. And clearer. And it looks to me like a car! Yes, that's what I see Lulu. It's got your name on it! There is clearly a car in your future. In the color of your choice.

"Why else have we been working so hard on these driving lessons?"

CHAPTER 7

THE INCIDENT IN SARDINIA

I T TOOK SOME TIME for Lulu to feel close to normal. She sat on the deck as the yacht steamed for Sardinia, staring out at the sea. Emma came and sat with her for a while, and, at different times, so did Milo and Connor. Each was trying to find the magic combination of syllables that would make her feel better.

Though Emma also spent time searching for a functioning Internet connection. It was pure reflex on her part, however, since she knew it was just about impossible to locate one here.

Just talking about what happened at dinner made Lulu feel horribly embarrassed. She had behaved like a baby, she decided, bawling like a five year-old. When anyone asked her how she was doing, even in an off-hand manner, she could feel the awful flush spreading up her cheeks.

It felt better just to sit there and stare out at the horizon line, with the salt air on her face. She tried to pretend that whole conversation had never happened. But she couldn't excise Ben's venomous whisper — that her mother was dying and she was a terrible daughter not to be there. She was a heartless monster, having fun on a yacht halfway around the globe. Yet, somehow, the words had a little less sting each time she went over them.

Meanwhile, Lulu kept ruminating about a conversation she'd had with mummy a few months ago. She realized only later that it was a sort of demarcation line. Everything earlier was BC — before the cancer; before her world was upended and sadness subsumed her.

Though mummy didn't tell her about the diagnosis until almost three weeks later, Lulu later figured out the first tests results must have come in shortly before mummy sat down with her to have this talk. She was already becoming increasingly distracted.

This discussion had been pointed, though, and Lulu remembered it in sharp detail. It was the first time mummy had talked about her about going out to spend the entire summer with Milo in Los Angeles. It seemed to come out of the blue, and Lulu had been adamant in resisting the very notion — she knew she would hate Los Angeles and all the people in it. It would have been embarrassing, Lulu thought, if she didn't.

As usual, mummy sat quietly and let Lulu make her entire case. But this time she overrode all of Lulu's arguments. "Darling, I now realize that it was wrong of me not to have you spend more time with your father out in L.A.," mummy began. That brought Lulu up short. This subject had never come up before.

"You have no idea what it's like out there," she continued. "You've been listening to Granny and all these people here talk about it. And they loathe it. Not just the place — they have never spent time there, so they have basis for what they're saying — but the very idea of the place." She paused and took a breath, as if trying to figure out the next logical step of her argument. "It's the antithesis of everything that Granny and Pop-pop believe in. It's only about the now. There's no past tense."

In an almost absent-minded fashion, she reached out and began gently smoothing back Lulu's hair. "You know how people today talk about Silicon Valley and Internet start-ups, or businesses like Uber or Airbnb, as 'disrupters.' They're disrupting the established order of things. Well, Hollywood is the Ur version of that. It made modern life modern. And it unsettled everyone who had a stake in the status quo — meaning just about everyone you know." She laughed. "Did I ever tell you, darling, that in the first six months after I moved back to Boston from L.A., I was asked where I went to college more often than in the entire seven years I spent in L.A. And no one in Hollywood ever asked if my father was Judge Sturges. They had never heard of Trever Sturges. No one cared about things like that there." She shook her head in mock dismay.

Her voice grew more serious. "This visit is going to be so interesting for you, Lulu — apart from it being an amazing experience." Her smile seemed a little wistful. "But you need to make sure you see it clearly. Don't let all the things you've been hearing about it cloud your vision."

She paused to consider it. "When you're unsure about how to see something clearly, how to really understand it, you need to look at it like you're putting together a puzzle."

That's essentially what she did every day as a conservator, mummy pointed out. Decorative art objects would arrive at her work table as a crate of pottery shards, for example, and she would have to figure out the correct way the pieces fit together.

"First, you need to be sure you have all the pieces. You might not — some key piece might be missing, or hidden away from you. When that happens — because it often does," she added, "it seems inevitable that the one piece you are missing is the key. This is virtually a rule of thumb!" She was laughing as she said this.

"Then you have to figure out the right way the pieces to fit together. 'Cause there is always one right way."

Sometimes, mummy explained, she was sure two pieces fit together perfectly. So she would begin assembling all the other pieces around this first pairing. But then no other piece could work with the form she had created. So she would have to start afresh, going through all the pieces again — since that original combination wasn't right. Just one piece in the wrong place, Mummy emphasized, could prevent you from assembling the whole object. And finally seeing what it should really look like.

Lulu circled around this discussion over and over, as she stared out on the Mediterranean. She knew mummy was trying to say that Hollywood could be confusing. So Lulu needed to make sure she saw all the pieces of it clearly. And mummy was also, Lulu now realized, talking about using this technique in all aspects of her life.

As for understanding Hollywood, Lulu decided that it also helped that she had parts of Abe's diary with her on the boat and was reading it. She discussed this with Milo.

"It's strange, Lulu," Milo had responded, "But I was also thinking that it's good you're reading it right now. What Ben said and did was vicious. It should never have happened. But I can only hope that Abe's diary shows you how terrible people behave — have always behaved —

in Hollywood. I know there is one incident where Abe throws someone out of a dinner. I know I was a pale imitation of what he did to that guy. The big players then never looked back at the wreckage they left behind.

"Abe was my father, your grandfather, but he was also a miserable excuse for a human being. When he got older, and was pushed out of the studio, he didn't mellow. He did the opposite. He got meaner — his tongue was even more deadly."

"I was just reading about Rita Hayworth," Lulu said, "Abe annihilates her husband."

"He had that skill set," Milo said ruefully. "Though I might still have an exaggerated view of Abe's cruelty — since I was so helpless before him throughout most of my childhood. There was really no one to defend me. Certainly my mother couldn't.

"Ben is an awful guy, but he's like a pale carbon copy of Abe — a faded duplicate made on a Xerox machine that needs toner. There was a Harold Ramis movie, years ago, 'Multiplicity.' About a guy who has clones of himself made — so he can accomplish more every day. It starred Michael Keaton. But the gimmick is that each clone is less sharp.

"That's sort of what I think of Ben. He's just not smart enough to be as cruel as Abe. My father had a real genius for cruelty. An instinct to go straight for the thing that would wound you the most. Then stay on it until he broke you. He was all id. It may not have been so apparent to you, and certainly not last night, but at least Ben has the veneer of a super-ego.

"Growing up with Abe made me so aware of the powerless. That's why I still, to this day, almost automatically look for the least important person in the room — and walk right over. Because, that person was me for a big chunk of my life. And, believe me, nobody cared. That's what Hollywood is about.

"I never want you to feel this way. You need to know that I love you very much. As much as your mother does. And we'll both do anything we can to make sure you never experience unhappiness like that.

"I know this can't begin to make up for the fact that I've lived so far away for so long — and I was so selfish in being out of touch. But there is at least one good reason why it was better for you to grow up outside of Hollywood, on the other side of the country. You're better able now to deal with the way people actually behave here. It's not just the cruel ones like Ben — or my father — it's the many, many people who are feckless and uncaring. They drive right through and don't look back. The system just allows them to act like this.

"Now you have some perspective on it — and Abe's diary should help. And you always need to remember how much both your mother and I care about you and care about what happens to you."

The conversation helped Lulu get her bearings. Just as important, though, Milo had managed to get a message through to mummy that afternoon, and she sent a positive progress report. Lulu felt better. This mattered most to her — far more than the keys to a silver Audi convertible that she got on her birthday the next day.

She had told Milo that her dream car would be silver on the outside with a navy blue leather interior. She didn't explain that those were the colors of the roadster Granny was driving in a photo from long ago that sat beside her bed.

"That's exactly what you're getting then," he had promised, in a voice only she could hear, while everyone around the table cheered as she blew out the candles.

Ultimately, it was also hard to feel continually blue when the surroundings were dazzlingly beautiful. By the second day off Sardinia, just outside Porto Cervo near the Cala di Volpe, Lulu woke feeling brighter about everything.

She lay in her bunk, thinking about the day before, for she wanted to go over it all carefully. It had ended with rejoicing. Last night after dinner, she, Connor and Emma had teamed with Xan and Rob at charades — and triumphed. Xan had been particularly uproarious when trying to convey the movie title, "The Spy Who Loved Me." At one point, when it seemed most everyone was in stitches, Lulu had glanced over and seen that Francesca, alone, was having a less-than-good time.

Lulu felt again that her stepmother was irritated by not being the center of attention — a role she was usually accorded. Feeling ignored was an unfamiliar, and obviously unsettling, sensation for her. When Connor sat next to Lulu at dinner, she saw that a shiver of irritation rippled across her stepmother's face. It was quickly veiled, but Lulu saw it. She decided that Francesca may have believed that at least her former co-star would be hovering around her. She clearly expected that he would be paying court to her in the manner she had grown so accustomed to.

But Connor had spent most of the morning huddled with Nate, and their conversation had continued throughout lunch. Then he spent much of the afternoon with Lulu and Emma. He'd looked for the girls soon after lunch. Emma, with typical resourcefulness, had heard from a crew member about an isolated beach nearby and they'd all decided to go. Mark joined them after he saw Russell packing up cookies, peaches, bread and cheese. He packed this into hampers, along with bottles of water, suntan lotions and thick beach towels. The group had taken three jet-skis and spent the rest of the afternoon swimming and snorkeling in the little lagoon that Frank, the captain, had located.

After a few hours they stretched out on the towels, savoring the peaches, which, Lulu decided, were juicier than any she had ever had, voluptuous with the aroma of summer. Emma and Lulu continued their running conversation about favorite movies and Lulu wanted Mark to tell his "Star is Born" story — so Connor would hear.

"I love telling it," Mark responded. "I don't need a lot of convincing here, kiddo. Well, Connor, it might surprise you to know that one of my favorite movies is the Judy Garland version of 'A Star Is Born' — Moss Hart's fantastic revision of Dorothy Parker and Alan Campbell's terrific original. It's one of the greatest movies ever made, as far as I'm concerned. That and "What's Up Doc."

"There's a regular midnight screening of 'A Star Is Born,' at a Boston movie revival house called the Brattle. Lulu and I have figured out that we probably have sat in the same audience there, watching old movies, at least a dozen times. Maybe even a seat apart. Very '12 Monkeys.'

"In any case, I went there with about three friends one night. There's a largely gay crowd for this one. It's not quite the sing-along 'Sound of Music' at the Hollywood Bowl — no one's dressed like Judy when she sings "Born in a Trunk" like the Bowl audience gets tricked out as nuns or the Von Trapp children. But you get the idea.

"So the crowd is kind of rowdy — in a good way. And everyone is really into it. But right at the end, just as Judy declares, "My name ... is Mrs. Norman Maine," a guy stands up in the back and screams, 'No, MY name is Mrs. Norman Maine." He runs down the aisle, takes a flying leap and crashes through the screen.

"The place goes crazy. The lights go up and management comes in. Just about everyone in the audience is clearly wishing they had had enough moxie to do this. Believe me, they all would like to be Mrs. Norman Maine! But, honey, none of us was so bat-shit crazy to do it."

Connor was laughing. Though Lulu and Emma had both now heard this story twice before, they exploded in laughter. Lulu knew this was a story that mummy would love.

"It took them almost a week to fix the screen. And the midnight showings were suspended for like two months. But when they started up again, the place was packed — more crowded than ever before."

They continued on to other favorite films. Lulu, as usual, lauded "Some Like It Hot," a movie that Granny had introduced her to three years before. Only Mark had seen it. And he didn't agree with her. In fact, he insisted, it wasn't even the best Marilyn Monroe film. That was, quite obviously, "Gentlemen Prefer Blondes."

"Marilyn needs to be in color," he insisted, "Those acres of downy, creamy flesh were made for Technicolor.

"You know, she had that in her contract — that she had to be shot in color. But the director, Billy Wilder, was able to convince her that 'Some Like It Hot' had to be black and white — since color would have made Tony Curtis and Jack Lemon look like drag queens. As if! They were standing next to Marilyn Monroe!"

Connor said he had never even seen a Marilyn Monroe film. But then he realized he had. "She was in one with Olivier, right?" he asked Mark. "I saw about half of that once. We wanted to see how Olivier handled his scenes with her."

Emma still defended "Titanic" — it was her absolute favorite. Connor soon joined in, arguing for "2001." But then he switched, insisting, "'The Godfather' — hands down."

As the sun sank toward the horizon, bathing everyone and everything in a rosy glow — Milo had explained to her this was called the "golden hour" in movie-making — Milo, Francesca, Xan, Nate and Gwen zipped by in the hacker. Xan, not Nikko, was at the wheel, though he was sitting next to her. Rob was wheeling and dancing around them on a jet-ski — leaping over the hacker's foamy wake or running loopy S curves alongside. They were all laughing in the golden light, and waved at the four on the beach as they passed. Emma pulled out her phone to video them as they skittered by. She, Connor, Mark and even Lulu found themselves caught up in the exuberance of the moment — all basking in the warm radiance before the sun disappeared for the day.

Soon after, one of the crew jet-skied over to remind them it was time to come in from the beach. They packed up what was left of the food, gathered up all the towels and lotions and headed back toward the boat.

Before this outing, Lulu had decided that these 10 days on the boat might have been trying for Francesca. She had to share the limelight continually with Rob and Xan — whose star power firmly outranked hers. And now even her former co-star was not dancing attendance.

As she lay in her bunk, Lulu wondered what Francesca would do address this issue. Her stepmother was not the sort of person who could let something like being overlooked and ignored continue. She was also not one for small gestures

They were all due to go ashore right after breakfast. It was somewhat early for this sort of expedition, but with the heat so oppressive in the middle of the day, they had decided it would be best to be back on the boat for a long afternoon swim.

Nate, as usual, had opted not to come onshore until lunch. He had brought one special suitcase full of movie DVDs — most not yet out, but also recent releases he had missed and needed to catch up on. So he was spending these two weeks methodically going through them. Lulu decided this time of the morning was the moment Nate most savored. When the movies had not yet disappointed him — the edit hadn't looked sloppy, the script made sense and every actor's performance was beyond expectations. Nate watched movies most of the day. Then, each night after dinner, they all watched at least two films with him — though sometimes charades came first. If it had been up to Nate, of course charades would never have come first.

For Nate, Lulu realized, nothing was as alluring as watching a movie. No matter how storied the city the boat was anchored near, how stunning the ruins. He'd been there, done that in virtually all these celebrated ports, in any case. He had been making these summer trips for years — as had Milo.

Yet Milo — as well as Ted that first week — was jazzed to revisit the sites he had seen before, sometimes many times before. Lulu decided that the two old friends were engaged in a virtual competition to point out the most surprising statue or the most tantalizing grilled squid. Ted made suggestions in his usual off-hand manner, seeming to discount his ideas even as he offered them. But Lulu noticed the others usually followed Ted's suggestions. Even Jake — who rarely joined their sightseeing expeditions and even more rarely cared about what anyone else was saying. For Ted was offering not just his own ideas, but those of generations of seasoned travelers — his parents and grandparents before him.

The Wellings, Lulu had decided, were a well-traveled family. Her Sturges great-great-grandfather and his brothers may have taken the Grand Tour, as most wealthy sons of the Gilded Age had, but they could not have approached the level of travel that Ted's family had luxuriated in. Though both the Sturgeses and the Wellings had used seasons of the year as verbs — "summering" at the Baur au Lac in Zurich, for example, with their own valet and lady's maids, and a private railroad car just for their trunks — Ted's family had inhaled the exotic sights and sounds to a stunning degree.

Ted was just continuing this family tradition. Lulu finally stopped being surprised when the proprietor of a tiny trattoria in an obscure port rushed over to Ted as the group entered, joyfully greeting "Teodoro." Usually, the owner would sing out that "piccolo Teodoro" had returned and then his wife, and in many cases, his sons and daughters, would emerge from the kitchen to welcome back the American they had known for decades.

The platters of food then paraded out of the kitchen were never items listed on the menu. The wines were also special, kept for the establishment's most valued patrons. Lulu could not help noticing that Ted usually pressed a good deal of money into the hands of the owner as they were leaving. Yet she felt that their welcome had been too genuinely warm for this to be the decisive factor.

Ted always played down these sorts of receptions, as he did most of his own travel suggestions. Milo tried to do this as well, but he could not achieve that same level of insouciance. For Milo clearly delighted in introducing Francesca to his favorite little restaurant tucked down an alley of a small port, or an amazing view that he had discovered years ago.

He seemed intent on making new memories with her — and Lulu. It was as if, Lulu thought, he wanted to imprint fresh, joyful memories over his own past. To have something positive and radiant to look back on.

And Francesca, Lulu realized, though a big star in Italy since age 18, had never been able to experience her native land like this — leisurely and randomly. It was Milo, not Francesca, who knew the way to a celebrated watering hole or the best paintings in the local museum. She had clearly been focused on building her career.

As Lulu got out of bed, she wondered again what sort of grand gesture her stepmother would use to re-assert her own stardom. And if it would happen today. Lulu tried to move quietly to avoid waking Emma.

Lulu was wearing her most faded Levi's and a Hanes T-shirt. She had quickly figured out the etiquette on these trips on shore, whether for a guided tour of ancient ruins or shopping in a white-washed village. The basic uniform was jeans, the more worn in the better, and white T-shirts. Most everyone wore faded blue jeans — except Ted, who wore his standard white pair.

Baseball caps were the hat of choice. All the actors wore them pulled down low, almost to their eyebrows. Running shoes were pro forma, socks were not. The actors seemed to favor the Converse sneakers without laces —

which Francesca had in baby blue and navy, Connor in white and Rob and Alexandra in black. Maybe there was some unspoken agreement that they didn't want to be slowed down tying their shoelaces.

For little seemed to slow them down. Rob, Alexandra and Francesca all walked at a surprisingly fast clip whether on a sightseeing stroll or window shopping. But Lulu quickly realized it was a defensive stride.

Francesca, Lulu now realized, was a far bigger star in her native Italy then in America. Her stepmother had a sexy-kitten strut, marked by a touch of indolence, when she strolled through Beverly Hills. In Italy, however, her pace reached a fast forced-march tempo — close to triple time.

Alexandra and Rob both knew that being recognized could cause something approaching bedlam, so each had adopted a studied casualness on shore. Her mass of long golden curls were plaited into braid, then scrunched through a baseball cap, which sat low over her eyes. Instead of her usual perfect posture, she would slouch, hands shoved into her jean pockets. She wore huge black sunglasses, which covered virtually the top half of her face.

Rob worked at being even more nondescript. He had become an international star at age 20, when he dazzled screen audiences as the poor boy who overcame great odds to win an Olympic gold medal — based on a true, but now forgotten, story. He had long ago accepted that his immense fame curtailed his movements.

Perhaps as a defense, he had developed an extraordinary sixth sense for spotting professional photographers. He would finger the most innocuous of loiterers, standing off to the side under an awning, or motoring with friends on a shabby pleasure boat. After three days of this, Lulu finally stopped being surprised that the people Rob fixated on were, nine times out of 10, paparazzi, waiting for their money shot. Tourists taking cell phones pictures were expected, but the people he was obsessed by would, it seemed inevitably, suddenly whip out a large powerful camera with a lens that meant business.

So Rob tried ever harder not to stand out. He usually pulled the baseball cap so low that Lulu was sure it blocked his vision. On the hottest of days, he would have on a gray cotton hoodie. He was known for his trademark lope on screen, but when walking with them, Rob's gait was more of a scuttle.

Lulu noticed that, probably as a longstanding habit, Rob and Xan rarely walked together — or even close to each other — on all shore expeditions. In fact, they were usually on opposite sides of the group. This was especially marked since, on the boat, Rob was usually glued to Alexandra's side.

Lulu thought it might be more than not wanting to help photographers get a two-shot. It may also have been that Xan liked this space between them. Lulu sometimes sensed a deep boredom in Alexandra. Lulu could see that the actress was jazzed when people recognized her — she basked in the public's glow. Rob had spent years striving to escape his fame, but she was just beginning to taste its joys. She lit up whenever people recognized her, luxuriating in her own stardom. Lula had seen that the solitary pleasures of scuba diving and snorkeling that Rob sought out didn't begin to excite Xan the way crowds did.

Lulu also noticed that the fast pace didn't hamper the actresses' ability to shop. Even at martial double-time quick step, Francesca and Xan displayed remarkable skill at spotting an enticing item. They possessed an acute clothing radar. The group would be trotting to reach the boat or a tour guide, when Xan would suddenly say, "That navy jacket is great" or Francesca would comment, "Those white pants are fabulous." Then, no matter how late or rushed the group was, the women could find time to go in, try it on and, usually, buy it.

Xan, in particular, could be ruthless when it came to obtaining an item she wanted. Timetables were something to be ignored. "I just do what I want," she once advised Lulu, "and everything else falls into place." Lulu only wished it were that easy. But maybe an ability to shape time as if it were Playdoh was one component of stardom.

In any case, both actresses displayed better clothing radar than Emma or even Gwen on their walks through town — an ability that impressed Lulu.

While Lulu was eating breakfast with Nate and Gwen, the rest of the group slowly emerged for their expedition. First Emma sat down, then Jake and Mark. Even Mark was not too talkative until after his first cup of café au lait. Rob and Xan emerged and ordered their usual organic protein drinks. All were in the appropriate t-shirts and jeans, ready for an early departure.

But when her stepmother came up on deck, Lulu was stunned. Francesca had abandoned all the clothing rules. She clearly had no intention of being under the radar.

Francesca was wearing a blindingly white linen dress, with a form-fitting, halter top and a wide, pleated skirt. It reminded Lulu of a dress that Grace Kelly wore in "To Catch a Thief" — cool and crisp, yet sexy. Francesca's wavy dark hair was not scrunched up and hidden in a baseball cap. Rather, it cascaded around her shoulders, like a Botticelli Venus. If Sandro's Venus had raven dark hair. She wore a pale, wide-brimmed straw hat, with a white silk band, and also carried a small vintage parasol, white with pink chrysanthemums, as added protection against the sun. She had on pink and silver platform wedge sandals that only she could make graceful. And did.

Francesca might just as well have placed a neon sign above her head, with an arrow of bright white bulbs, pointing downward as the sign flashed: "Movie Star Here."

"Wow, Chesca," Rob said with his usual over-enthusiasm. "You look fantastic. What a stunning dress! It's perfect for you!" He seemed barely able to contain his delight. His thousand-watt smile beamed. Lulu knew it was typical of his joy in the moment, but she wondered when it was going to occur to him how likely Francesco was to stand out — a thought usually uppermost in his mind.

Milo had been up earlier, and was now talking to the captain, but when he finally re-appeared for breakfast, he did an obvious double-take to acknowledge Francesca's dress. "Adorable, darling," he said, as he kissed her hello, "but is that really how you want to play this?"

She gave him an innocent look, refusing the bait. "I so love the Casa de Volpe," she said. "I felt like celebrating being here with you — with all of you." Her last words were meant for all of them, and her eyes swept across their faces. Lulu thought she seemed to linger a beat on Connor, who had just come up on deck.

As the group walked down the cobblestone, heads began to swerve. In her dazzling white dress and hat, Francesca would have stood out even if she weren't a famous actress, Lulu thought. But the clothes intensified her star power. Passersby would look at the dress, then take a second look when they realized who she was. Then they would begin to take in just who she was walking with.

Soon, it was more than heads swerving. People began to fall into step behind them, trailing at a not-too-discreet distance. Lulu was, as usual, toward the back of the group, and she could see the rumor take physical shape as it traveled through the neighborhood. People from side streets were hurrying toward them, those who had been window shopping turned in a flurry of movement as the rumor skipped along the street just ahead of them. People emerged from store doorways and faces gazed out from shop windows, iPhones were whipped out and the buzz of cameras clicking sounded like locusts. A lot of them. She heard murmurs of "Francesca" and "Frateli" as people were rushing over.

As the rumor gained momentum, she began to hear "Alexandra Hobart" pronounced as if one word. Then, almost as the sort of gasp, the word "Tracey" arose from various locations.

As the crowd grew, Lulu worried that she might be swept away by this gathering tide. Jake and Mark had peeled off well before this commotion gained speed. Mark had noticed a blanket that might work for a guest bedroom, so they went to check it out. But Lulu decided she shouldn't be lagging toward the back here. She didn't want to get pushed aside and cut off.

She pushed forward to be nearer to Milo. The growing crowd was both trailing them and surrounding them. Suddenly, men with massive telephoto lenses were muscling through, cameras clicking like gun shots. Lulu was buffeted as the fans, photographers and gawkers filled the narrow street. She was getting scared she might lose her footing.

All these people seemed to be trapped in a magnetic beam, irresistibly drawn to the stars they had recognized. Maybe, Lulu thought, this is why fans acted as if everyone else, the others in the group or the entourage, were merely in the way, and could be elbowed aside.

Lulu always wondered what this was about. Did they think celebrity could rub off? Or that star power was contagious, something they could catch — like the flu? Did they imagine lasting friendship, a deep connection, could develop in this fleeting moment? Lulu felt this avid desire for proximity, for contact, was unsettling. But perhaps, she decided, her view was colored by the fact that she was often the person being elbowed aside.

Milo put his arm around Francesca in a protective gesture, pulling her tight against him. Lulu, who was pushing hard to get closer and was already in their downdraft, could hear him say, "Let's get over to Prada," which was in the next bank of stores. Gwen had moved to Francesca's other side, to help shield her in some way. Rob and Xan, their heads bowed as if walking into gale-force winds, were now clamped together, his arm around her, his hand gripping her shoulder. Nikko, the steward who usually shadowed Rob, was now glued to his other side. Russell, who would usually trail behind the group, carrying extra water and snacks as well as basic first aid supplies, was now fastened to Xan and talking into a short-wave radio. Emma was pressed against Russ, at her mother's heels.

Lulu could see this but was still being buffeted as she fought to reach Milo. Even as she did, Connor, who was off to her left and slightly behind her, moved closer, saying loudly, "I'm getting Lulu out of here." He leaned forward to grab her hand and quickly began pulling her sideways through the jostling throng. She clutched his arm with her other hand and held on tight, scared she might lose her grip and be swept away.

He moved fast, weaving through the crowd like a linebacker, so she had no time to focus on her fear. She concentrated on being a football. As they cut through, people in the crowd seemed eager to give way. They were fiercely intent on moving the opposite direction, toward the stars – especially Rob. Anyone moving away from the celebrities meant fewer people blocking their effort to attain that stardom. Everything and everyone else was incidental.

Once Lulu had escaped the crowd's grip, she looked back, and saw that Milo, Francesca and the others were almost at Prada. They were the tip of what looked like an unwieldy flying wedge formation. And that wedge was expanding, as more and more people heard about the megawatt celebrities in their midst. Lulu could see a trio of policemen running on an angle directly toward the crowd, aiming to intersect at the tip of the wedge

She realized she was shaking — and still clinging to Connor's hand with both of hers. Then he was hugging her tightly. It felt comforting, even protective. "That was way too close," he said, murmuring into the top of her head. He suddenly took a step back, "We need to get away from this mess now. We shouldn't stay around here." He laughed suddenly. "It's insane really. This epitomizes everything I want. If 'Chessmen' stays strong, and then 'Dead Drop' comes together, I'll have this to look forward to — but only if I'm really, really lucky."

She started laughing with him. They were buoyed by the giddiness that comes from evading a close call, sharing the near-euphoria created by eluding danger. "You're an amazing girl, you know, Lulu. I don't think you know just how amazing. My first thought in that craziness was that I needed to get you out of there.

"Of all the people I've met in Hollywood," he continued, his eyes now serious, "you're the only one who actually asks me about me — not my next project, or what movie offers have come in. About me. That means a great deal. It shouldn't sound so special. But it is. Most people I meet here only care about what I do. To you, it doesn't seem to matter. You don't understand how special you are."

Lulu basked in his potent charm as he focused his attention on her. She had given up trying to figure it out. She only knew that, in this moment, she had stopped feeling self-conscious and out of sync, as she so often did.

"I sort of do when I'm with you." She didn't realize she had said it aloud. But his smile deepened, until it was as dazzling as the Mediterranean sunshine. His charm was palpable. She felt drawn even closer. He reached out to stroke her hair

Four more policemen ran by, headed toward the mob. Francis Linton, the yacht captain, and another steward were keeping pace with them. Nate was several steps behind. Linton stopped when he saw Connor and Lulu, motioning to the policemen and the others to continue on toward the throng. But he and Levinson peeled off to head toward Lulu and Connor.

"This will all be fine," were the first words Linton said, once he was within earshot. He seemed too cool and collected to have just been sprinting toward an unruly mob. Lulu noticed he was clutching a walkie-talkie in his left hand and there was a stubby baton attached to his belt.

"We spoke to the Prada store manager," Linton explained, "and we're going to take them all out the back door. There is an alley there that we can use. It might be best, though, if you both head back to the boat now.

Once we get them out of there and back on board we intend to get out of the area fairly quickly."

"Thanks, Frank," Connor said. "We were just about to do just that."

"And Mr. Levinson," Linton turned to Nate, "It might be best if you did that as well. There's really not much you can do if you come with us at this point. And that way, I can know you're safe on the boat and away from all this." He motioned toward the crush of people, which was still growing. "We have a plan now, so it is relatively under control. And once they are out, we need to get them — get all of you — away. It will be madness for us to stay in Puerto Cervo any longer than we have to — now that everyone has identified your party and probably figured out our boat. If you don't mind, sir, it's far better this way. I am sure Ms. Hedges will understand."

His walkie-talkie crackled and the captain paused as he held it up to his ear. His jaw set as he listened. "The store manager is concerned that the crowd is getting so large that they might break the windows," Linton told them after he signed off. "They're pressing too hard against the glass. The police are getting worried that people could get hurt — crushed or trampled or maybe impaled on shards of glass. I thought shop glass was supposed to be unbreakable, even bulletproof. We have to start this evacuation now. I need to get over there." He started running. "I'll see you back at the boat," he called over his shoulder.

As they walked back, Nate picked up his continuing conversation with Connor about "Dead Drop." The trio soon ran into Jake and Mark, who had been walking in their direction, trying to hook up with the group as planned. Connor quickly filled them in on what they'd missed.

"Thank God I saw that blanket," Mark said. "I always knew that shopping was life-saving. It's as important as going to gym. Maybe more important. We need to keep in shape for it just the same way. I am going to forever look on this blanket as our lucky talisman, Jake."

"How did this all happen, anyway?" Jake asked. He looked pointedly at Connor. "What was the deal with Francesca this morning? What's up with her?"

Lulu wondered why Connor, as Francesca's former co-star, was somehow expected to have special insights into what made her tick. Good luck with that!

Connor looked blandly back. "I have no idea," he said. "It was pretty trippy though. Maybe it's about being home in Italy. It's been a while for her. But who knows with these things?" he added with a shrug.

Jake looked at him a beat more before he dropped it. He had other things he wanted to talk about.

"Things are crazy all over," Jake began. He turned to Nate, "Have you talked to Fred recently? I was talking with him late last night. He told me that Lefferts has been flipping out. He's furious about Roger running over-budget.

"Fred said it was way too much like the old days. He's beginning to think that Harry might be a little too furious. He's wondering if something might be up with Tessa."

Jake paused and again looked directly at Connor. As if he was expecting some sort of reaction from the actor. He failed to get one.

"Anyways," Jake continued, "Now, Roger's almost six weeks behind schedule. They'd built in extra days, just so this wouldn't happen. But first it was rain for more than a week. And then that insane incident with the extra. And now Emily is looking so terrible in the dailies that Lefferts wants to shut the whole thing down. He keeps yelling that he's paying her too much for her to look so lousy. He's ranting about firing Roger and replacing Jules."

"Roger I can understand," Nate said casually. "But Jules? He's one of the best DP's out there. His lighting is phenomenal. If he can't make Emily look good something must be wrong — with her. Listen, the last time I saw her, she looked like a Shar-Pei. She'd clearly missed her Botox appointment. More like her last five appointments."

Lulu had to school herself not to say anything. But even after a summer of comments like this, she still felt shocked by how these men, even Milo, talked about actresses. They were discussed like a commodity. If Granny had been here, though, Lulu knew she wouldn't have stayed silent. Granny could always be relied on to cite her own mother, Lily Thayer, who had been a baby suffragette. These men would have heard what for.

"And what incident with the extra?" Nate had moved on from Jules. "I'm not up to speed here."

Jake looked only too happy to tell him. He so clearly enjoyed knowing things before others did – and particularly enjoyed letting everyone know he knew.

"Roger spent about three days last week on a huge crowd scene – see, this is related!" Harris laughed at his own joke. "He's shooting in Union Station, closes it down for five nights, and stages it with literally hundreds of extras. He's too much of a 'filmmaker' to use CGI!

"Who died," Nate interjected, "and made him Cecil fucking DeMille? He can't even figure out where to put the camera in a two-shot. Fire Jules! Jules should fire him!"

"So they've been setting up for about three hours," Harris continued, "and the shot is finally ready and they turn around – and can't find Nick. He had been standing there, the PA had been wrangling. But now he's nowhere to be seen.

"They're looking for him frantically. Then, after like a half-hour, Roger sees, in the far corner, way in the back — there's a woman wearing a pale yellow straw hat and a bright yellow dress. Lemon meringue yellow. It hits him like cartoon character being hit with a mallet."

Nate started to laugh and shake his head after Jake mentioned the word "yellow." Jake pauses, turning to Connor. "Nick has a thing about yellow."

"Nick?" Connor asked. "A thing?"

Nate turned to annotate the conversation for Connor, and also, incidentally, for Lulu. "We're talking about Nick Copley," Nate said, "He's starring in Roger's movie. And there's a reason why Nick loves those old Warner Bros. cartoons so much. He's secretly Daffy Duck. I know the word on him is "eccentric" but that's a euphemism for 'out of his mind.'"

Nate turned back to Jake, who continued. "Yeah, and one of his crazy things is that he absolutely loathes yellow. Don't ask me why. But he hates it so much, Fred tells me, that there's a clause in his contract — if anyone on the set is wearing yellow, he can leave. And some assistant to the assistant costumer somehow missed this memo — and I'm sure this time there actually was a memo — and she puts one of the extras in a yellow dress. Frankly, I don't know where she'd even find a yellow dress on that set."

Nate is laughing so hard that he is almost wheezing. "That is so right!" he said. Connor was now laughing as well.

"It took them a while even then to figure it out. But they finally hear Nick had left the set. He had the teamster drive him to the Roger Room, a bar he likes on La Cienega. By the time they tracked him down he was on his third scotch. Though it may have been more, since he was doing Three Stooges routines for this cute bartender when they found him. So they had to wrap that day. And the three nights at Union Station turned into six. And the bartender got a walk-on.

"So this, on top of everything else, drives Lefferts nuts.

"He just opened up on Roger. The flamethrowers went from 'scorch' to 'incinerate.'

"Fred is also worried now since he saw that Roger has no idea how to deal with this. It got so insane yesterday, Fred told me, that Harry kicked Roger out of his own office. Harry was sitting in his New York sanctum, on the speaker with Roger and Fred, who are sitting in Roger's L.A. office. And Harry is getting more and more furious. Out-of-control furious.

"But Roger keeps offering up explanations, Fred says, instead of just letting Harry go off. So not the way to play it. Excuses just make Harry crazier. The screaming builds to a crescendo. Fred was thinking that not just the people with offices on that floor, but everyone with offices in the building can hear it. Maybe even everyone in the next building over.

"Lefferts, meanwhile, can't believe this guy is explaining instead of just apologizing. He eviscerates him. Then he steps over the ledge. "GET OUT OF MY OFFICE!" he started bellowing, "GET OUT OF MY OFFICE!" Fred said they could hear him frothing at the mouth. So Roger, who is sitting in Los Angeles, in his own office mind you, finally stands up and walks out."

"Fred just sat there, speechless. Which is saying something."

They were all laughing, now. Even Lulu. Though she was also thinking that this was some wacky work environment.

"Listen," Nate said, "Harry has hated Roger for years. Loathes him. It goes back to before the Architectural Digest story?"

"What Architectural Digest story?" Jake asked. Lulu could see it bothered Harris to have to admit this: A story he didn't know.

"It must be about five or six years ago," Nate begins, "It was when 15 Central Park West opened. Roger and Francine were like the first people to move in. They finally had an excuse to give up their place at the Sherry — which they had prized for years because Jack Warner's apartment had been on the floor above theirs. But that place is so over.

"So they get a palatial spread at 15, on a high floor, something above 30, and they do it up in grand style.

Barbara Barry helps with the layout. Architectural Digest asks to do a story — since he's such a big-time director and the building is so hot. And the apartment really does look terrific. So the AD spread runs, and they are indeed the talk of the town — in both L.A. and New York.

"Harry is talking about it too, but in another way. He's livid. He sends Roger an itemized bill. Because you could see in the photos that Roger furnished the entire apartment from his films. Harry spots a sofa in particular, as well as four club chairs that he had asked about a while back."

"So what happened?" Connor asked, laughing as hard as the others.

"They sent Harry a certified check," Nate said. "The very next day. By special courier. And they gave Lefferts the club chairs for Christmas that year. But that's the sort of thing Harry never forgets. This is the first film Roger has set up at Lucent since it happened. It's an amazing script that Copley is perfect for. And we can all see it — if they ever finish the shoot."

Nate turned to Connor. "This can't be the first time you've heard stories about Lefferts?" he asked.

"No. I've heard some," Ericson replied evenly, "Sounds like quite a guy." Lulu thought his tone sounded guarded.

Jake was looking at him as well — a speculative stare. "I'd have thought you heard more than a few stories about Harry," Jake said. "I got the impression you might have been hearing quite a lot of them in recent months. From Tessa, no? You know her, don't you?"

"The stories about Lefferts are endless," Nate said, almost cutting Jake off. "He's a legendary screamer. My personal favorite is the one about a job applicant who had a coronary. He couldn't answer all the questions that Harry was firing out him — too scared, probably. Then, when Harry started yelling at him to get out, he couldn't get up from his chair.

"Harry has these special white Mies Barcelona chairs, in brass instead of chrome. And this guy was big — really big. And sweating. So he's struggling to pull himself up out of that low-slung X seat, and Harry is using him for vocal target practice. Physical target practice as well — since the spittle is spewing across that big Gordon Bunshaft desk he keeps so bare. The guy had never experienced anything like this — I'm sure it's not covered in your standard interview prep. They don't teach how to protect yourself from verbal knee-capping. He has a coronary right there during the job interview.

"He was ultimately okay. He didn't die or anything. They got him to the hospital and he was out in a day or two. But it did take four people to maneuver that stretcher out of the office. Two of Harry's assistants had to help. He was furious because they had to leave the phones and email unattended."

Jake, Mark and Connor were all laughing hard by this time. Jake was wiping his eyes. Even Nate was laughing at his own story. Lulu also laughed — though she still felt sorry for that poor applicant.

They had maintained a brisk pace throughout this conversation. As they neared the pier, they could see the hacker waiting. Lulu had noticed that Connor had kept his hat pulled down almost to his eyebrows ever since they escaped the mob. He didn't raise it until they were in the speedboat, scudding across the harbor to the yacht.

Jake turned to Nate once they were in the speedboat. "Did you hear the latest on Ben?" he asked. He was speaking quietly, perhaps thinking the hacker's engine would drown out their voices, and Lulu wouldn't be able to hear. But she did.

"He actually closed a deal. He just signed Cassidy," Jake continued. "It came together fast. Sam's next project was supposed to shoot in New Zealand and Thailand, and he decided he didn't want to be so far away for so long. So he suddenly had an opening in his schedule and was available. Ben is already starting the revisions — the guy is going to be older, with a teenage daughter. For about two days, I heard, the studio was pressing him to turn the part into a girl. They thought that would work. But then he got Cassidy, so they dropped that."

Stephanie was on deck to meet them. She had snacks laid out, as well as bottles of water and pitchers of iced tea and lemonade. There was an open bottle of Domaine

Ott on ice. She said they had just heard from the captain that the others were now safely out of Prada and heading back to the boat. They were taking a circuitous route, so it might be as long as a half-hour or 45 minutes.

Mark poured a glass of rosé for Jake, and then one for himself. He motioned with the bottle to Nate, who nodded in assent. But Connor shook his head no, and reached for a bottle of water. Lulu picked up the pitcher of iced tea. Her hands were still a little shaky, so Connor took it from her and poured her a glass. It embarrassed her a little. He smiled as he handed the glass to her, though, and she couldn't help but smile back.

"So would you guys please explain to me what happened with Tim?" Nate was already pouring himself a second glass. He was addressing both Jake and Mark, but looking at Jake. They waited for him to continue. "He left Sophie last week, you know."

"It's about time," Jake sighed happily. "I wasn't sure if it was out yet. This has been going on for months."

"Sophie reached Gwen late last night. Near hysterics — not that she's ever far from them," Nate continued, "It shouldn't have been such a surprise. But it sounded like she's the only one who doesn't know her husband is gay. I always knew she was dizzy, maybe even daffy — but how stupid is she?"

"She knew," Jake said. "Of course she knew. She just didn't see why he should want to leave. She kept insisting that he should stay with her at least until the baby. What does his happiness matter? It's already been so complicated for him to address this. He does really care about her. But the thing is that he really is in love with Eddy — has been for quite a while now. Yet she was doing everything she could to make this harder for him.

"What seemed to matter most to her," Jake let the scorn show in his voice, "was that OK! has the deal to run the first baby pictures. But I'm sure she'll calm down when she realizes she can renegotiate the prices even higher with this cockamamie scandal she's created. If she plays this right, she could get a reality TV show out of it. She'd get the greatest numbers — since she's out of her mind."

"Eddy is a terrific guy," Mark said, "He's the opposite of high-maintenance. So, right there, Tim is immediately in a better place. Just the fact that Eddy's hung in there through this insanity shows you this is will turn out great for both of them. And for Sophie and the baby as well. "

Mark and Jake headed down to their cabin. Nate went below as well, since he wanted to take a shower after his sprint toward the Prada store. Lulu and Connor stayed on deck, hovering around the food.

To hide her momentary awkwardness, Lulu stared intently at the mixed nuts and started picking out the cashews. She was giving herself an internal pep talk: What would Jazzy do?

"Here, you missed one." Connor fished out a cashew that she had overlooked. She held out her hand. There was that smile again — a smile that you had to respond to. "You really are incredible," he said, picking up the thread of their earlier conversation.

"I thought I was 'amazing.'" She tried to sound aloof and collected.

"That too," he laughed. "Most girls would have had hysterics."

"I was with you," she said. She willed herself to keep looking him in the eye. "I always feel better when I'm with you. I don't know what it is, exactly. But when I'm with you, I'm not as self-conscious. I don't worry as much. I somehow feel I'm as capable as you seem to think I am. That I can handle anything."

She paused to smile at him. He had this knack of reassuring her. She heard the sound of a speedboat approaching the boat. So she hurried the rest, wanting to say it before the others arrived. She took a gulp of air as she gathered up her courage. Yet she spoke even more softly, "It feels so wonderful whenever I'm with you. I'm so glad you're here on the boat with me. I'm so happy we met."

"I'm glad, too," he said. She hadn't felt him moving, but they were now standing close together, their bodies nearly touching. Yet Lulu realized she didn't feel nervous. This felt so right to her, so natural. She had promised herself, after Tom Haverferd behaved so beastly, that she would not do anything unless she thought she was really in love. And she was sure Abby had said it would feel like this. She realized she had been holding her breath, as if breathing too hard would break the spell. "And it's a constant surprise to me that you don't realize how beautiful you are." He pushed her hair back off her face. "Because you are, you know, Lulu. Beautiful."

He was running his thumb along her jaw, tracing its outline. "I never knew a blush could be so adorable," he said softly. She could hear the smile in his voice. But she couldn't focus on the words, just the touch of his fingers as they traced the outlines of her face.

The voices of the passengers on the boat below were getting louder. "Thanks for saving me today," she whispered, as she put her arms around him and shyly reached up to kiss him. Connor's arms tightened quickly around her and his features swam before her, she thought, jumbled together like a Picasso cubist portrait as his face drew closer. Then she stopped thinking. His kiss was like a lightning bolt of joy. The current seemed to flash down to her fingers and toes and then reverse course. She felt tingly, off-balance, almost giddy and exuberantly happy. She was breathless, but every ounce of her body wanted his kiss to go on forever. It carried a promise of shimmering adventure and intense fun.

As the voices from below grew clearer, however, Connor's hold slackened. He took a step away from her and turned around — just in time to greet Francesca as she stepped onto the deck.

Only her stepmother bore any evidence of the riot they had all been through — her dress was torn in two places and her parasol was gone. But Lulu could see Francesca looked far from chastened. In fact, there was an angry sparkle in her eye.

As for Xan, she was carrying three overflowing shopping bags from Prada.

CHAPTER 8

THE SCREENING ON THE YACHT

O VER THE LAST FOUR DAYS of their boat trip, the "Incident at Porto Cervo" became a storied touchstone of all conversations. The narrative arc, Lulu noted, developed sweep and power, and details were honed and polished as carefully as facets on an important jewel from JAR.

That half-hour wait in Prada soon possessed an undercurrent of danger that U.S. diplomats experienced when trapped for days in a besieged embassy far from their native land. The exit from the boutique gained the trappings of an elaborately timed P.O.W escape, out of a World War II movie, or the Iranian hostages' escape in "Argo." Details were equally fanciful. The circuitous route back to the boat took on the evasive maneuvers of the most complicated Cold War cat-and-mouse thriller. Even reaching sanctuary inside Prada was now revealed to be as perilous as scaling the north face of K-2.

And there were no cameos in this scenario. Everyone had a starring role — with equally outsized emotions to play. It was surprising, Lulu decided, just how many individual dramas were contained in the swirl of events.

Rob, for example, had helped Xan evade a particularly nefarious trio of photographers, just as the shore party gained the Prada entrance. He also masterfully made sure that the paparazzi were denied a clean shot of the couple. Xan was still dazzled by the ingenuity he had displayed. Rob and Xan both recounted this in granular detail — though Lulu noted that their close call sounded closer each time.

Once they were all in the boutique, Gwen had devised some much desired privacy. By artfully moving clothes racks and carefully positioning the shoppers trapped in the store with them, she was able to design a secure space beyond the sightlines for most of the throng outside — even those pressed against the windows. As Gwen explained it, she had little trouble convincing everyone else in the store to do exactly as she envisioned.

Jake, meanwhile, seemed to have been in continual contact with the captain via walkie-talkie, to make sure everything was proceeding smoothly. Frank, as Mark explained it, had relied on Harris's okay for every step the group took as they headed back to the safety of the ship.

Francesca ratcheted up the drama quotient as she insisted that Milo had rescued her from an exquisite danger — her fans' obsessive adoration. When she described the day's events, her jaw-dropping, movie-star outfit didn't rate a mention. Instead, she focused on her Italian fans' passionate devotion, which could so readily tilt toward violence. And she fervently lauded her husband's cool daring and tactical prowess during what had become, in her version, a riot.

By the next day, her narration starred not just Milo but the entire group — they had all gallantly come together to save her from her too-ardent fan base. Even Connor had played a significant role in coming to her aid. Without her traveling companions' quick thinking, she insisted, it could easily have ended in a "Suddenly Last Summer" moment — with her as Sebastian.

From Francesca's perspective, the entire group had now bonded tightly over this terrifying experience. They had gone through the fire together, undergoing trials that outsiders could never fully appreciate, or even comprehend, and emerged safely out the other side. True friendship had been tempered by these flames, and it would nurture them all in the future. She pledged to maintain this closeness long after the trip ended and they had returned to L.A.

For Lulu, Francesca's assertions sounded like the pledges you make at the end of summer camp — the vows of eternal friendship made by little girls. Lulu had made these pledges herself when she was younger — only to see them wither as the air turned cold. She wasn't sure, though, that Francesca would have acknowledged this comparison.

As the trip continued, Lulu also began to feel that she could never get a moment alone with Connor after their kiss on deck. It was true that the actor was often locked in movie discussions with Nate — deep conversations that Milo usually joined. Lulu sometimes sat nearby and listened, but only briefly, since the talk was largely movie jargon — of cutting continuity or characters' arcs. She could see, however, that Connor was soaking it up.

But when he was not bathing in this movie argot, Francesca was a constant presence. She fluttered around Connor, drawn to his flame and delighting in his company. He seemed to delight in her delight, though her actions blocked anyone else who sought to draw close — particularly Lulu.

If Lulu casually pointed something out to Connor, and he walked over to chat with her and Emma, Francesca would soon join their conversation. If Lulu was getting a Coke while Connor was at the bar, Francesca needed a refresher. If Mark was telling her another hysterical story and Connor paused to listen, Francesca was soon there, listening as well. She never failed to hit her mark.

The evenings offered no opportunity either. After dinner the entire group settled into the saloon to watch movies. They were methodically working through Nate's movie stash. Milo and Nate, along with Uncle Ted the first week, used a casual shorthand when analyzing the film they had just seen. Lulu realized that Milo and Nate shared the easy banter of old friends — if not quite the patois her father used with Uncle Ted. Rob and Xan had quickly gotten into the rhythm of these marathon screenings and both clearly enjoyed dissecting each picture. The conversation would start as the credits rolled.

Rob delighted in this discussion, and Lulu felt that this was one time where Xan's enthusiasm appeared genuinely to equal his. The conversation sometimes seemed to be the real attraction for Xan, even more than the movies. She drank in the film analysis from a director or producer's point of view. For each approached a movie from a different perspective — with Milo, Ted and Nate often focusing on the structure or pace and cutting, while Rob and Xan zoned in on the performances. Even when Rob talked about lighting and editing, which Lulu soon realized he knew a lot about, it was usually through the prism of the actors' skills — or lack thereof.

The first few nights of the trip, Francesca had eagerly joined in this conversation, staying up late into the evening. But by mid-week, she was usually asleep on the sofa before the second feature ended. Sometimes even before it had started. By the second week, she was heading down to her cabin as the opening credits of the second movie rolled.

But everyone else indulged in the nightly movie marathon. The crew's night shift, overseen by the omnipresent Russell, was fully occupied taking care of the movie-watchers' requests for drinks and late night snacks. They usually went through platters of grilled cheese and tomato sandwiches (no crusts), trays of triple-cream brie and Eppoisses de Bourgogne with pear slices and French bread toast points, or bowls of berries and sliced peaches. At some point, far into the night, there would be an ice cream break, with yet more fresh berries. Xan was partial to grapefruit ices, which the chief had begun fashioning into ever more fanciful shapes for her. Meanwhile, the group was going through so much champagne and rosé that Milo said he was glad that he had brought along an extra three cases of each.

Connor, on his first night aboard, had sat through all three features, talking with Nate, Milo, Xan and Rob. But on his second night, he'd left soon after the second feature started, apologizing that he was running on fumes after the South of France. The night before had been too long, he said, and he needed to catch up on sleep. He clearly reveled in the conversation, but, as he explained, he was still so tired he felt punch drunk by the end of the second feature.

It was well into the second feature of their triple bill the second night after the riot when Lulu realized she was cold. Even triple layers of the cashmere throws from a pile stacked in the saloon weren't doing the trick. She decided to run down to her cabin and get her cardigan — she had forgotten to bring it up to dinner.

The movie was a French action thriller that had roared through Cannes a few months ago but was not due to be released in the U.S. until next spring. Lulu left the saloon just as preparations for a bank heist were being laid out. She ran down the stairs leading to her cabin, hoping to get back before the robbery started.

She sped down the hallway, slowing only slightly as she approached the intersection with the long corridor. She picked up speed again as she turned the corner — and ran smack into Connor.

She had been looking down as she hurtled down the corridor, and was caught off guard. He had seen her rounding the corner, though, so had time to put his hands out and catch her at mid-stride. This staved off a head-on collision, but she still managed to jolt him hard. "Whoa," he was laughing, as she came to a halt in front of him. He was wearing one of the boat's terry cloth robes and slippers. "What's up?"

"Gosh," she panted. "I am so sorry! I am going to my cabin to grab a sweater — it's even colder than usual in the saloon tonight and those blankets are no use. I'm trying to get back before the heist starts."

"You better move it then," he advised. "Come on, I'll walk you."

Lulu was silent as they walked toward her cabin. She knew what she wanted to say though — now she just had to say it. She and Abby had spent more than two weeks figuring out the right words that would reveal whether Jamie had feelings for her. Whether he even liked her. Because the signals just weren't clear enough for Abby.

Lulu had been ruminating about this over the last two days. And, she had to admit, even before. As she had replayed those conversations with Abby in her head, Lulu had wished she could call her best friend for a quick pep talk. But this was going to have to be done without her.

"I'm glad I ran into you though." Lulu thought about how that sounded and course-corrected. "I mean, not physically run into you — I'm sorry about that. But just run into you. I've been wanting to talk with you alone for the last two days, since we were interrupted up on deck. I have been thinking about it a great deal."

Usually, when speaking with him, Lulu felt at ease, less nervous and unsure than she often did in conversation. But not this time. She paused as she gathered her courage.

"I have really been thinking about you a lot, Connor. The thing is, I, I feel so wonderful when I am with you. I feel like I am the person I always wanted to be. The best possible version of me. And... and... it happens because of you."

They had reached the door of her cabin. Lulu opened it, and they both went in. She stood with her back to the door for support. Then she went for it. "I really care about you. It's exciting and amazing. I am not all that experienced at this — at feeling like this — but I know how I feel about you and I know how much I want to be with you. How much I like you."

He looked into her eyes with an amused, slightly skeptical look. "Lulu, I thought you were in a hurry to grab your jumper and get back to the movie?"

"I was," Lulu was not deterred. "I am. But I really want to talk with you. When we were interrupted the other day, I felt there was so much I wanted to say. So much more I needed to say." Lulu felt her courage failing her, "I keep thinking about it."

"We were indeed interrupted," he said. That golden smile lurked behind his eyes. He flicked her chin in an offhand manner and then cupped her face almost casually with his hand. His other hand was at the small of her back. "So where were we?" There was a lazy, offhand tone in his voice. "I can't quite remember. Were we here?" He kissed her forehead just above her right eyebrow. It felt electric. "No? Well, maybe we were here?" He kissed the outside edge of her cheekbone. "Or maybe here?" He tipped her head gently so he could kiss the arc of her long neck. She tried to maintain a similar offhand manner, but was finding it hard to hold an indifferent pose. "Or here?" He kissed the hollow of her throat. Lulu had no idea one kiss could excite her so powerfully. But she did now. She focused on keeping her breathing steady. His movements, meanwhile, remained slow and lazy. "Or it may have been higher, closer to here." She could hear the smile in his voice and feel his breath on her throat. His mouth traveled up her neck as he gently moved her hair behind her ear, so he could kiss a tattooing pulse she didn't know was right under her earlobe. "Or maybe here?" He kissed the corner of her mouth. "Ah, I remember now," he said, with a laugh that was even more lazy, "I believe we were right here." Finally, in a motion that Lulu had been aching for, he kissed her on the lips, a long deep kiss. She pressed herself more closely against him.

He pulled back, but the smile was still lurking in his eyes. "Yes, I do think that might be where we left off," he said. "Is that what you remember too?"

"I'm not so sure," she said. "It seems familiar, but I can't tell yet. Why don't you try it again? Maybe this time it will come back to me."

His arms tightened around her again. He was about to say something, when they heard voices in the hallway. Sandy was speaking to someone, "Have you seen Mr. Ericson? Did he head back up to the saloon by any chance? He ordered this bottle and the berries and cream. And an extra bucket of ice. But he doesn't seem to be in his cabin now. Should I leave it there for him? Or would it be better if I check upstairs first?"

"No, just leave it in his room if he's not there now," Russell answered him. "And make sure there's also enough ice around the champagne, so it stays chilled. Once you do that, come back up to the saloon please. They seem particularly hungry tonight. I need all hands there now."

"Shite," Connor said under his breath. "I, I need to get back to my room. I was having such trouble getting to sleep, I ordered something to drink and a snack, to see if it would help. I need to get some sleep, Lulu. And you need to get back to the movie. If you don't give me a report on it, I'd be lost tomorrow.

"But this is to be continued." He held her so tightly she had trouble breathing, and gave her a quick hard kiss. Her lips felt bruised. "Though maybe not here on the boat. Listen Lulu," he said, "this is one big boat. But it is still not large enough for all the oversized egos aboard. So many are trapped in a confined space that it might not be the right place for this. Above all, I want you to be sure. Very sure. You know, I hope, that I think every particle of you is adorable. Every square inch. I've made that about as clear as I can." His hands traveled up her body as he kissed her again, this time soft and lingering. "But you are the one that has to be sure here."

The heist was already over when Lulu finally got back to the movie. She came in time to see the mismatched gang of robbers, who had pulled off an intricate heist, begin a roundelay of betrayals and recriminations. Lulu had a hard time following the action, though. Her mind kept going back to the scene in her cabin.

The next morning, Lulu could barely remember what the third movie was about. When Connor sat down next to her at breakfast, asking both Emma and her about the films he had missed — their usual drill — Emma supplied much of the plot lines. As Connor continued to quiz them about the movies and the conversations they'd had after each one, Lulu was surprised how casual he sounded. His tone was so bland and matter of fact.

She had forgotten how good an actor he was.

Chapter 9

THE ESTATE IN BEVERLY HILLS

THE DAY AFTER LULU GOT BACK to Los Angeles, her mother called with the news — her latest test results had come back clean and the prognosis was officially positive. The ice-cold knot, which Lulu now realized had been sitting on her chest for the entire summer, dissolved.

She started to cry, as she seemed to do so often when speaking to her mother. But these tears were different, tasting of solace rather than anger and despair.

Until then, Lulu had coped with the possible terror lying in wait for her by trying desperately not to think about it. For back in May, during one conversation between mummy and Aunt Grace that Lulu was clearly not supposed to hear, she had learned that the cancer might have spread to two lymph nodes. Lulu was never quite sure she had heard correctly, and she had never heard those three words mentioned again — before or since. But the fear they brought had hovered, like the bat in a vampire movie.

Now, however, as her mother talked about these good results, Lulu could hear the unfeigned joy in her voice. It was a tone, Lulu realized, that she hadn't heard since last winter. The chemo, though grueling, was pronounced a success, her mother said, and all traces of the cancer had been eradicated. That was such good news, mummy said, since she never wanted to go through anything like this again.

Lulu waited for the words "lymph nodes" to emerge — but they never did. Lulu felt waves of relief roll over her.

"Darling," her mother was saying, "Did you hear me? It's all extremely positive. And I am feeling much stronger every day. So this is all to the good — since you've been having such a wonderful time this summer with your father. And that really was so important — for you as well as for him.

"Your father and I emailed earlier today, and you're going to fly back next week. We'll be there to pick you up at Logan. I have missed you so, Lulu – I can't even begin to tell you how much. But it's all over now. We are going to have a spectacular fall!"

After she hung up, Lulu immediately texted Abby. Lulu knew her best friend would understand her radio silence these two months once she read this text. Mummy's cancer had been so terrifying for Lulu that she had made all sorts of deals with herself – as long as she didn't type the word, for example, it wasn't real. It couldn't hurt her, or affect her life. At the same time, however, her mother's cancer was the one solid fact, above all else, that obsessed her. It may have been too upsetting to text her friends – yet it was still the thing she herself couldn't stop thinking about.

Her other obsession – Connor – was also not something she wanted to discuss. Not even, she realized, with her best friend. She was worried that Abby might say this was just a crush on an actor.

Yet Lulu knew what she was feeling was real. And she was ready, more than ready, to act on it. She could never have imagined not consulting with Abby every step of the way on something like this. But she did not want to hesitate or be talked out of it – which she somehow felt Abby might try. So the words Connor and Ericson – or any hint of this situation – were not in her text to Abby.

Lulu knew that someone like Jazzy, for example, could pull this off easily. So she just had to adapt that mind-set. It shouldn't be so hard, she told herself. After all, Lulu had just spent two weeks sharing a cabin with Jazzy's BFF. Lulu now knew why that was true. She also had a firm grasp of how these girls operated.

Lulu had been sitting in the den, on one of the oversized plum leather club chairs, while talking to her mother. It was amazing, she thought once she had hung up the phone, how Francesca could take such cozy furniture and assemble a room that was so cold. It took a certain skill, she decided, to create such soulless interiors. Even the garden, was remarkably uninviting. Shouldn't this have been at least a hint to Milo?

The den was right off the imposing, double-height foyer, and Lulu wanted to stay close to the front door, just steps away. Connor had texted her earlier that he was coming over to help Francesca run through some lines. Lulu had asked him to come by earlier – and planned to be the one who opened the door. From the den, she could get to the door well before the majordomo, who was down in the screening room, and the housekeeper, who was with the cook, going through the pantry supplies in the kitchen, four rooms away.

Francesca was up in her bedroom, lying down, at the other end of the house, and Lulu could see from the light on the phone console that Milo was talking on the phone in his office. It was now or never, Lulu had decided. She wasn't going to be in Los Angeles much longer – and she felt she might die if she didn't play this out.

When she heard the bell, Lulu took a deep breath and ran to open the door.

"Connor!," she said, inserting an inflection of surprise in her voice. "It's been far too long!" She started laughing, and so did he – a flicker of that giddiness they had shared in Puerto Cervo. She pulled him into the hallway to give him a welcoming hug – holding on a beat too long. She said softly into his ear, "I really have missed you, you know." Her tone would have done Jazzy proud – sincere, yet somehow teasingly laced with sex. It still surprised her how easy this inflection was.

She took a step back, smiling at him all the while. "It's feels so strange not to be eating with you at every meal. Or at least seeing you whenever I look up," she continued. "Life on that boat was sure something I could get used to. I wanted to go to the beach the other day – and I was so bummed that Russell wasn't around to pack a hamper."

"I know just how you feel, Lulu," he laughed. "I need someone like Russell to run my life. Especially now – it's bloody barmy. There were two of him, you know. There had to be, since he never went to sleep – serving grilled cheese and tomato sandwiches are 4 a.m. and breakfast at 8:00. I'd take just one of them. They could keep the other."

"But even more than Russell, mostly I've been missing you." She paused a beat, hesitating before finally plunging ahead, "especially because I so want to finish what we started on the boat. I can't think of anything I want to do more." His smile met hers. "I've been thinking about it just about all the time."

He didn't ask what she was talking about or pretend he didn't understand. "I've been thinking about it, too, Lulu," he said, with that lazy smile. He focused it on her, and she could not help but think, as usual, that she was the most important person in the world to him.

"Let's go up to my room." She felt somewhat breathless as she said it.

His smile somehow shifted, subtly, into one of sly anticipation. She wondered how he was able to do this — to engage in a virtual conversation though carefully modulated smiles. It was almost uncanny. But she had already taken his hand to lead him up the stairs. "We can just pretend we're back on the boat," she said, willing herself to maintain a casual tone.

They walked into her bedroom and she turned to close the door. He pulled her close before she had a chance.

"So, Lulu, I think I was saying that I never knew blushing could be so beguiling." His smile deepened as he leaned toward her, gently pushing her hair back off her face. "So, so beguiling." He began slowly caressing her neck. Lulu could feel his breath on her skin. "And though this summer has been barmy, completely surreal at some points, it's also happened to be one of the most brill of my life. And you're a big part of that." His other hand moved gently up her arm. "A very big part. You've helped ground me in this madhouse."

Her body tingled as Connor's caresses grew stronger. It was remarkable, she thought, she felt excited yet exquisitely relaxed. He began kissing her — soft, light kisses, like butterfly wings landing on her forehead, her eyes, her nose, cheeks and, finally, her mouth.

They were now sitting on the bed, her arms around him. Connor had shifted position so slowly and sinuously that she had been almost unaware of any movement. She felt they were drifting together, back on the boat, rocked by some internal surf. He was stroking her back, long seductive motions. Then his hands were under her T-shirt. She peeled it off and pressed against him. In every way, she wanted to be as close to him as possible, to fulfill this connection. He unhooked her bra and he teased it off her as she lay back on the bed. Then he was on top of her, kissing her, caressing her. She had thought about this so often, but nothing she had imagined came close to the way she felt right now, tantalized and exhilarated.

Even as she experienced it, Lulu felt somehow outside of herself, watching this scene on the bed play out with an ease beyond anything she imagined. She felt her body responding, as if Connor possessed some secret code. She tugged on his T-shirt to pull it over his head.

He paused to look down at her with that same soft smile. This time, it seemed to promise all the wonder, the fun that lay just ahead — literally. "Let me do this." She wasn't sure he had said the words — their connection seemed so strong. He twisted and arched his back, pulling his shirt off.

She found herself laughing. There was a giddiness, but also something deeper — and far more pleasurable. She heard herself repeating his name, "Connor, oh, Connor." As he bent over her again, she ran her hands through his hair. But she found it hard to focus on anything beyond his caresses and her body's instinctive responses. Their fingers were tightly interlaced as his mouth moved down her stomach, leaving a trail of fire on her skin.

Suddenly, the door banged open. Francesca was at the threshold, screaming. Time was suspended into a sort of stop-action slow motion. That part of Lulu which had been watching from outside the scene was amazed. She was both in the scene and watching it.

At first, though she saw her stepmother's mouth moving, it felt like a silent movie being played out. All Lulu could focus on was that Francesca was wearing that same unflattering chiffon top — the one with small yellow flowers scattered across a sea-blue field. What was it with this blouse?

But as the harangue continued, Lulu began deciphering words amid a fierce jumble of Italian and

English sounds. The gist was obvious. Then the words started unspooling as lacerating clauses, which formed into vitriolic sentences.

"You conniving whore! Maledetta puttana!!" Francesca shouted, "Merdaccia schifosa!! I've been watching you, troia! Lurida troia! Throwing yourself at him. You think I couldn't see what was happening on the boat, bastarda di una schifosa? You think I didn't know what you are? Maledetta stronza! Puttana non sei altro che una schifosa puttana!"

She was screaming furiously, her anger out of control. Unlike most incidents involving Francesca, Lulu realized, her stepmother wasn't artfully staging this scene. She wasn't just acting angry. No, this was the real Francesca — maybe one of the first real moments that Lulu had ever experienced with her stepmother.

Lulu was stunned at the force of Francesca's fury, cowering almost instinctively. Connor had sat up, partially blocking her from Francesca's view, as if to shield her from the rage. He held out his hands, fingers splayed, in what looked like an attempt to absorb some of this anger. "Wait a minute, Chesca. Hold on," he said cajolingly, "Slow down a minute."

"You are disgusting, mi fai schifo!," Francesca continued, stalking toward the bed. Lulu was stunned that her stepmother's voice was getting louder. She hadn't thought that was humanly possible. "I never wanted you here in the first place, zoccola bastarda!"

"Chesca, what's going on? What's happened?? Chesca!" Lulu could hear Milo's voice, then the thud of footsteps as he raced up the stairs. "What is it? What's going on?"

But her stepmother could focus only on her own fury. She didn't hear Milo — even when he reached Lulu's landing. He paused at the doorway, looking both stunned and bereft.

"Jesus Christ! What in hell! Lulu!" He gasped out her name, his voice sounding strangled, "Jesus!"

"Chesca, what's going on!" It was an exclamation, not a question. With two strides, he was standing beside his wife. "What are you doing? Why are you screaming at Lulu? He's the one you should be screaming at. He's to blame. She's a girl — a little girl. He's the adult here. He's to bl–." He stopping abruptly and stood there, starring at Francesca.

She had turned to face him. Francesca had finally stopped screaming, just as Milo ran out of words. His silence enveloped the room, smothering her rage. Milo stared at his wife, with a terrible stunned expression.

The only movement Lulu saw was the pulse throbbing in her father's temple. His skin grew mottled as his jaw hardened. His gaze focused diamond sharp as, almost unconsciously, he swung his right shoulder back and raised his hand high. Francesca winced involuntarily, as if anticipating a blow. Her face, crimson just seconds before, had drained of all color.

ALLISON SILVER

But Milo slowly lowered his arm. His entire body
seemed to deflate, as his face flooded with a terrible
sadness. It seemed to take all his will to keep looking
Francesca in the eye. "I thought we were happy." His
tone was almost plaintive.

Suddenly, Lulu understood. She gasped and then
seemed unable to catch her breath. It felt like the wind
had been knocked out of her. She shrank back to the far
corner of the bed, as far from Connor as possible,
clutching a pillow tightly to her chest, as if it were
a shield.

She felt too numb even to cry. She was furious with
herself — for not having realized what was going on. How
could she have been such a naïve dolt, such a silly little
girl. She lacerated herself inwardly. Then, right behind
that ice-cold anger with herself was a wave of crushing
embarrassment. How could she have ever believed that
she loved him and wanted, above all else, to give herself to
him? She was even more ashamed that she ever imagined
that he genuinely cared about her. How could he, when
he was hooking up with Francesca? And who knows who
else? She also felt a consuming sorrow that she had so
misread Connor and misunderstood what was going on
between them. That was when the tears finally started.

Through her tears, however, Lulu could finally see
what she had been unable to comprehend this whole
summer. Connor, she realized, had probably been
hooking up with Francesca long before Lulu arrived

in Los Angeles, perhaps ever since the film they made together two years ago.

Maybe that was why he had been out on the deck during that party in Malibu — waiting to meet up with Francesca. And why her stepmother seemed so thoroughly irritated when he wasn't paying enough attention to her on the boat. And why she made sure Lulu never spent time alone with him there.

As her father turned toward the bed, Lulu thought she had never seen him look so old. It was as if he aged a decade in these past few minutes. "Please get dressed, Louise," he said in a near-whisper. "We need to talk — downstairs."

His voice was steely when he turned to Connor. "I can't even say your name," he said, "You're a monster, a predator." He took a deep breath. "I've known what you've been doing around town. With Tessa, with Hannah, with Cyd, with Maisie, with..." There was a long pause. "Most of it, anyway. But don't kid yourself about what's happened here — she's a girl. A little girl! I might run into you again, but I won't ever see you — much less talk to you."

Connor shook his head and sighed. "You're wrong," he said quietly. "I care about Lulu. I care about her a great deal. What I feel for her is different. It's real. And she's not the five-year-old who moved back East with her mother. That little girl is gone, Milo. Lulu is old enough to have real feelings for me. Just like I have for her." He looked back at Lulu, with a sad smile, as he stood up and put on his shirt. She could feel his eyes on her but couldn't bear to look at him, much less meet his gaze. A gaze she had hungered for just minutes ago. Instead, she hung her head in embarrassment.

But she could still see, out of the corner of her eye, that he didn't once look toward Francesca as he left the room. Even he couldn't pull off a graceful exit.

As Lulu reached down for her T-shirt, which was on the floor beside the bed, Milo turned back to Francesca. Again, it seemed a struggle even to look at her. There was a simmering silence.

Until Milo broke it. "I'm going to leave for the set tomorrow," he said, "instead of next week. I'll drop Lulu off on the way. We'll talk in a few weeks, when we both have some perspective. I don't know how repairable this is — or should be."

Jagged tears were running down Francesca's cheeks, and she wiped her nose with the back of one hand. This was nothing like the dramatic, tempest-tossed storm of tears that Lulu had sometimes seen from her stepmother. Lulu knew that she was again seeing the real Francesca — not a carefully constructed set piece orchestrated by a supremely self-involved actress. "Milo, please, Io non vivo senza di te. I can't live without you," her words emerged as a harsh croak. "Ti adoro. Tu sei tutto per me."

"Don't, Francesca," he said. His tone was more sad than angry. "Not now."

She reached out in a supplicatory gesture. He looked at her hands, without responding. "I can't do this now."

Lulu had pulled on her T-shirt on and buttoned her jeans. As she got off the bed, Milo walked over and put his arms around her. "It'll be all right," he said softly. He seemed to lean on her, though, as they walked out of the room.

Lulu felt no solace from his words. She continued to cry in embarrassment and frustration. "I feel like such a dolt," she whispered, "I, I thought he cared about me the way I cared about him. I was such an unbelievable idiot."

"Hush, Lulu. Shush." He hugged her more tightly as they walked into his office. "Don't talk like that. Ever. But especially not now." She sat down in one of the big arm chairs, folding her heron-legs under her as he closed the door. When he turned around, she was struck anew by how he had aged this last half-hour. She could never have imagined him so deflated.

"All I care is that you're okay," he said. "You are, right?"

She nodded her head.

"Always know, Lulu," he began, "how much I love you. That is the number one important thing." He took her hands in both of his and looked directly at her. "Nothing else even comes close. Everything else is ephemeral.

"And we're okay, right?" He sat down and waited for her to answer before he continued. "I am so, so sorry for the sadness you are feeling right now. I would give anything, anything, if I could ease some part of the hurt — the heartache — that Connor has caused you." He was stroking her cheek softly. "This is the worst kind of pain. I know how terrible it feels. It hurts so much, you think you can't survive it. But you do. You get through it. They say things like this help build character — but you already had enough character! So now you have some to spare. Which will be good in the long run — you just have to get there."

He smiled at her. Lulu saw a palpable wave of sadness break over him. But he physically shook it off, the way a dog shakes water off its coat. "And you need to understand this, Lulu. Connor can't actually tell what's real at this point. His life is crazy right now. He's in that Forum of the 12 Caesars moment. He's the one guy everyone wants. In every possible way.

"So he's irresistible." He let out a sigh that seemed involuntary. "And everyone wants him: women and men, straight and gay, young and old, film studios and cable networks, name directors and big-deal fashion designers, brand endorsements and publicity firms. Because being with him, being attached to him, puts them at the white-hot center. And that's where all these people long to be. It's what keeps them feeling alive.

"With everyone chasing after him — it's hard for Connor to decipher what's authentic and what's artificial. Virtually impossible. Your entire sense of perception goes out of whack. And you operate by your own rules.

"You should hold on to the fact, sweetie, that despite all this, he saw what was real in you. You are so unlike everyone he runs into at this point. There is nothing phony about you. You're clear as a bell. You are a lifeline for him — a lifeline to any authenticity, to any sort of real emotion."

Lulu knew her father was trying to make her feel better, trying to lessen her hurt and embarrassment, but it wasn't working. She tried to concentrate on his words though, and realized his tone had changed, as if he were purposefully distancing himself. "How he deals with this success is what counts in the long run," Milo said. "He might never figure out what the important things really are."

He went back into explanation mode, his comfort zone. "Years ago, a women I know, a fifth-rate actress but a first-rate beauty, was engaged to a lovely guy. He was a civilian — rich but not in the business. And he wanted to get married and have kids with her. Had been waiting years for her to agree. She was finally about to — but then she was offered a role by... I think it was Kubrick. That was the bright, shiny object she was chasing. Nothing else mattered. So she walked out on her fiancé and their relationship. The part was too important to her. Kubrick was too important to her."

He paused a beat, and Lulu could sense he was rifling through the files in his brain. "She married someone else. Then she divorced that guy and married someone else. I'm not sure who she's with now. But whenever I ran into her, I don't think there's an inch of her that's real. Not physically – which might also be true – but emotionally. I'm not sure she would even feel regret for the thing she lost – that genuine happiness and sense of contentment she shared with her first fiancé. She can't tell the difference any more. Hollywood swallowed her up."

His smile wavered slightly. "We, on the other hand, are both going to be fine," he said even more softly. He seemed to be speaking to himself as much as Lulu. "We are, my little contessa." His voice was gentle as he said her childhood nickname, sweetness mixing in the sorrow. "It looks so hard right now. But we'll both get through this. That's the magic of time." He paused again, and seemed to be gathering his strength. "I have to go talk to Francesca. We need to discuss some things, since you and I are getting on a plane tomorrow to head back East. Maybe we'll get a ride in the jet. I'm not sure. But either way, I want to leave early – because of the time difference.

"Always remember it meant so much to me that you stayed here all summer." He reached out again to cup her face with his hands. "I want this to be a regular thing for us — father and daughter. I know how much you love your mother — and how much Claire loves you. But I'd like to be part of your life — and have you share a big part of mine."

He hesitated a minute. When he started speaking again, his voice was quieter still. "Sometimes, I'm sure you must think I treat you like a little girl, Lulu. You always are going to be my little girl, you know — even when you're 30. But I..., I... also think he may have been right about this." He avoided saying Connor's name.

"It may be true that it's because part of me will always see you as that five-year-old who left L.A. with her mother so many years ago. I only know that the fact I have you in my life now is the one thing I don't want to lose. Everything else is ephemeral as far as I am concerned." His voice hardened. "Everything.

"Leaving tomorrow is all good, actually," he sought to reassure her. And maybe also himself. But she was not assuaged — his sadness was tangible and her own felt insurmountable. "I still have lots of prep to do for the shoot. I need to see the locations and check the sets. The pictures Mayer sent me are out of date — at least I hope so. And we're due to start production soon — though we haven't fully set the shooting schedule. Much less locked it.

"Meanwhile, you'll be able to see your mother by tomorrow night. That will be terrific for you — and her."

He reached out to stroke Lulu's hair tenderly. "Don't worry, contessa. It will be all right. I promise." Lulu thought he was promising himself as much as her. "I know you want to go back to your room. You need to start packing, right? So give me about 15 minutes before you head up. We should be out of it by then."

But Lulu sat in her father's office for almost 45 minutes, reflecting on what had just happened in her bedroom. In addition to an unbearable sense of heartbreak, she felt she was in mourning for something — though she wasn't sure quite what.

CHAPTER 10

THE TARMAC AT THE JETPORT

MILO AND LULU were sitting in the car on the jetport runway early Thursday. He had arranged for them to travel on a company jet with Tessa Lefferts, who was flying in with a friend for fashion week in New York. Since Milo was getting a lift, he and Lulu had arrived early. He explained to Lulu the night before that he didn't want to cut it close at Burbank.

Milo had decided yesterday that it would be easier to travel on the jet. He was bringing along a lot of luggage —

since he was planning to be away for almost four months. He didn't foresee any weekend trips back to L.A.

These travel logistics would work for Lulu as well. She could get off with the two women in New York, at the Marine Air Terminal at LaGuardia Airport. The shuttle to Boston took off directly from there – so she didn't even have to go to a different terminal to board it. Meanwhile, the studio pilots could fly Milo down to North Carolina to drop him off, and then head back to New York, where they would have downtime waiting for Tessa.

Neither Lulu nor her father had mentioned Francesca that morning. Lulu hadn't seen her stepmother since she had walked out of the bedroom. But Francesca's presence seemed to weigh on them both.

On the way to Burbank, Lulu had filled the anxious silence by describing last night's phone conversation with mummy. Her mother had sounded so joyful when she heard Lulu was coming back a week earlier than planned. Lulu omitted telling her father how glad she herself was to be going home early. She didn't mention how forlorn she felt about Connor. How embarrassed she was. She also blamed herself for this sadness in her father's eyes, a certain grimness about his mouth.

As they sat in the car, waiting on the tarmac, her father finally tackled the subject they had been avoiding. "She wanted to come with us today, you know." Lulu didn't ask who. "She doesn't think we should be apart right now. She was ready to get on the plane this morning and stay with me in North Carolina for the entire shoot." There was a pause. When he continued his voice was quieter. "She kept saying, over and over, how terribly sorry she was. She kept talking about how much our marriage means to her, how much she wants to make it work."

There was another, longer pause. "I told her we both needed this time apart, to give us some perspective. And right now, frankly, I need to concentrate on the movie, at least these first weeks. It's a complicated shoot, and I have to give it the attention it needs and deserves."

He took a deep breath. "I also told her that I wasn't sure there was anything worth salvaging," he said softly, "But if there is, it'll still be there in a month or two.

"She already had the names of two couples therapists she wants us to sit down with. But I told her we each need to figure out what we want before we even take that step. We'll see what happens, Lulu, I'm not sure at this point."

He took another deep breath. "You should also know, Lulu, that she wanted to come down this morning and apologize to you in person. She wants to tell you how sorry she is about what she said — how she cares about you and wants you to understand that. I advised her today wasn't such a good idea — aside from the fact we needed to get out to Burbank. In any case, I think everyone's feelings are still too raw this morning.

"But I get the impression that she is going to write you a letter. She asked for your address. I think you might be getting it soon. And, knowing her, there could be a gift involved." He smiled briefly.

"We left it that she may come down in about five or six weeks — probably around mid-October. We'll see where we stand then. By that time, I'll also have more time for her."

He took a deep breath before mentioning an even more difficult subject. "As for Connor, don't be surprised if you hear from him again. You'll have to decide how you really feel. And what you want to do."

Lulu didn't say anything about the text she had received from Connor last night, asking her to hear him out. She had hit delete. It had taken her far longer than usual to fall asleep. Close to midnight, she had decided that the word to best describe this summer was confusion. At some point, she decided, she had gotten in way over her head. It was like she had been walking step by step toward the deep end — then, suddenly, the bottom fell out from under her. She was looking forward to going home, getting life back to normal.

A limousine pulled up near the jet and Evie Rothman got out. She was wearing her usual thigh-length caftan, this one a milk chocolate brown silk, over slim tan trousers, with chocolate brown patent leather Tod's. She was carrying, as usual, a Hermes Birkin bag — this one was matte crocodile in a chocolate brown that matched her top.

She waved and walked over, smiling broadly as they got out of their car. "Tessa told me you were coming with. I was so glad! We're going in for the fashion shows so we're going to have a terrific time. And now the flight will be terrific too — since we'll have the time to catch up!"

Her smile turned vulpine. "You'll have enough time, Milo, to tell me exactly what happened in Porto Cervo." Her tone was light, but Lulu could see how voraciously she sought these details. "I want to know just what happened with Rob! I'm assuming this little incident was all about him, right?"

Milo laughed gamely. "Evie," he said, as he kissed her hello. "I can trust you not to miss anything! You're right, as usual. He's just too big a star to walk anywhere without causing a riot. You certainly know your cast of characters!"

"And Evie, you remember my daughter Lulu? You met her just after she arrived this summer I think. Well, the summer's over and I'm taking her back home now, before I go down to the location in North Carolina."

"Of course I remember Lulu," Evie said, smiling brightly as she kissed Lulu hello. Lulu could see only vague recognition in her eyes. "Well young lady, you must have had quite a summer. I'm sure you had fun in Los Angeles."

She didn't even pretend to wait for an answer. "Milo, have you heard the latest about Candace? The details have been too, too delicious. She checked herself into rehab. She didn't even bother to wait to come home and do it here. She went to one right outside London. That was her solution to this mess. The reshoots have had to be pushed back. But she's already found a new boyfriend there! Some spikey British rock star, complete down to the serious heroin problem.

"Mel's furious. The public line on her disappearance is exhaustion — as usual. But the word is drugs. She's insisting it's a serious drug rehab center. Though everything I've heard makes it sound more like a high-end spa. Meanwhile the picture's unfinished."

She barely paused for breath. "As for Jim, he's never looked back. He's seeing Maisie Anderson. Her career's taking off — weren't you recently considering her for something, Milo? He seems so happy to be out of that craziness."

She analyzed all the finer points. They were still at it when a navy Mercedes Maybach pulled up alongside the plane, roughly 10 minutes after their official departure time. The driver raced to open the door, but the tall, voluptuous woman who emerged moved at a languid pace. She wore her black hair in a loose thick plait down her back and was dressed for riding. But it was unlike any riding outfit Lulu had ever worn – or seen.

The woman was wearing robin's egg blue moleskin jodhpurs, a sapphire blue tweed hacking jacket with a navy velvet collar and knee-high riding boots in shiny black crocodile. A green and aqua Hermes foulard ascot was tucked into the neckline of her crisp white blouse, and she was carrying an oversized Birkin bag in navy blue crocodile. The driver had taken a luggage-size, baby blue leather Kelly bag, the size of a large carpet bag, out of the trunk.

"Hello Sam," the women said to the crewmember who picked up the large Hermes bag. "Thanks so much for your help." Her voice had a slight lilt.

She strolled over to the group, which was now standing at the foot of the stairway up to the plane. "Evie!" she said, greeting the older woman with a warm hug. As she turned to Milo and Lulu, the reason for her choice of color was obvious. She had pushed her dark sunglasses up off her face as she approached and the limpid blue of her eyes, fringed by thick black lashes, was startling. It was even more striking against her milk-white complexion. Blue must be her favorite color, Lulu decided, since her eyes somehow mirrored and echoed all the blues she was wearing. But if all she ever wore was blue, Lulu thought, this could get old quickly.

Milo kissed the woman hello. "Tessa, thanks so much for making space for us," he said, "I really appreciate it!"

"Please Milo," Tessa said with a smile and slight shake of her head. "You're the reason we have these planes. It's about a master of the art like you. I should be thanking you for taking me." Her smile deepened.

"That's sweet of you, Tessa. And please be sure to tell Harry thanks as well.

"I'm not sure you've ever met my daughter, Lulu." Milo paused, "Lulu, this is Mrs. Lefferts." Lulu shook hands, looking into what must be the bluest eyes she had ever seen. "Lulu spent the summer with me, but now she's heading back to her mother and school."

"Lovely to meet you, Lulu," Tessa said. The Irish lilt was even more noticeable. "The whole summer! That must have been fabulous." She smiled brightly at the teenager, "Did you have fun?"

ACKNOWLEDGEMENTS

This book has been a long time in development. It was a three-step process.

First, my mother, Helen Paltis Silver, loved movies. Like so many of her enthusiasms, it was infectious and I was happily smitten. Hers was a fierce and wide-ranging passion – from "Children of Paradise" to "Duck Soup" to "The Wild Bunch." Once, when I was a little girl, in the days before Netflix and streaming, she had me go to bed early so she could wake me up at 1 a.m. to watch "Twentieth Century." That was my vivid introduction to Carole Lombard's delicious laugh and the wonder of a Ben Hecht and Charles MacArthur screenplay.

Second, at Yale I was still so movie-mad that I somehow convinced my history senior essay adviser, Professor John Morton Blum, to let me focus on how Hollywood changed the expected development of a writer's life. One of the three Algonquin Round Table writers I wrote about was Charles Brackett, an East Coast Brahmin who ended up in Hollywood working with Billy Wilder. (MacArthur was another.) I tracked down Brackett's papers, including a remarkable diary that he kept throughout his years in Hollywood, from the 1930s to the 1960s. His daughter, Liz Moore, let me spend my Christmas vacation plowing through them. They were jaw-dropping.

Third was living in Los Angeles, while I was the editor of The Los Angeles Times Sunday "Opinion" section. My brother, the producer Joel Silver, opened the door to the backrooms and boiler rooms of Hollywood. I was close to many people in the movie business, and I was often stunned by how similar it was to the world Brackett had described. His diary served as a sort of prism, refracting and focusing everything I saw. People regularly lamented changes in the movie business. But, at least when I was there, much of the structure and hierarchy seemed staggeringly similar. Brackett, for example, writes about trying to close a deal with Cary Grant, and the same story could easily have been written about Warren Beatty, or Brad Pitt, or perhaps Jennifer Lawrence.

I tried to convey this through Abe Fleischman's diary entries. It was Brackett's diary that inspired me here. I was jazzed that I could place Abe at, for example, a dinner party at producer Jerry Wald's house and know the guests were many of the same people who had actually sat down for dinner there. Knowing how Brackett's day as a producer was structured gave me the freedom to riff on what a studio head would be doing in that era. This also made me feel as if I had closed a circle – using information that I first learned in college.

The "Matts" in my life also came through for me here – as they have so often before. It was kismet that Matt Mahurin, whose political illustrations have dazzled me since I first worked with him at The Los Angeles

Times "Opinion" section, found the time to do my book jacket image. I can only hope readers judge my book by his swell cover. Matt Wuerker, a maestro of cartoon art who worked with me at Politico, contributed the nifty drawings at the beginning of each chapter.

Many friends read this novel, or various iterations of it, and all gave me encouragement and input. Many offered astute comments, including Maria Gallagher, Suzanne Garment, Chris Hart, Christopher Knight, Mike Lillis, Sean MacPherson, Bruce McCall, Polly McCall, Alix Madigan, Evangeline Morphos, Paul Rudnick, Janny Scott, Matt Wuerker and Nadia Zilkha. Charles R. Morris and Tom Powers, though unfamiliar with the world I was describing, offered wise counsel. Neal Gabler's savvy advice caused me to revise a key plot point of the story and, I hope, improve it.

If it got better through the various drafts it was because of them.

If it did not, that is all on me.

And, of course, I would like to thank Bobby Woods and his team at Marmont Lane, who literally made this book happen.

About the Author

Allison Silver is the executive editor of Reuters Opinion. She has served as the Opinion editor at Politico, the editor of The Los Angeles Times Sunday "Opinion" section, an editor at The New York Times "Week in Review" and founding editor of The Washington Independent. She was also Politics Producer for "Charlie Rose." She is the co-author of "20th Century Travel" (Taschen). She lives in New York City.

MARMONT LANE BOOKS WOULD LIKE TO THANK TOM ANDRE, ANDREW GOLOMB, AND MAUREEN FEWEL FOR THEIR ASSISTANCE IN THE MAKING OF THIS BOOK.

MARMONT LANE
BOOKS

MARMONTLANE.COM

www.ingramcontent.com/pod-product-compliance
Lightning Source LLC
Chambersburg PA
CBHW070200260626
47160CB00002B/406